SCARLETT FINN

Also by Scarlett Finn

GO NOVELS
GO WITH IT
GO IT ALONE
GO ALL OUT
GO ALL IN
GO FULL CIRCLE

EXILE
HIDE & SEEK
KISS CHASE

WRECK & RUIN
RUIN ME
RUIN HIM

**THE BRANDED
SERIES**
BRANDED
SCARRED
MARKED

**FORBIDDEN
PREQUEL DUET**
ALL. ONLY.
ONLY YOURS

THE FORBIDDEN NOVELS
FORBIDDEN DESIRE
FORBIDDEN WANT
FORBIDDEN WISH
FORBIDDEN NEED
FORBIDDEN BOND

**BOMBSHELLS & BILLIONAIRES
(ROXIVERSE)**
NOTHING TO HIDE
NOTHING TO LOSE
NOTHING IN BETWEEN: ONE
NOTHING TO DECLARE
NOTHING TO US
NOTHING IN BETWEEN: TWO
NOTHING TO SAY
NOTHING TO GAIN
NOTHING IN BETWEEN: THREE
NOTHING TO YOU
NOTHING TO THIS PREQUEL: ONE WILD NIGHT
NOTHING TO THIS
NOTHING IN BETWEEN: FOUR
NOTHING TO DO
NOTHING TO NO ONE
NOTHING TO FEAR
NOTHING TO DENY
NOTHING TO BEAT
NOTHING TO THE WEDDING
NOTHING TO TELL
NOTHING TO IT
NOTHING TO SEE
NOTHING TO WIN
NOTHING TO OFFER
NOTHING TO PROVE

**LOVE AGAINST THE ODDS
STANDALONE COLLECTION**
SWEET SEAS
HEIR'S AFFAIR
RESCUED
MAESTRO'S MUSE
GETTING TRICKY
THIRTEEN
REMEMBER WHEN...
RELUCTANT SUSPICION
XY FACTOR

KINDRED SERIES
RAVEN
SWALLOW
CUCKOO
SWIFT
FALCON
FINCH

MISTAKE DUET
MISTAKE ME NOT
SLEIGHT MISTAKE

LOST & FOUND
LOST
FOUND

**THE EXPLICIT
SERIES**
EXPLICIT INSTRUCTION
EXPLICIT DETAIL
EXPLICIT MEMORY

TO DIE FOR...
TO DIE FOR TRUTH
TO DIE FOR HONOR
TO DIE FOR VIRTUE
TO DIE FOR DUTY
TO DIE FOR LOVE

**RISQUÉ & HARROW
INTERTWINED**
TAKE A RISK
FIGHTING FATE
RISK IT ALL
FIGHTING BACK
GAME OF RISK

ONE

Lacie

"PREGNANT?" Lacie asked.

"Everyone will think I'm such a hussy."

"Well—"

"What?" Sorcha snapped.

"I didn't say anything," Lacie said, placing a calming hand over her best friend's knee.

The women sat together on Lacie's moss-green couch in the middle of her living room; the piece positioned like an island. An enviable notion.

"How am I going to explain this to my father?" Sorcha asked.

The peace of her day had been shattered when Sorcha phoned from the car to say she was on her way over.

Lacie hadn't lived in her apartment for long, but she enjoyed the quiet street and the unassuming neighbors. Making a final decision had been easy when she'd been introduced to the trapdoor in the bedroom floor, which led to a secret cellar. The mystery of it appealed to her curious side.

Sorcha had been on at Lacie about certain throw pillows that were required to "disguise the couch" that came with the apartment. Ordinarily Sorcha was observant about the most benign things. The sincerity of her friend's panic was amplified when Lacie realized Sorcha hadn't commented on the throw pillows she'd finally gotten around to purchasing. Having now heard the news, Lacie could understand why.

"I don't understand how it's possible," Lacie said. Sorcha narrowed her eyes. "I mean I understand how but… I didn't know you'd been with anyone."

"It's Bruce's," Sorcha said.

"What?" Lacie exhaled. "But I thought… he left town when you broke up… that was about…"

"Three months ago," Sorcha said.

"It took you three months to notice?"

"I think I was trying to pretend it wasn't happening," Sorcha said. "I got a test, in fact I got a few. They all came back positive."

"When did you take them?"

"This morning," Sorcha said, retrieving her purse from the floor behind her feet to dump the contents on the center cushion of the couch.

Dozens of the pregnancy tests lay between them. Though Sorcha waited for a reaction, Lacie had nothing.

"Wow," Lacie said, overwhelmed by the white plastic sticks scattered amongst Sorcha's usual purse paraphernalia. "You got more than a few."

"How am I supposed to tell my father?" Sorcha asked. "I'm Catholic! He'll go crazy."

"He can't think you're still a virgin," Lacie said. "You're twenty-eight."

"I don't… I doubt he does believe that, but we don't talk about it. He'll expect me to get married! How can I get married when I don't have a baby daddy, or rather a groom?"

"Will Bruce marry you?" Lacie asked.

She and Sorcha had been close friends since they met in college. Lacie was new to the country at that time; Sorcha had educated her in all things American. While Sorcha was tall, elegant, and perfect, Lacie was a few inches shorter, much less refined, and far less confident with the opposite sex. Sorcha simply had to walk into a room to get the attention of every man there, which had always been fine with Lacie. She wasn't sure what to do when a male paid her any attention, but then she had different priorities.

Sorcha Reynolds was the eldest of two daughters to Lawrence and Amelia Reynolds. They were high society, and Sorcha still slurped from her silver spoon occasionally. As a result, Lacie was used to digging Sorcha out of any dirty pit she found herself in. Except, this time, there was little she could do for her friend.

"He won't have a choice when I get hold of him," Sorcha said.

"Are you sure you would want to marry him? He always seemed a little self-absorbed to me."

"And thus ends your introduction to the pretty boy. He's hot, and he's rich, he doesn't need a decent personality."

"Is that your opinion or your mother's?"

"What else can I do, Lace?" Sorcha said, snatching Lacie's hands to pull them to her lap. "I have to at least find him. I have to tell him."

"There are options if you don't want to…"

Sorcha was visibly startled. "I wouldn't have thought that was your type of thing."

"We're not talking about me," Lacie said, steering away from the subject of her sex life, which had been non-existent for more than a while. "This would be your decision."

"I don't know," Sorcha said on a long inhale. "I'm terrified of my father, but I'm twenty-eight, what if this is it? My last chance."

"Last chance at what?" Lacie said on a laugh.

"You know," Sorcha said. "I have to find Bruce. We have to get married before my father finds out about this."

"Okay. So where is he?"

Sorcha slumped back on the couch in the most unladylike pose Lacie had ever seen her in; usually Sorcha was the epitome of poise. "I have no idea."

"Can you call his work?"

"And say what?" she said. "He told me he got a big promotion somewhere. He's not even working for Lewis Fund and Investment anymore."

"What about family?"

"I never met them," she said. "I suppose I could ask my mother but… I don't really want to talk to my family about this until… you know."

"So you don't have a clue where he is," Lacie said, trying to find a different route of information for her friend. "Hey, what about that guy?"

"What guy?"

"I don't remember his name, I never met him… The guy you were seeing when I was in the UK."

"What guy, I don't—oh, you mean Shep." Sorcha's blanched expression regained some of its rosy hue as a smile curled her lips. "He really was something… it's just a shame about…"

"About what?"

"I told you," Sorcha said. "The man was useless in bed. I tell you it's a waste on someone as hot as he was."

"Didn't you say he was some kind of investigator?"

Sorcha sat bolt upright. "That's right. Yes, he

does private investigations."

"Hire him. He can track Bruce down for you."

"I can't," Sorcha grumbled. "He was really pissed when I broke up with him. I can't go back to him now and ask him to look up another of my ex-boyfriends."

"Isn't it better that than facing your father without knowing where Bruce is?"

Sorcha considered it for a moment. "You could hire him."

"Hire who?"

"Shep," Sorcha said. "Just tell him I referred you. He'll want to help when he hears my name."

"And what do I tell him?"

"Tell him you need to find an old boyfriend. He's hardly going to ask any questions about your motives. All he has to do is find Bruce. So it's not like you'll have to actually talk to Bruce. Shep can give you the information, and then you give it to me. Bingo, everyone's happy."

"I don't like it," Lacie said.

"It'll be easy. All you have to do is go down there give him the name, the money, and the information. After that, he can phone you with the results. Boom, done. One conversation."

"Sorcha, how can you be sure he'll—"

"Money," Sorcha said, raking in her purse. Producing a pen then her check book, Sorcha scrawled out the details. "I'll pay you, and you pay him."

"But what about—"

"That ought to be enough."

Lacie glanced at the check her friend had handed over. "Ten thousand? You think it will cost ten thousand dollars to find out where someone is?"

"I don't care about the money," Sorcha said. "But Shep will never turn down money, he'll see that, and all his other questions will go away."

"I'm not sure about this."

"Trust me," Sorcha said. "I'd really owe you if you help me out."

How could Lacie say no to her best friend who'd found herself in this pickle. They'd been through a lot together, and Sorcha was always there when she needed a friend. Boom, done. One conversation… she could handle that.

TWO

Ryder

RYDER OPENED THE top drawer, and then the middle one, raking through each in turn. It was a sad situation when one investigator had to poach off another. But being that he was poaching from Seth Sheppard, the world's laziest investigator, he didn't half mind. Shep took his fee and then some, sleeping with most of the wives who came in for information on their cheating husbands. On top of that, Sheppard had stolen more than a few potential customers from Ryder and his partner Jamie. Undercutting them on price only to lump extras on the final bill. Usually, Shep's information wasn't extensive or accurate either.

This time Ryder had happily taken a job from the husband of a former client of Sheppard's. The client, Rich Gillespie, wasn't interested in whether his wife knew he was cheating. He was interested in information Sheppard may have found regarding some dodgy business deals. Deals related to a certain white powder that supplemented the respectable Mr. and Mrs.

Gillespie's income.

Ryder knew Sheppard's habits. Like clockwork, Sheppard had left to go on a "job," which meant hanging out at a pool hall a few streets over. Sheppard's nineteen-year-old assistant, Tiffany, toddled out a few minutes later, heading to the nail salon in the mall. Tiffany took as much advantage of the client's money as Sheppard. Ryder figured they were sleeping together too.

Knowing all these facts, Ryder watched from his truck as events played out just as he predicted. Sheppard should have noticed him sitting there. The fact that he didn't spoke to his inherent detecting skills, or lack thereof. Ryder waited a respectable time then got out of his car, crossed the street, and walked into Sheppard Investigations like he owned the place. The small entryway opened from the glass storefront. Their reception consisted of a desk, computer, and a few personal items of Tiffany's. In the corner were four plastic chairs, and a fake ficus. Sheppard really was the last of the big spenders.

On the back wall, there were two doors, one led to a small restroom, the other Sheppard's office. In the office, piles of files, paperwork, discarded magazines and newspapers, lay in every corner. It was a wonder Sheppard got any business at all.

Never known for loitering, Ryder ignored the mess and got searching. When the filing cabinets weren't fruitful, he went to the desk angled in one corner in front of a closet. Seating himself in the leather captain's chair, Ryder hunted through the drawers for the Rich Gillespie file. When raking through the last drawer, he heard the squeak of hinges. He anticipated Sheppard or his assistant had come back early but was wrong.

The brunette in the doorway displayed the same disgust he too had on his face when walking in. He'd put her height at five six, maybe five seven. Her sun-bleached hair hung in loose waves around her shoulders. When her attention landed on him, he noticed striking green eyes that were a little unsure of themselves. Whatever it was, or wasn't, his dick jumped to attention in two seconds flat. What it was ready for, he didn't know. The woman was still a clear twenty feet away. He didn't know her name, her business, what she felt like… what she tasted like. He hadn't had such an impulsive and instant reaction to a stranger in, well… ever.

"I'm sorry," she said in smooth honeyed tones. "There was no one out there, and—"

"What can I help you with?" he asked.

This was a woman with business; business she was apparently taking to Sheppard, or so she thought.

"I don't know. I need to find someone."

"Well, you came to the right guy," Ryder said, though wanted to point out she'd come to the wrong office.

An investigator was an investigator. Yet Ryder couldn't imagine stretching the definition to encompass Sheppard.

"Can I…?" she asked, taking another step, pointing at the seat opposite him at the desk.

"Um… yeah."

This might be risky, but he couldn't tell the woman in the little blue dress that she'd caught him in the middle of a little B&E.

She crossed the room and took the seat, smoothing her dress over her knees. All the while not making eye contact.

"This is the easy part. I've heard it all. Don't worry about saying anything you might think is inappropriate or shocking."

After a few fortifying breaths, she looked at him. "I have to find a man."

"Need a little matchmaking?" he asked.

On her next breath, her expression relaxed. With her more at ease, his dick tried to jump through his zipper again. Thank God there was a desk between them… or not.

"I've never done this before. I don't exactly know how—"

"It's easy. You tell me who you're looking for, give me as much information about possible whereabouts as you can, and then I go to work."

"Okay," she said. "I'm looking for a man called Bruce Booth. He used to work for Lewis Fund and Investment in town."

"I know them," Ryder said.

Linking his fingers, he rested his forearms on Sheppard's desk. The pose wasn't typical, but for some reason, he was concerned his hands would act on their own. Overcome with the need to touch, to feel, his fingers tingled. He'd have to lunge over the desk to do it. That wasn't exactly professional, though was probably the norm for the man who usually occupied this chair.

"He got a promotion, or a better job, or… something. He left town and I need to know where he is."

"What about his family? Friends?"

Her eyes slunk to the corner behind him; a classic sign that she was hiding something. "I'm trying to stay under the radar."

"Right," Ryder said. "Does he owe you money?"

Her brows came together in a show of curiosity rather than irritation. "Why would you—?"

"Sometimes people don't want to be found, and a guy in his industry…"

"Oh no, it's nothing like that," she said, shifting to the edge of the chair, flattening her fingers on the desk.

Her nails were short and neat, but there was a

faint sign of color around her cuticles. A smoky dust not quite removed. She'd awoken his dick the minute she walked in, now his mind was buzzing with a dozen questions. What was behind those mesmerizing eyes? Where did the chalk on her fingers come from?

"Listen, Dusty, I don't care about your motives. I need to know if I'm getting into anything illegal or that's likely to give me trouble."

"Dusty?" she asked, wrinkling her nose.

Her whole face was expressive. She shifted the angle of her head. The pout of her lips. The gap between her eyelids. The muscles of her cheeks. Her forehead. Like a child curious about a world they knew nothing of. How her expression would change if he kissed her? How would those wide, inquisitive eyes look when he sheathed himself inside of her?

"Mr. Sheppard?"

It took him a good eight seconds to realize she was talking to him. "Sorry, what?"

"I can completely understand that you wouldn't want to jeopardize yourself or your business by getting into any trouble. But, perhaps, this would be an appropriate time to tell you that a good friend of mine referred me to you."

"A friend?" he asked, wondering if he was about to be made.

"Yes," she said and blinked as though sorting through her thoughts before speaking. "I wouldn't want this to be awkward. I can assure you that I would never bring any aggravation to your door. I'm assured that your services are top notch, so I…"

He hadn't noticed the small strap over her shoulder attached to a tiny bag under her arm. She slid it down into view and opened the clasp to draw out a slip of paper, a check.

"I didn't know if I should make it out to you

personally, or if I should make it payable to a company name."

She pushed the check the width of the desk. For the first time since she'd entered, he took his eyes away to look at the paper under her fingertips.

"Whoa," he said when he read it. "This is way too much."

"Like I said, I want to go under the radar and it's important."

When he took his attention from the check, their eyes locked, she didn't blink. The tip of her pink tongue darted out to moisten her lips. Her shoulder came up as her head tilted. That innocent little expression… He gritted his teeth against the pain in his jeans. Had she ever been taken? A woman like her couldn't be real.

She sure wasn't like the women he was used to. Those women knew what they were and how to use their sexuality to their advantage. That worked for him. He got off and didn't feel guilty about not calling the next day. Both parties knew what they were getting into. Either this woman in front of him took a different angle completely and did it to leave men like him panting like desperate dogs, or she had no idea how luscious she was.

"If it's not about money, it's about sex," Ryder said, watching her mouth when her lips parted, then she wriggled in her seat. Jesus, this woman was going to have him shooting his load in his pants if she moved again. A man couldn't be with a woman like her. She didn't sit still, her eyes, her mouth, her neck… Her body loosened, and he had another first: he wished he was that goddamn chair. "He's your boyfriend."

Words were on the tip of her tongue, but she held them in. A curious frown flashed to her face only to be erased when her eyes rolled upward. Her lips moved silently, and then her gaze fell back to his.

"You could say that," she said.

"This guy ran out on you?"

"Mr. Sheppard, I appreciate that we're acquainted by proxy but it's a very difficult situation to explain."

"Acquainted by proxy," he said, reminding himself of the referral.

"I do hope that your break-up won't flavor your angle on this case."

"My break-up."

"Yes," she said. "I told you Sorcha referred me."

"Sorcha," he said, wondering when he'd become a parrot.

"She is very sorry about the way things ended between you."

"Sorcha."

"Yes, Sorcha Reynolds…" she said. "She assured me that you would be fair. I would hope that the fee would settle any misgivings you may have about working on my behalf."

Again, Ryder read the zeroes on the check. "Will Sorcha be involved in this case?"

"Oh no," she said. "No. She'll stay far away from this. She's on vacation at the moment, she left just this morning."

Ryder would hate to see these zeroes in Sheppard's bank account. Given the chance, Shep would take it. He'd do his best to sample this delectable client too, even in spite of the previous relationship with her friend.

Ryder couldn't refuse her. If he did, the chances were she'd show up on his actual doorstep. He didn't want her to know he was in Sheppard's place unlawfully. What choice did he have? The woman needed honesty and guidance that Sheppard would give for an overinflated price while pawing her.

Ryder had no intention of cashing the check.

Chances were that a quick computer search would locate this Booth guy. He folded the check in half and slid it into his back pocket as he stood up. She fumbled with her bag and pounced to her feet. Five seven, but he hadn't noticed if she was wearing heels. At six two, he was used to towering over women. Usually, he'd prefer his women taller. By itself, height difference didn't usually prompt him to feel protective. But he wanted to tuck this woman close and keep her there for as long as possible.

"We're having a problem with our phone connection," he said. "Our phones and our internet are down. Do you have a pen?" She nodded and retrieved a pen and a receipt from her bag to hand them over to him. He tore it in two, wrote down his cell number, then handed it all back to her. "Write down your number."

She nodded and scribbled it down. "You'll call me?"

He took the number. "As soon as I have something," he said. "One more thing, what's your name?"

"Lacie," she said. "Lacie Hart."

"It's a pleasure," he said, extending his hand.

Immediately, he wanted to take it back. She tilted her head to the side like a confused puppy, examining the offer for a second before her hand leaped to his. His fingers hadn't curled all the way around hers when his dick pulsed again. Busy mentally chastising himself for his reaction to the simple touch, he wasn't ready for the moment their eyes met.

Neither was she. He saw her feel what he felt. A heat zinged through him, and their hands sprang apart. Damn, that was unsettling.

"Miss Hart," he said, pressing his hand to his chest, quelling his urge to grab hold of her.

"Mr. Sheppard."

She thought he was Shep. Fuck, he'd forgotten about that. If that zap was anything to go by, this sensation wouldn't disappear in a hurry... He'd known her five minutes and was already in deep. This ought to be interesting.

THREE

Lacie

DRYING HER HANDS, Lacie was satisfied that her heart rate had returned to normal. After that meeting with Sheppard, she'd come home, taken a shower, and worked. Her way of trying to forget the chemical reaction that had fizzed in her belly from the moment his dark eyes first touched hers. Seth Sheppard seemed uneasy but confident. Cool but aware.

His certainty wasn't what made her fizz. It was the heat in his eyes. Pure, unadulterated desire. Though unvoiced, somehow, she'd known what was on his mind, which wasn't like her at all.

Under normal circumstances, such an understanding would torment her anxiety, but this time was different. This time she was disgusted with her own body's reaction to the knowledge of his longing. Part of her wanted to skirt that desk, straddle his lap, and let actions say what words didn't. In her entire life, she had never been bold. She'd certainly never wondered what a stranger would look like naked or if he would let her touch, to trace his lines with her vocational fingertips.

Throwing the towel to the back of the couch, she drove her fists into her eyes trying to erase her own traitorous libido. For months, she hadn't been with a man… no, years. Did she still remember? Yes, the sensation of impotent frustration as her lover grunted and rutted over her for a few minutes before collapsing in a heap at her side. She wouldn't make a sound, and he wouldn't even notice.

Sorcha had said Sheppard was good-looking; Lacie was used to good-looking men. She was used to men of flash and no substance. Sorcha had told her Sheppard was useless in bed, so why was she thinking these thoughts? Sheppard was her friend's ex-lover. Lacie would never go there, not in a million years. Sheppard would have to compare them. If a man was used to prime venison like Sorcha, he'd never be satisfied with Lacie, the fast-food burger by comparison.

Except she'd never go there. The unspoken code wouldn't allow her to lust over her best friend's cast off. The man was shallow and not at all her type. Yet she closed her eyes again to relive the moment their eyes met over their joined hands. It was physical, visceral. So much more intimate than a handshake, but she didn't know what it was.

Sorcha was on vacation and would be until this was over. Her best friend had never been a good liar. She wouldn't want to be near her father, mother, or sister because she'd drop herself in it. No doubt about that.

Darkness formed around the gray clouds. Lacie figured she should think about eating. The thought of anything made her stomach roil. Descending to the floor, she lay flat on her back dropping a hand over her eyes. She liked the floor, she liked firm, unyielding surfaces that offered security and stability. The squeal of her phone came from within her purse that lay only inches away.

She reached over to retrieve it. The number on-screen was unfamiliar. Hello?"

"Miss Hart," the deep male voice sent a shiver down her spine. "I'm the investigator you spoke to this afternoon."

"Yes," she said, annoyed that her thoughts had somehow conjured him. "That was very quick. Have you found him?"

"I've got a couple of hits. But I can't ID him. Do you have a picture that you could send?"

"A picture," she said, lifting her torso to prop herself against the front of the couch. "If you give me the addresses, I can check them out for myself."

Amusement floated in his tone. "That's not how this works," he said. His voice had gone from drilling her deep to light-hearted. "You gave me a very big check today. I intend to earn it."

"I don't have a picture," she said. "Honestly, if you give me the addresses, I can check them out. If it's not him then I'll get in touch, and—"

"One address is relatively local," he said. "The other is not. I appreciate that you are hesitant to give me the details. But I won't send a woman such as yourself into unknown territory."

"Bruce isn't violent," she said, wondering what *"a woman such as yourself"* meant.

"Not the one you know maybe. But I could be giving you dud addresses and maybe those Bruces aren't as docile."

"That's a point," she conceded. "Is it your plan to go there?"

"To the addresses? Yes. But there's no point in me staking them out if I don't know who I'm looking for."

"I'll come with you," she said. No response. "We

might not know each other very well, but Sorcha trusts you, and I have no reason not to. It's about the only thing I can think that will solve the problem."

"This guy was your boyfriend?"

"I can assure you that you're not being drawn into a lovers tiff."

"That's not what concerns me," he said.

"What are your concerns?" she asked.

There was a pause before he asked, "When can you leave?"

"Ready when you are," she said.

"I can pick you up if you give me your address."

"That is very generous of you. I could meet you at your office if—"

"No," he said. "I'm not at work. If you're uncomfortable giving me your address—"

"It's nothing like that. Sorcha trusts you. I just wouldn't want you going out of your way on my behalf. If there are any expenses incurred—"

"I think your check today will cover everything. Give me your address." She did. "I'll be fifteen minutes."

FOUR

Lacie

IN FACT, he was nine minutes. A dark pick-up truck lumbered to the curb. He got out, but she was already running down the stoop from her communal entrance.

"You're on the first floor," he said, putting a hand to the small of her back to guide her to the truck.

"I would've thought you would drive something more inconspicuous."

"I go for comfort over discretion in cases like this. Space to stretch out can be an advantage."

He helped her up into the cab then rounded to his own side. In the time it took him to get in and start the engine, she looked around in wonder.

"This thing is huge."

"Size matters," he said, winking then pulling out of the space. "Are you ready to tell me what this guy did to you?

"It's not like that, it's… complicated."

"It's revenge or reconciliation," he said. "They are the only two reasons a woman wants to go after an ex. Sometimes it's compensation. Rarely. Most women let money stuff go; men chase the woman for that."

"You must see everything in your line of work," she said. "It's a fascinating insight to human character."

"Are you a psychologist or something?"

"No," she said, pushing her head back to the headrest only to find she barely reached it.

"So what do you do?"

"I'm a sculptor," she said.

"What?"

"I know. Most people don't understand it. I've been in love with shape, and form, and proportion all my life. I like angles and curves, planes, and ridges. Watching the clay take shape is what I love; it's what I've always loved."

"You can't make much money."

"Money isn't everything, Mr. Sheppard," she said. "But I've been lucky enough to draw some attention to my work. I've had a few wealthy patrons, and I have several commissions on going at the moment."

"So you don't need compensation from Booth… is it revenge?"

"Are my motives significant?" she asked.

"I don't suppose they are."

"How long have you been doing this?"

"A few years now," he said.

"Do you enjoy it?"

"I do. I like a good puzzle."

"Who is your typical client?"

"There isn't such a thing," he said. "We get all sorts. It's one of the good things about this line of work: the variety. We get a lot of couples, one trying to catch the other out, looking for proof of infidelity."

"Do you enjoy those cases?"

"I'm good at what I do which means I can pick and choose which cases I want to take. If I think something will go sour, I can turn it away. I'm not interested in helping damage anyone. But if you're doing something wrong, it's not my fault that you get caught, even if I am the one doing the catching."

"I can't imagine that."

"What?" he asked.

Lacie examined the dark sky around them. Their jet-black vehicle pierced the ink of night. Black chased black, perpetually enveloping and succumbing to each other.

"Being in a marriage where one party has to go to a third party to seek fault," she said.

"You're a romantic?"

"Oh no," she said, her smile stretching. When he glanced in her direction, the truck swerved out and her hands leaped for stability. His grip on the wheel tightened to bring them back into the correct lane. "Are you okay?"

"Yeah," he said.

"Are you sure?" she asked, placing her hand to his bare forearm. A static sting zapped her, and she snatched her hand away.

"You're electric," he said. Keeping his focus on the road, his knuckles turned white around the steering wheel. "If you're not a romantic, what are you?"

"I believe romance exists," she said. "Somewhere out there."

"Bruce doesn't romance you?"

"What about you?" she asked, deflecting his question.

"Not much time for romance in my line of work."

"It's sad, isn't it?" she said. "The world we live in. Everyone's so materialistic and practical. We ignore our instincts."

"I believe in instinct. Instinct has kept me alive."

"Alive?"

"Instinct is a requirement in the Marines."

"I had no idea," she said. "Sorcha never said anything… though I wasn't in the country while you two were together."

"Out of the country?"

"My family live in the UK," she said. "I was over there for a couple of months at the start of the year."

"But you live over here now?"

"Yes," she said. "I went to school here. Like I said, I was lucky enough to have support here."

"It must be difficult to be away from your family."

"Sometimes," she said. "But we talk regularly, and we email. I like my life. And I get my freedom over here."

"Freedom?"

"It's a long story," she said. "What about you? Do you have family?"

"Not much in the traditional sense. But I have colleagues I consider family."

"Do you miss her very much?" Lacie asked.

"Miss who?"

"I know you took the break-up hard. Sorcha is a dynamic and an alluring woman. Was it awful for you?"

"It might be best to stay off that subject," he said.

"Yes," she agreed. "Of course, I'm sorry. Do we have far to drive?"

"Another ten miles or so," he said. "Not long."

She nodded and took her attention outside again. Maybe talking wasn't so wise. She didn't want to like this man any more than she already did. To like him would be betraying a friend. Plus, she wasn't exactly being honest herself. The fewer lies she told, the better.

"You didn't tell me if it was revenge or reconciliation," he said, taking an exit and driving back toward streetlights.

"It's neither," she said. "Well, I suppose…"

"You don't sound very sure yourself," he said. "I don't see a man walking away from a woman such as yourself voluntarily. Did he steal something from you?"

"What does that mean?" she asked.

"What?"

"That's the second time you've said a '*woman such as yourself*,' what kind of woman am I?"

He signaled onto a busy road, and they drove for a few hundred yards. "You're beautiful."

"I would disagree, but that's not what you meant."

"How do you know?"

"The first time you said it was in relation to Bruce being violent, that has nothing to do with beauty."

"You'd disagree?" he said, wearing a frown. "You don't think you're beautiful."

"What I think is not important," she said.

Signaling again, he drove into a parking area in front of a three-story apartment block, each with its own terrace.

Pulling into a parking space, he killed the lights and engine, then brought all his attention around to her. "If you're not beautiful, what are you?" he asked.

"You haven't uncovered a deep seeded self-loathing. I don't think I'm ugly, but I wouldn't put myself anything above passable."

He scoffed a laugh. The light in his eyes was unthreatening this time, not desire, but… some kind of disbelieving joy.

"I almost crashed the truck back there because you smiled."

"Because I smiled?" she asked.

"Yeah, Dusty, the first time I see your smile, and I almost drove off the road. I've never crashed a vehicle in my life."

"I thought you had a tick."

"Not until I met you."

"Well," she said. "I'm not entirely sure what to say."

"Bruce never told you that you were beautiful?" he asked.

"No," she said. "I can certainly say he did not."

To process the exchange, she took her focus outward, so she hadn't anticipated his hand touching her face. He smoothed his thumb back and forth on her cheek to soothe her startled reaction to the contact. It left a fizzing trail in its wake. Only this time neither of them were surprised, this time she was ready for it. They both were.

"Bruce is a lucky guy."

The bubbles in her gut turned to lead. Pushing away from him, she plastered herself against the passenger door.

"Charming me won't distress Sorcha," Lacie said. "Men have tried it before."

"What?"

"She's moved on, Mr. Sheppard. I'm sorry."

"Sheppard," he muttered. His hand fell away, and his head hit the headrest with a thump.

"I am sorry," she said.

"Whatever," he said. "I'm going to take a look around. Wait here."

Shoving out of the car, he slammed the door, and the reverberation made her uneasy. Watching him stalk across the parking bays, she felt the sting of pity. Sorcha intoxicated men and Lacie had seen more than a few embarrass themselves when Sorcha ended their relationship. It was a shame for them, but it was a shame for Sorcha too.

Suitors would line up around the block yet none

of them measured up and Lacie usually had to agree with Sorcha's conclusions about potential futures with these men. Men wanted to parade her, they wanted to show her off, and eventually she would make someone the perfect trophy wife. Lacie didn't envy her friend's position.

Except choice had been blown out of the water for her friend. Lacie's pity welled. Sorcha would end up with Bruce because she wouldn't disappoint or embarrass her parents. The burden was unimaginable. A lot had been expected of Lacie too, but her parents would embrace her choices, even if they didn't agree with them.

Her parents had been mortified when she wanted to study in the US. Her uncle had married a woman from the States. At the time she moved, Lacie hadn't known them well. Lacie was sure to this day that her parents only consented because Aunt Elise agreed to look after her. Uncle Wilbur had died only a year after she'd moved, drawing her and Elise closer.

Sorcha's chance to choose her own suitor had been eliminated because of one careless choice. Sorcha could be reckless, but to find yourself pregnant had to be the epitome of poor sense.

How someone could be so overcome with passion was a complete mystery. Either she'd been doing it wrong this whole time or she just wasn't the type of woman that men lost their head over. She'd certainly never worried about being unprotected. In Lacie's experience, the very conversation about protection served as the sum total of foreplay.

The driver's door opened, startling her out of her reverie. "Come on."

"What?" she asked.

"I've got the apartment number. Come with me."

"You want me to come with you?" she asked.

"How else do you plan to ID this guy?"

"Oh, uh… I thought I could just look, you know, from afar."

"You want to find this guy, but you don't want to talk to him? What are you doing? Arranging a hit?"

"No!" she squealed. "Who knows what he's doing in there? What if he's with another woman?"

"Then he's in for a shock."

"Oh, God," she whispered, releasing her seatbelt, and slinking out of the truck.

Sorcha had assured her that she wouldn't need to see Bruce. But Sheppard was right, there was no good reason for her to refuse without telling him the truth, and she couldn't do that to Sorcha or to Sheppard. Clearly, he was still hung up on Sorcha. Lacie couldn't tell him that Sorcha was pregnant with another man's child or that she intended to marry him.

"What's the matter with you?" he asked.

He stood at the bottom of the stairs, and she was still slinking across the parking lot. This was awful. Bruce would think that she was insane, and he would be right. Why would your ex's friend hunt you down with a private detective who also happened to be another ex?

"What number is it?" she asked. "I'll go up myself."

"Like you said, this guy might not be happy to see you," he said, taking her arm to drag her up the stairs.

"I doubt he'll be any happier that I'm showing up with another man."

"He doesn't have to worry. If there was romance between us, Dusty, I wouldn't be taking you anywhere near any of your exes. I'd be clearing up any mess for you while you were safe in my bed a dozen miles from here."

His frown hadn't shifted. He focused straight ahead moving with a determined gait, yet for some reason Lacie was touched by the sentiment. Though she knew it wasn't specifically for her, it was nice to know that such fierce resolve to protect existed.

She was still going when he stopped, so she pinged back against him as though his gravity was a bungee rope connecting them. "Are you going to leave me here?" she asked when he lifted his hand to knock.

He stopped and looked down at her. "Do you want me to leave you here?" he asked. She shook her head without thinking her reaction would probably encourage more questions than she could answer. "Are you sure your ex isn't violent?"

"We don't even know if he's here."

"That wasn't the question I asked," he said.

That frown was still there. It read of a severe anger… and something else she couldn't identify. Her hand ascended, but she wasn't sure where it was going or what it was doing. There wasn't time to find out because the door he'd been about to knock on opened.

The man, in his late fifties, looked between the pair loitering outside his doorway. "Get away from my door if you want to get all gooey eyed over each other," he asserted. "I won't have this in our building. This is a respectable neighborhood."

"Do you live here?" he asked.

"No," the guy said. "I'm just here in my bathrobe at nine p.m. for kicks."

"The buzzer said Booth, and we—"

"That's me," the man said. "What is it? What do you want?"

"Sorry," he said. "We've got the wrong place. Sorry for the intrusion."

He didn't say anything else, just grabbed hold of her arm to pull her down the stairs, and brusquely boosted her into the truck.

"Where next?" she asked when he slammed into

the driver's seat.

"Put your seatbelt on," he said, screeching back out onto the road.

FIVE

Ryder

THIS WOMAN HAD been sent to him by Satan himself, she was a test, or a punishment for the wrongs he'd done in his life. Ryder couldn't fathom any other explanation. She just sat there stinking out the place with that fruity scent she exuded from every pore. His dick was past the point of aching. The sharp pain worsened every time she wriggled.

"Do you have any boiled sweets?" she asked. "Hard candy?"

"What?"

"I need something to suck on."

His knuckles cracked as he tightened his hold on the wheel and eased off the gas. His frustration made him want to speed up, but this woman had a habit of catching him off guard with the simplest maneuver. He doubted she'd want his suggestion of what she could wrap her mouth around.

"Well?" she said. "My mouth is dry. Do you have any—"

"Try the glove box."

She reached forward with those dainty fingers and popped open the compartment. His mind was on the fall of her hair when she screamed and bounced up in her chair pulling her feet up under her.

"Jesus!" he hollered and swerved them to the next lane between a couple of screeching cars blaring their horns.

He brought them to a lurching halt on the shoulder.

"Sorry," she said, panting with her hand against her heart. "I'm sorry. I'm really sorry."

"What the hell's the matter with you?" he demanded. "You don't scream like that when a guy is driving with the boner of the century! My mind ain't on the ball! You get it! Don't scream like that! What the hell happened?"

Though her hand remained over her heart, her attention was firmly on his lap. "I'm sorry," she said.

He cursed his revelation. "What is it?" he demanded.

The pulse point in her throat hammered. "Nothing, I just—"

"What is there a snake in there or something?"

He reached over and lifted the driver's manual to see the Beretta nestled in plain sight.

"No, I—I'm British."

Such a simple explanation, his anger dissolved, and he smiled at her. "You've never seen a weapon?"

"Of course I have," she said. "I watch movies."

"You don't have to worry. It's perfectly safe."

"I wasn't expecting it," she said. "I'm looking for a humbug and I come across that humdinger instead."

"It won't hurt you. I can show you how to use it sometime if you like. A woman should know how to defend herself."

"I have a rape alarm," she said.

"That's a good start. But chances are, if the guy is holding a gun, you're not going to get much of a chance to pull the pin."

"I love living in this country. There are so many ways in which your society is virtuous but…"

"You're not a fan of the second amendment."

"I believe in each to their own," she said.

Her feet slithered down from the seat; her shin made contact with his forearm because he was still holding the compartment flap. It slid across her knee to her thigh. Although she wore skinny jeans, the contact wasn't any less potent with a denim barrier. Or rather, he had to believe that it wasn't. The shock of awareness that bled to his every nerve had him sitting immediately upright again. Easing his hips down to try alleviating the pressure in his groin, he groaned and closed his eyes to the agony. It was all he could do to try to relieve it… baseball, burnt toast, England.

"Is that normal?" she asked.

When his eyes popped, he saw her looking at him with that tilted head innocence again. "The gun?"

"Your discomfort," she said. "You don't look happy."

"Let's just get on the road."

"Can I help?" she asked, and he groaned again. "I mean… do you take medication or something?"

"The kind of relief I need, you don't get on prescription."

He put the truck back into gear and slammed the glove box as he merged back into traffic.

"What were you looking for back there?" she asked a few minutes later. "When you left me here."

"Back door," Ryder said.

"What kind of back door?"

"It's always best to get the lay of the land when you don't know what you're walking into. If possible, you should always have at least two exit scenarios. It's a good idea to check for cover, which may also provide cover for others. It's good to know what you're walking into."

"Did you think he was going to hurt us?"

"I would have no way of knowing that," he said. "But it's worth preparing for the worst. There is also the possibility that your boy might want to make his own sharp exit."

"You think he was going to run from me?"

"I don't know anything," Ryder said. "I usually make more of an effort to interrogate or manipulate my clients into giving me specific information."

"But you just accepted my refusal to?"

"You're beautiful," he said. "Plus, I'd rather walk into the unknown than leave a woman such as yourself to walk in blind. If you're squeamish at the sight of a gun, I'd hate to think how you would react to someone attempting to physically hurt you."

"You did it again."

"Did what?"

"You said it, 'a woman such as yourself,' what does that mean? And it's nothing to do with my looks because you just referred to that as a separate entity."

"You're… do I have to answer that? Surely if I accept your refusal, you should accept mine."

Her laugh bred a smile and she nodded. "I suppose I should accept that as fair."

"Thank God for that," he said on his own smile.

Stealing glances at her, he managed to stay in lane and check out her smile. Knowing he'd put that happiness on her face made a ball of warmth form around his heart. The satisfaction at something so simple wasn't anything he'd experienced before.

"You know you're nothing like she said."

"Who?" he asked.

"Sorcha," she said, extinguishing the heat in his

chest. "When she told me about you I expected… something else."

"Every time we relax you bring up Sorcha. Maybe you and I should start afresh on our own… draw our own conclusions."

"Our business won't take long," Lacie said. "And it's nice to keep things in perspective."

"Meaning?"

"You're Sorcha's ex. I don't want to forget that."

Great, yeah, she didn't know who he really was. But it was worse than that. Because she thought he was her friend's ex, she would never let herself relax in his company. That meant she wouldn't be open to accepting him as a man making a play for her. In her view, Sorcha got there first. He could tell she was a woman of principle. And, in truth, he got it. He wouldn't go with any of his guys' exes.

"There's something I should tell you," he said ready to bite the bullet. They were in a vehicle in the middle of nowhere, which reduced the chance she would run away from him on spec… Reduced it but didn't eliminate it.

"What's that?" she asked apparently not hearing him because she was pointing to the stilled red lights burning the night on the road ahead.

"Traffic."

"It's not going very fast," she said as they rolled to a stop behind the car in their lane.

"It's not going anywhere at all," he said, pulling on the parking brake. "Wait here." Ready to leave the truck, she stalled him when her hands leaped to his forearm.

"You can't leave me here," she said.

"You'll be safe. If something scares you, hit the horn and I'll come right back," he said. "I won't be long."

"What if the traffic moves?"

"The keys are in the ignition."

"You want me to drive this?" she asked, looking around as though he'd just asked her to climb Everest.

"It's easy," he said. "Just like any other vehicle. I trust you… and it's insured."

"I'm British," she said.

"You have your license for here though, don't you?"

"Well, yeah but… we're not used to… size."

The corner of his lips curled. "You hang with me, you better get used to it."

Maybe he was throwing her in at the deep end, but he got out and walked away. When he was on the shoulder, he glanced back to see her clambering over the center console, turning on the internal light by mistake then rubbing her head. Once settled, she looked around at all the bells and whistles. She'd be fine.

SIX

Lacie

LACIE BEGUN to panic; he'd been gone for more than half an hour. All sorts of possibilities flitted through her mind. A car could have hit him. Maybe another driver's road rage got him into a fight or maybe he'd gone for something to eat and abandoned her.

While she sat there almost motionless, traffic piled up around her, packing them in from behind. She'd had to drive a small amount, a couple of feet at a time, though it took a while to get comfortable with controlling this mammoth.

The passenger door opened and he slid into the space she'd previously occupied. "See you're a natural," he said.

"You scared me," she said. "You've been gone for ages."

"It'll take us a few minutes, but if you can get onto the shoulder there's an exit about a mile and half up—"

"The shoulder?" she said. "We've moved ten feet in half an hour."

"There's a tanker spill," he said. "About eight miles down. It doesn't look like anyone will be going far for a while."

"You went eight miles in half an hour?"

"Didn't have to go that far," he said. "I met an official who gave me the information."

"Eight miles?" she said.

"I spoke to him a mile or so down the road."

"Is there another way?" she asked. "If we take the exit?"

"Might be," he said. "But I'm hungry. Are you hungry?"

"I suppose," she said.

"Let's get off this road and regroup, there's a steakhouse down there. What do you think?"

"Okay," she said. "But you should drive."

"I don't mind."

"I do," she said uncomfortable in the beast of a truck while its tamer sat there prone.

"Okay," he said. "Stay there."

In a flash, he was out of the vehicle, around it, and then the door at her side opened. He didn't give her the chance to exit, instead he lifted her out of the seat and across the center console into the seat he'd just vacated, and he'd done it as if she weighed the same as a bag of sugar.

"I would have been happy to get out," she said, reaching for her seatbelt to stop herself from looking at him.

"It's not safe out there on a highway like this."

"You went out in it."

"I'm not safe either," he said, getting them across and onto the shoulder much quicker than she would have.

They trundled down the shoulder at a steady, slow pace until they were on the exit slipway and free.

SEVEN

Ryder

THE STEAKHOUSE WAS next to a rest stop. They both ordered and ate while maintaining conversation. He'd told her about some cases he'd worked, keeping the details vague, and she'd laughed at his stories. The fact that she accepted everything he'd said brought him to the conclusion Sorcha hadn't disclosed too much about Sheppard's life.

At his mental reminder of the misidentification, Ryder stopped laughing at the joke she'd been telling about her aunt and the strawberry stain.

"Are you okay?" Lacie asked, covering his hand with her own. The air crackled, and he found himself once again cataloguing her every nuance and expression. "Did I upset you?"

"No," he said. "Sorry, I was thinking about something else."

"Is it because I mentioned Sorcha?" she asked. "Oh, I'm an idiot. I'm sorry."

"No," he said. "It's nothing about Sorcha. I'm

over that."

"You're over Sorcha?"

"Yeah," he said.

Cringing at the lie, he'd tried his best to avoid further deceit.

"You don't have to hide," she said with such sympathy the dinner he'd just eaten threatened to reappear. "It's okay. Sorcha and I have been friends for almost a decade. I've seen how losing her affects men like you."

"Like me?" he asked, jumping on her own previous question.

"Yes," she said, unfazed. "You're a good-looking man, you obviously have confidence, and strength, and a natural ability."

"A natural ability for what?"

"Drawing women in," she said. "Men like you are used to being coveted. It stings when someone rejects you, especially when that someone is Sorcha."

"You think a lot of your friend."

"I do," she said, sipping from her beer. "She's beautiful, and poised, and everything any man would look for. She deserves love." Lacie fidgeted with the corner of the napkin left on the table. "She's spent all this time looking for it and…"

"And?" he asked, sensing the depth behind what Lacie wasn't saying.

"Nothing," she said, pasting on a false smile. "Should we get back on the road?"

"It's late now. We're another couple of hours drive from the next address. Your friend likely won't be awake when we get there. I also can't guarantee what the roads will be like. Anyone avoiding the Interstate will be—"

"On the road we'll want. Okay."

"I'll take you home," he said, sliding to the end

of the booth while taking his wallet from his back pocket.

"I'll get this," she said, snatching up her purse. "It's not fair that you should cover expenses incurred while—"

"I had fun," he said, opening his wallet to pull out the bills needed to cover the cost of the meal. "This wasn't business." Her mouth opened, but from the way her eyes searched, he knew she had nothing to say. "Are you ready?"

On leaving the booth, she hooked her hand into his elbow and let him lead her outside. Now that they were used to the zing at physical contact, he got to like it. More than that, he liked that she wasn't afraid of it, or caught off-guard by it anymore.

"There's a motel," she said, pointing to the neon sign at the end of the lot. "Why don't we stay there?"

"I like a woman who's direct," he said, making her smile glitter again.

An ease had formed between them. Neither of them was unaware of the other nor had they dwelled on his last comment in the restaurant, which was good because he'd meant it.

"I'll pay for your room," she said. "It will save us waking up and starting the journey from scratch again. There was no point in driving this far just to turn back."

"If that's what you want, Dusty."

"Do you have other business?" she asked. He adjusted trajectory to head for the motel. "I would be happy to speak to your girlfriend and make her aware of the situation. I wouldn't want her to worry."

"I don't live with a girlfriend."

"Of course not," she said, shaking her head. "Do you live alone?"

"I live with my partner actually," he said then wanted to kick himself, he was supposed to be Sheppard.

"Oh," she said.

He didn't have to look at her to know she was smiling again. "Oh what?"

"Nothing," she said. Her free hand came up to cover her mouth as she averted her gaze to her feet.

"You can't say that with that look on your face and not explain yourself."

"Sorry," she said.

He halted in the shadow of the motel-office. "Tell me."

"I just…" she said, looking from left to right. "It kind of explains something that's all."

"Kind of explains what?"

"You're handsome, and you have appeal, and…"

"What?" he demanded.

She scrunched her expression. "Promise not to get angry?"

"I don't know," he said. "Tell me, and then we'll see."

"Sorcha mentioned the uh… the difficulty that you two had in bed, and I suppose if you don't swing that way—"

"Difficulty in bed?" he barked.

"Don't be offended," Lacie said, laying a hand on his chest, looking at him with that sympathy again. "Your sexuality is your business, and if you were going to test your heterosexuality with anyone Sorcha would be the prime candidate. Any man who isn't pleased by her must have an underlying reason."

Sheppard hadn't pleased Sorcha. Now the woman who'd plagued his mind, and his pants, all night believed he was gay and lousy in the sack. As Ryder formulated a response, his impatient body took over and stepped closer to urge her against the concrete motel-office wall. Her surprised gasp brought her chin up, giving him the perfect chance to capture her inhale with his mouth.

Her lips parted in the surprise; he used the opportunity to sweep his tongue against hers. Her rigid body relaxed at the same time those fingers on his chest curled into the cotton of his tee-shirt. This was primal, all instinct. Hot and wet, their mouths danced, testing texture, taste, resistance.

Laying a hand on the wall above her head, he pressed his weight to hers earning himself a desperate mew from her ravenous throat. That delectable little body pushed up, so he crouched to meet her unspoken demand, bringing them nearer to each other. Whatever had crackled between them now combusted. A growl rumbled from within him, he pushed deeper; lips, tongues, teeth clamored in desperation to mate, to be joined and never parted.

Someone nearby laughed. "Get a room!"

Ryder tore himself away, shamed at taking her so thoroughly in such a shadowy, squalid setting. The trouble was his eyes wouldn't focus. The hand he had on the wall above her head wasn't enough to keep him upright. So he rested the other on her waist; some of her weight shifted to him. Although his body still pinned hers, she was as in need of an anchor as him.

Blinking back to reality, he sought those plump, pillowy lips now red and swollen after his attack. Gritting his teeth, he tried to quell the animal in him that wanted to complete the transaction right there. Her eyes weren't open yet, she was suspended as though in wait for part two.

Sliding his hand from the wall, he touched her cheek with the back of his fingers. Obviously, she was having as much trouble with re-entry to reality.

"I want to have sex with you," she whispered.

His shoulders straightened. He wondered if he hadn't fallen somewhere, hit his head, and tumbled into his perfect fantasy. If he had, he didn't want to wake up.

"I like honesty in a woman," he said.

Still stroking her face, his other hand slid up her waist. Hooking the hand behind her shoulder against the wall, he drew her into his arms.

"That's bad," she murmured.

"Baby, it's okay."

Her eyes popped open, stricken with grief and horror. "No," she said. "No, it's not."

"It's okay."

Keeping her body trapped between his and the wall was meant to keep them grounded. Right now, he was floating with her. His entire universe became about those wide green eyes and the silent whispers from those engorged lips.

His mind and his body hadn't reengaged communication. He lowered his head and kissed her again. Softly, hiding the passion that bubbled between them, she needed comfort, and reassurance. She let him kiss her like that, like a boyfriend who'd kissed her a million times before, as though it was the most normal thing in the world for him to press his lips to hers.

"This has never happened to me," she confessed. His hand moved from her face to her hair. The impulse to touch her was automatic; it was so all encompassing that he was overwhelmed with the urge just to be, just to exist with this woman.

"It's okay," he said again. "We'll take our time."

"No," she said, shaking her head. "No. We can't. But… you don't understand."

"Tell me."

His lips touched her temple, her brow, her hairline.

"I've never wanted to go to bed with a man before," she said. "I've never…"

His hand was still on the wall hooked behind her shoulder. He shifted it further around her to pillow her head against his knuckles rather than the concrete wall. The maneuver had the bonus of bringing her chest flusher with his.

"Are you telling me you've never—?"

"No," she said. "I've had sex. I just… it's been something they've wanted."

"You've never felt desire?" he asked. "Passion for a partner?"

She shook her head. Her silken hair rubbed his knuckles; he parted them to let the strands tickle between his digits.

"I'm flattered," he said. "I've known it since the moment I met you."

"What?"

"That I want to take you to bed."

"That's why it's so sad," she said, blinking those imploring eyes.

"Sad," he said. "It's not sad. I'm not only interested in using you for sex if that's what you think."

"That's not what I think."

"I'm not gay—"

"I noticed," she whispered.

She managed a smile then drew her lower lip between her teeth, which made him want to mimic the action.

"I'm not involved."

"We can never… I can't believe the first time I start to understand what all the fuss is about and it's… never mind."

Pressuring her palms to his chest, she wanted him to release her, but he wasn't ready to move yet.

"We don't have to jump straight in the sack," he said. "This feeling won't go away. It'll get better with the more time we spend together. We can get to know each other and see where this goes."

"You're trying to look after me," she said,

relaxing her arms again. "Why do you do that?"

"What?"

"Look after me," she said. "You buy me dinner. You won't let me out of the car on the road because it's dangerous. You went to check out the block before we went inside, and you wouldn't give me the addresses in case they were dangerous. Why do you look after me?"

"You're special," he said. "Don't ask me to explain it because I can't. You're hard on yourself but see the best in people. I have a feeling you've been used to standing on your own two feet for a while. You're not used to deferring to anyone. You look after yourself, and yet… there's an innocence about you, you let people take advantage of you far too easily."

"It's such a cruel irony," she said then took a deep breath, further crushing her breasts against his chest.

"Irony?"

"That the one man I finally find myself interested in isn't available."

"I'm available, baby," he said.

"Not to me."

"Because of Bruce?"

"Bru… no, not because of him."

"You don't have to fear me. I'll prove myself. You don't have to take Sorcha's…" and just like that he understood. "You won't date me," he said. She shook her head. "Because of Sorcha."

"She's my best friend," Lacie said. On another deep breath, her body sagged. "It's late."

She eased him away and he couldn't do a thing to stop her. If he told her the truth now, she'd run a mile for sure. She probably wouldn't believe him because if Sheppard had been here now instead of him, Ryder would guarantee that Sheppard would lie. Shep would say anything to get a woman he wanted into bed.

Ryder clenched his fists. An uncharacteristic flare of rage bolted through him. Normally he'd just avoid Sheppard, and usually he felt more shame for the loser than anger. Sheppard played women, but he didn't discriminate. Shep would play anyone to better his own ends.

"I'm going to get a room and take a long bath," she said. "Will I see you here in the morning?"

"I'm not going to ditch you."

He took his truck keys from his pocket and held them toward her, but she only looked at them. Taking her hand from her side, he dropped the keys to her palm then curled her fingers around them.

Ryder edged in the direction of the motel-office door. "I'll go in and get two rooms next to each other."

"No one knows we're here. I hardly think there will be any trouble—"

"People don't expect trouble," he said. "Do you know where you are? Do you know the area?"

"Well, no, but—"

"I don't know it well enough," he said. "I'll get the rooms."

"No, I'll get my—"

"It's covered," he said, going for the office door, but she kept his hand.

"You're doing it again."

"What?" he asked pleased to see her discomfort fade and her smile return.

"Looking after me."

He brought the petal soft skin of her knuckles up to his lips. "Stay in the window where I can see you."

EIGHT

Lacie

THE FOLLOWING MORNING, Lacie had just put her feet in her shoes when there was a knock on the door. Hooking her bag over her head, she opened it to see her companion holding a white tee-shirt and a cardboard tray with two cups bearing a coffeeshop logo.

"You brought coffee," Lacie said.

His eyes were covered with reflective aviators, but his lips turned upward. "Do you want one?"

Moving backward, she let him into her motel room then closed the door behind him. "Thanks. Were you paying enough attention at dinner to remember how I take my coffee?"

"Just milk," he said. "I'm a detective."

"True."

"You shouldn't do that," he said, setting the tray on the unit by the TV.

"Do what?" she asked, taking the cup he'd twisted from the tray.

"Open the door when you don't know who is on the other side of it."

"You're the only person who knows I'm here."

"Which should make you more careful," he replied.

"I think if you were going to attack me, you'd have done it last night."

"I sort of did," he said. "But anyone seeing you walk in here knows you're here. You don't have to know them personally for them to want to get in."

"You were just through the wall. What's the tee-shirt for?" she asked, noticing that the tee-shirt he wore that day was charcoal instead of the black he'd worn last night.

"I didn't know if you'd want to change today," he said, holding it toward her.

"You bought it for me?"

"I didn't buy it. I always have a few essentials in the truck."

"You want me to wear your tee-shirt?"

"Your call," he said then reached behind him into his back pocket to produce a still sealed toothbrush.

"You are prepared aren't you," she said, taking the brush. "Will you wait for me?"

When he nodded, she went toward the bathroom but paused when a thought struck her. Sure enough, when she picked up her purse, the truck keys he'd handed her last night were still there. Holding them in her palm, she spun to present them to him with the question in her countenance.

"Yeah," he said. "Quite a novelty breaking into your own vehicle. I appreciated the chance to polish my skills."

"You could have come here for them."

"That would've taken the sheen off my generosity."

She tutted and threw them to him, he caught them without thought. "I'll be two minutes."

NINE

Lacie

THEY GOT ON the road not long later and stopped at a drive-thru for breakfast. He'd commented that most of the women he knew didn't eat breakfast. Lacie wasn't sure if she should take his observation as an insult or not.

The day was glorious. Sun baked through the windscreen and white fluff-ball clouds meandered across the blanket of blue behind them.

"It has rained every day this month," she said. "I wonder why today is so glorious."

"Maybe it's the company," he said, which earned him a smile.

"We should put on some music," she said. "Do you have any CDs?"

"CDs? What century are we in? My iPod is in the duffel bag behind my seat."

Leaning back a little, she rolled her seat into a bit more of a recline to see the black bag he referred to. "Do you mind if I…?"

"Knock yourself out," he said.

"Are there any guns in there?" she asked him.

"Are you planning to shoot me?"

"No, but I would hate to do it by accident, especially with you being the driver and all."

One side of his mouth slid up, and she was overcome with the urge to taste that corner which was pleased with her comment. She wasn't sure if he had said anything, but when he glanced at her once, then took another look, the other side of his mouth joined the first.

"What are you looking at?" he teased.

"Hmm?"

"That look, what is that look for?"

"I was thinking about your mouth," she said absently.

Her head still swam with the notion as she relaxed into the cradle of her seat.

"Were you now," he said. "Anything in particular?"

"Nothing I should say out loud," she whispered.

When he glanced her way again, she smiled. "You shouldn't stop speaking your mind now."

"My mind can get me into trouble."

"Not with me," he said. "I like your mind a lot. A lot."

She continued her scrutiny of his profile even after his long-fingered hand squeezed her knee, then relaxed slightly further up closer to her inner thigh.

With the gentle rocking motion of the truck, her eyelids grew heavier over the next few minutes. Secure in the knowledge his attention was on the road, she kept examining him.

"You offer a very comprehensive service," she said.

His lips twitched up before he laughed, a deep rumble from somewhere in his chest. The vibration traveled through his fingers to her thighs. Squeezing her legs closer, she trapped his fingers between them, making their connection all the more intimate. But he didn't move his hand, in fact he increased his grip either to show her he meant to stay the course, or to stop himself from moving higher still.

"My comprehensive behavior with you has nothing to do with any service, at least not any I charge for."

"I'm not rich, you know."

"What do you—"

"The check," she said. "If you think that I'm rolling in—"

"You think I'm interested in your money," he said, digging his fingers into her flesh.

"I didn't say that. But Sorcha told me how you—"

"I thought we were starting afresh," he said. "You and me, no assumptions."

"I shouldn't flirt with you the way I just did. What I said last night still stands."

His phone on the center console began to buzz. Silently, he cursed and switched lanes until he hit the shoulder. On stopping the truck, he answered the phone.

"Yeah," he said into the device.

Lacie reached behind the driver's seat and managed to get the bag open. She took the time to be careful because he hadn't answered her question about guns. Maybe if there was music on, she wouldn't feel the need to fill the silence, and therefore could stop herself from flirting with him.

Flirting wasn't usually in her nature. But he was different, or maybe this was different. Lacie didn't know why, but an ache in her chest linked to her thigh, which now felt cold and abandoned without the weight of his hand. While his words into the phone might have been quiet and non-specific, they were adamant.

Groping under the towel and first aid kit in the duffel bag, Lacie rummaged until she found a box shape. Assuming the iPod must be in a case, she pulled it out only to shower a dozen condoms all over them in the front seat.

"Oh," she exclaimed.

He picked a couple from his leg, and though she tried to be contrite, he grinned. "I've got to go, something's come up."

He didn't wait another moment to disconnect the call.

"I'm sorry."

"Don't be," he said, resting his elbow on the shoulder of his seat to sweep her hair from her face. "All you had to do was ask."

"It was an accident."

"I know."

"What do you have all of them for anyway?"

"Like I said, I like to be prepared."

His fingers ran into her hair. They slipped to the back of her head and angled her to meet his mouth. The kiss that they'd shared last night was such an anomaly that she was sure she dreamed the whole thing in a drunken stupor. Which was sort of wishful thinking, given she'd only had one beer.

"What was that for?" she asked.

He kissed each corner of her mouth then her jaw. "I was thinking about your mouth," he murmured then once again pressed his mouth to hers.

Familiarity bred between them, Lacie couldn't explain it. She barely understood what was happening. When his tongue touched the seam of her lips they opened automatically, as though she had granted him entry dozens of times before.

"We should get on the road," she said. His other hand found her hip and skimmed upward to where she had tied his tee-shirt at her waist. "And we shouldn't do that again."

"Okay," he said, taking his time examining her body.

Lacie couldn't imagine that it looked much different to how it had when she'd come out of the motel bathroom this morning. When she glanced down to decipher what held his intent interest, she gasped. The heavy ache in her breasts climaxed in a sharp, tingling sensation where her skin met the soft cotton of his tee-shirt. The illusion that the sensation was only in her mind was shattered by the clear outline of her hard nipples lilting up toward him, begging the care he'd given her mouth.

"May I?" he asked.

"What?" she panted.

But his mouth had shifted lower to kiss her chin. She was so caught off guard that his trek down her throat sent her head backward, thrusting her chest up for attention, which he gratefully gave.

"Oh my God!" she squeaked when he breathed her in through the fabric.

Lacie snatched at the back of his head. Although she hadn't intended to, her fingers curled into his hair, holding him firm. She didn't know if she wanted him to stay or leave. His growl told her how he interpreted the act. Her fingers twisted deeper of their own volition. With her free hand, she braced against the door to keep herself in place when his teeth nipped at her.

Her eyes rolled back in her head. "Oh God," she whispered.

His hand took the position of his mouth when he moved over to spoil her other breast with the same attention. Wriggling back in her seat, she squeaked again. This was wrong, all wrong, but it felt absolutely incredible. A thought flashed in her mind. Like a flood of ice-water down her back, her eyes opened to frigid reality.

"Did you do this with Sorcha?" she asked surprised at how husky her voice came out.

His mouth left its post, but he remained in her cleavage. Desire fogged his eyes, but she could see something else, anger maybe, or hurt. Sharply, he sat up. Her whole body screamed for his return.

Glaring out of the front windshield, he drove his fingers through his hair a few times. Biting her lip, Lacie didn't know what to say. Her impulse was to placate, except she couldn't apologize. Her thought had been honest. She couldn't console him because she was fixed in her loyalty to Sorcha, no matter how gray things had been moments ago.

"We should go," she said.

The traitorous tingle remained inside her. For some reason, her desperation beseeched him to look at her. He didn't.

He slammed the car into gear, and with one glance at the lanes, he screeched out onto the road. The condoms shot around the car every which way. To conceal the burn in her eyes, Lacie tried to gather those of them that she could reach. She'd disappointed him, but she was a disappointment to herself. She would be to Sorcha too, if her friend ever learned what had gone on between them. Lacie couldn't work out why this was so difficult, but it was.

TEN

Lacie

THEY WERE ON the road again, but the ease that had cocooned the journey before their pause was gone. As they neared their destination, the cotton wool clouds had become decidedly gloomy. Gray clouds grew thicker. By the time they took the exit toward denser population, thunder rumbled above. The temperature in the cab hadn't changed, yet a chill swept through. She wrapped her arms around herself, in hope that when she rubbed her skin, she'd generate heat.

The urban area seemed to be mostly dilapidated. Groups of kids who should be at school gathered on corners near convenience stores, or in dumpster-filled alleys, taunting the hobo's huddled in their damp cardboard dwellings.

"Are we close?" she asked.

"Just at the end of the street," he answered flatly.

"This doesn't seem like the type of place Bruce would hang around."

"Do you want to forget it?"

"We're here now," she said, prickled that he wouldn't look at her or address her with familiarity. She'd built the dam, she couldn't complain that he was respecting it. "Do you think it's him?"

"I don't know him."

"So? I don't—"

"Listen, I'm hoping for you, baby. I've got my fingers crossed. This guy just signed a new lease a couple of weeks ago, and he paid six months up front. I'll get you back to your lover-boy. Be patient."

"Seth," she said.

He pulled his arm away from her reach to steer into a parking spot and killed the engine. "I'm going to look around."

"You're going to leave me here?"

"Just for a minute."

"Seth—" she started, but he was out of the truck before the word was finished.

A blue plastic bag swept into the street, then spun in the air as it was caught in the eddy of a passing car. Her legs were stiff, her shoulders ached, and the air around the cab was stale.

From experience she knew the recce could take some time, so she popped the handle and eased out, stretching her toes to the concrete. Her legs sprang back to life, eager for the exercise she gave them now.

After pacing the length of the car a couple of times, she ventured toward the corner a few yards away. The air was thick and muggy. A sticky heat clung to her limbs, pushing her chest, constricting her. She felt deprived of the fresh, clean air she'd craved while stuck in the car.

Just as Lacie decided to return to their sanctuary, a shadow swept past her, and that chill returned. Looking back to the path she'd abandoned, she saw nothing. Now she couldn't get back to the vehicle fast enough. When she turned, she was met with a wall of tee-shirt clad male chest. She got as far as the gasp of air on the wave of an oncoming scream when she saw his bullet stern eyes.

"Don't do that!" she exclaimed, smacking his chest.

"Didn't I tell you to stay in the car?" he griped.

"No," she said, finding herself once again in his grip so he could drag her down the street. "Actually, you didn't."

"I did yesterday."

"That was yesterday."

"Until otherwise notified, consider my authority as absolute, and all orders remain current."

"Orders," she said.

Sandwiching her between him and the truck, he yanked her to a halt. "I come down that alleyway and you're not in the car, do you know what I think?" He didn't give her time to respond. "I think, where is my gun? I think, is she hurt? Does she need me? I have to get to her."

"You thought all that in those few seconds?"

"Damn it, Lace—"

"It's okay," she said, lifting her weight from the car. "I'm okay."

In the few seconds that followed, she read a dozen more questions in his eyes, but he didn't give them voice. "Let's get this over with."

On the way to the communal door, which was held open by a bare brick, he moved fast. So fast that she had to run to catch him up. She tried to snag his hand to slow him down, to ask for comfort in the bleak surroundings, but he snatched it away and took the concrete stairs two at a time until they reached the third floor.

"Seth," she called when they started down the stained hallway.

A barking dog, and a crying baby each vied for the attention Lacie sought, but her guide was already banging on a door. When she got to him her intention had been to speak, but he stepped away and thrust her in front of him right in the frame of the door. When there was no response, he reached over her head and banged on the door again. The dog's barking rose once more.

The door opened so suddenly that she almost fell backward, but she came up short against his chest. The man who opened the door was tall but skinny and his ice blue eyes dragged over her figure. She regretted not untying her tee-shirt from her waist because he certainly seemed to linger over her exposed midriff. A belly button wasn't something she'd ever thought to be self-conscious about. His tongue rolled out as he leered, and he could just as easily have been ogling her bare breasts.

"What can I do for you, Sweet-Cheeks?"

Either this stranger hadn't seen the man at her back, or the man she relied on had abandoned her. She didn't want to turn and check for fear that the ogler would take liberties while her eyes were averted.

"I'm looking for someone," she said.

"You just found him, Sweet-Cheeks. I'll be anything you want me to be."

"No, he's a friend—"

"Come on in," the stranger said. "I'm visiting. The man you're looking for is just in here."

He beckoned her inside. Despite not liking how he ogled her, she had no reason to refuse his invitation. So Lacie went into the apartment keeping her eyes front. The stranger went to close the door, but from the thump behind her, she assumed her travel companion was inviting himself in too. She couldn't say she was sorry he was at her back.

Of the two doors in front of her, Lacie didn't know which to choose, but she didn't have to wait long for an answer. The door on the left opened revealing two more men, one short and stocky, the other black and bulky.

"Lookie! Now there's a party!" the stocky guy said.

"Guess your wish came true, Jed," the black man said, nudging his friend. "You wanted fun last night, and look it's come looking for you."

An arm lolloped over her shoulders, propelling her toward the two men backing away from the internal door. In the new room, daylight seeped through the makeshift curtains: fuzzy blankets taped to the walls. Immediately, Lacie wanted to leave when she saw that there were five other men there, taking the total to eight. No Bruce in sight. The gang took one look at her and were on their feet in an instant.

"I don't think—" she started.

"Don't panic, Sweet-Cheeks, we'll take care of you," the guy with his arm over her shoulders said. The men moved closer, circling around to come at her from all angles. "Won't we, boys?"

A thwack made her spin. The group closed in on her, separating her from her travel companion, who, it appeared, had just dealt a punch to one guy. Another approached from his back and hit him with the butt of a gun. When the blood sprayed, Lacie screamed. But when she tried to run toward her friend, she was lifted off her feet, and suddenly they were going in opposite directions. The gang were taking her friend away, and she had no idea if he was unconscious or worse. Now she was alone.

ELEVEN

Ryder

CURSING HIMSELF for the amateur mistakes didn't help Lacie, who was out there alone. When he'd regained consciousness, he was in a room with bare floorboards, and nothing else. The cable ties around his wrists were attached to the cast iron radiator behind him.

He had no idea how long he'd been out. From the moment he'd opened his eyes, he'd tried to fathom his bearings. He'd been shocked back to reality by the sound of her terrified scream, which still shuddered up his spine. From that moment, he'd bloodied his wrists trying to liberate himself, only to discover that the cable ties were simply the first line of defense, a solid metal chain also held one wrist in place.

Ryder had counted eight of the lowlifes, but he had no way to gauge developments during his unconsciousness. The scum made no secret of what they wanted. Lacie would have no way of stopping them from taking it.

She screamed again and Ryder smacked his head

back against the radiator. The stinging reminder of the bloody welt his captors had given him didn't make him regret the deed; he deserved to be in pain. He would never be able to give Lacie back what the gang would take from her. No one would.

A scuffle came, and a shout, then a moment of silence. His blood chilled. Could they have taken it too far? Had she fought too hard? Could her torment be over in the worst possible way? After another shout there was some background noise that he couldn't identify.

Not being able to figure out what was happening frustrated him especially as the sound came closer and he didn't know what to prepare for. As he strained to hear, his eyes were blinded when the door opened unexpectedly.

Ryder didn't see anyone or anything, then she was thrown in, and the door slammed again. Her body remained motionless. She lay there on the floor, saying nothing, her face averted from him. Certain he could see the rise and fall of her chest, he convinced himself that she was okay, alive at least. But the longer she lay there silently, the more he worried he was imagining things.

"Lace," he said. "Lacie, baby, look at me. Come on now, baby, come on."

Her bent knees straightened at an excruciating pace then she flopped to her back, but he still couldn't see her properly, not with the lack of light.

"Are you okay?" she whispered. Her voice was hoarse. It pained him to know what had caused that trauma to her throat: she'd been screaming for her life.

"Me?" he asked. "Yes, I'm fine. Come over here, please, baby."

"I'm fine."

He didn't believe her. "Whatever they did to you, I swear I'll make them pay each and every one of them."

"Stop looking after me," she murmured without

moving a muscle.

"I failed when it counts, baby. I swear to you, baby—"He stopped when she dragged her torso up using only her core muscles.

"I was so scared that they'd hurt you," she said. "I didn't know where you were, or what they were doing, and I—"

"Lacie, stop it, please." Her tee-shirt was no longer tied, and though her back was angled toward him, he saw her pick up the hem and wipe her mouth. "Look at me."

When her hand fell away from her face, he knew she was considering his request. The room was empty except for them, she had to have heard him. This time was crucial. He couldn't let her pull away from him. She needed to know she had an ally, even if he'd been useless to her when it mattered most.

Slowly, she turned, wiping the back of her hand across her mouth. In his years of service, and his years since, he'd seen atrocities. But that beautiful face, the innocence of those eyes he'd witnessed for the first time yesterday, shocked him more than anything he'd seen in the past. Dark blood was swiped across her chin and a bruise already marred her cheek. He didn't miss the swollen egg forming at her hairline either.

"My God," he breathed. Again, she used the tee-shirt to wipe her mouth. When she lifted the material, she uncovered thick red lines on the delicate skin across her taut body. "What did they do to you?"

Her tangled hair shielded her face when she dropped her attention down. It lingered there increasing his apprehension. He didn't want her feeling any shame or guilt. Setting his focus on begging her to look at him, he opened his mouth. But in that same second her hands hit the floor, she crawled toward him. She didn't stop and came all the way to him until she sat in the vee of his thighs, and nestled her head under his chin, pressing her cheek to his chest.

"I'm sorry, baby," he murmured, kissing her hair.

Her legs stretched flat on the floor under his bent knee while his other knee provided her back support. A yell grew within him. In this state he could offer her no support. Holding her was impossible because of the ridiculous restraints on his wrists. He'd kill them. He'd kill them all. Turning his mouth against her again, he rubbed his cheek to her forehead hoping she would look at him.

When his gaze fell, he saw that the snap was off her unzipped jeans. "I'll kill them," he growled.

"I want to go home."

"I know, baby. I'll keep you safe. I swear, I'll never let you down again."

"Bruce is here," she whispered.

"He let them—"

"Not much he could do," she said. "He came in with another man a few minutes ago. They were wearing suits, respectable like."

"Did he recognize you?"

"I don't know," she said. "The man he came in with went crazy at the other guys. He said they'd compromised things."

"I don't care about them. I care about you. Did they touch you? Did they…?"

"The blood isn't mine," she said. "I bit him." She nestled closer. Wrapping her arms around him, she linked his detained hands with her free ones. "I warned him I would."

"You bit him," he said, feeling an odd burst of pride.

"I warned him," she said. "One of the others tried to get at me first, but there was an argument, and… I spat at the one trying to get into my jeans, so he hit me.

The other guy laughed but his friend… took off his belt and used it to…"

Understanding hit him when he married her statement with the long red welts he'd seen. "I'll kill them all."

"They're going to kill us," she said. "I made them so angry. I'm sorry I've made things worse and—"

"No," he said, using his chin to try to bring her attention up. "Look at me." Despite obvious reluctance, she eventually did, but seeing her injured face churned his rage to a primal wrath. "You fought. I am so proud of you, baby. You're a fighter."

"They're going to hurt us," she said.

Those glorious eyes, once filled with pure virtue, filled with tears she didn't want to shed.

Her lower lip quivered. When the sob escaped, she tried to take her eyes away, but he couldn't let her, she had to know that he was there with her. On impulse, he trapped her mouth under his. Maybe it wasn't the wisest thing to do after what she'd been through, but she welcomed him, pushing her body upward to get closer. She kissed him one way, then tilted her head the other to do it again.

Her hands ascended his back and went through his hair until she held his face in her palms. The force of her kiss pushed his head back against the metal behind him. She rose to her knees, urging herself closer, consuming him in desperation. Her body pressed to his as though she wanted to climb into his skin. If he could have delivered for her there and then, he would have.

A click came from the far side of the room. Both heard it simultaneously; she stopped kissing him. They breathed in time, their eyes holding the conversation their mouths couldn't. A splinter of light sent her spinning around, seating herself against him, her back to his front. Her hands splayed on his thighs as though she meant to protect him. The woman was a wonder, he'd let her down and yet she was getting herself between him and trouble and he was the one with the training.

The streak of light widened; all took time to adjust to the disparate illumination.

Lacie gasped on identifying the new entrant. "What the hell are you doing in here?" she snapped.

She was on her feet that Ryder only then noticed were bare.

"Lacie, it is you."

"Yes, it is me," she said, striding toward the door as though the soft woman who'd come apart against him was nothing more than a figment of his imagination. "What kind of company are you keeping these days, Bruce?"

"Don't shout," Bruce said, creeping around the door with his hands outstretched toward her.

"Lace," Ryder growled, unhappy that anyone was going to put their hands on her again.

Lacie apparently didn't share his concern because she had no fear of this new guy.

"Who's your friend?" Bruce asked.

"None of your business," she said. "What are you doing? What did you get yourself mixed up in?"

"What are you doing here?" Bruce asked, ignoring her questions. "These guys are for real; you could get yourself hurt."

"No shit," she said. "They're your friends."

"They are not my friends," he said. "I left town for a reason… How is Sorch?"

"Typical," Lacie tutted. "Do you think you can just erase the last three months?"

"Just tell me how she is," Bruce implored.

Lacie tipped up her chin and thrust her hands to her hips. "You don't want to know."

"Yes, I do," he said. "Please… is she here?"

Ryder processed the conversation and wanted to smack himself in the face. Lacie was here for Bruce but not for herself. Bruce was Sorcha's ex… she'd lied to him.

"No," Lacie said. "She's not here. Give me your pocketknife."

"What?" Bruce asked.

"The little Swiss thing you carry."

"How do you know I—"

"You opened the wine with it on Sorcha's birthday."

"If those guys—"

"Look at me, Booth," she said. "What do you think Sorcha's going to say when she hears about my day?"

"You can't tell her. You can't tell her I'm here. They'll hurt her."

"What is going on?" she asked. Bruce fumbled with something from his pocket and Lacie snatched it away from him. Without pause, she brought it to the wrist restraints. "What are you doing here, Bruce? Who are these people?"

"I left for a reason," Bruce said. "I left to keep Sorcha safe. They need me."

"Money," Ryder said. After Lacie slit the cable ties, despair flitted to her expression at the sight of the chain. Ryder took the knife from her and flicked out another attachment to use on the padlock. "You're working for them."

"What?" Lacie gasped, turning from her crouch to look at Bruce. "How could you—"

"We don't care," Ryder said, pulling Lacie to her feet at his side. Using the knife, he slit the edge of the blanket over the window to survey what he could of the street. At the same time, he linked his fingers between hers. "How many of them are still in there?"

Bruce answered. "The boss went to pick up a shipment, there are three guys in—"

"Fantastic," Ryder said, closing the knife and putting it into his own pocket.

When he started for the exit, Lacie pulled him back. "We can't go out there," she said.

"I won't let them hurt you."

"And what about you?" she asked. "You can't ask me to watch you get hurt again."

"Trust me," he said overjoyed that he could touch her again.

Lifting his hand to her cheek, she rubbed it against his palm only to freeze on noticing the state of his wrist.

"Oh my God," she said, reaching for the wound, but he pulled it away from her.

"Later," he said. "We'll fawn over each other later. Right now, I'm getting you out of here."

"If they know I was in here…" Bruce stuttered.

"Do you want me to beat you a little?" Ryder probed, silently begging the guy to agree.

"No one is hitting anyone," she said. "Your boss wanted rid of me. He was pissed I was even here. Just tell them I slipped out."

"He doesn't know about your friend," Bruce said.

"Good," she said. "Don't tell anyone."

"We're leaving," Ryder said and tried again to pass Bruce.

"I won't let them hurt you," Lacie said, planting her feet wide. "They can take whatever the hell they want from me. But I won't see you hurt. You're here because of me."

No one had ever defied him so totally and completely like this. Certainly no woman. Ryder could read the determination in her eyes. She really would let all those guys out there do whatever they wanted to her just to keep him safe. But that was his job.

He touched her again, warmed by her sentiment, but time now was for action. They'd appreciate each other when he could lock the door behind them and keep her safe in his bed. Ducking down, he tossed her over his shoulder. She screeched and punched at his back. If he had to fight with one hand on her pert little butt, then he would. Without restraints, there was nothing keeping him from protecting her. He'd meant what he said, he wouldn't let her down again. Never again.

"What's going on?" someone shouted.

She instantly went limp. "Put me down, I'll help you," she said. "I'm sorry."

"Not a chance, Dusty," he said and kissed her outer thigh.

Only one of the guys came at him. The other two were too surprised that he was bloodied, she was battered, yet they still had the confidence to fight with each other despite circumstances.

With one punch, he dispelled with the toad who came at him. One watched from the couch as the other rolled a reefer. Bruce was nowhere in sight. Ryder wasn't waiting. He ripped open the unlocked front door and took them down the corridor to the truck, which shockingly was still there, and still unlocked.

He tossed her into the back then rounded to the driver's seat. He didn't wait. He dug the spare key out from under the seat and put the pedal to the floor. They were free again, only an hour or so had passed since they'd entered that place, but everything was different. Nothing in his life would ever be the same after his road trip with Lacie Hart. This woman was… his.

TWELVE

Ryder

THE JOURNEY HOME seemed shorter than their outward trek despite his careful driving. Keeping within the speed limit and being courteous to other drivers may be the last things his adrenaline riddled body wanted to do, but he had a head wound and a battered woman in the car. The last thing either of them needed was to be pulled over by a cop. He didn't want to explain their injuries, he wasn't even sure he could.

Lacie had stayed in the back, lying out on the seats for over an hour. When she did move, the very first thing she did was open his duffel bag. Her first port of call were the alcohol wipes, which she used to clean the gouge on the back of his head. He'd hissed away from her, but she gripped his shoulder hauling him back. To soothe him, she kissed the side of his neck until he relaxed then carried on treating him.

Only after she patched him up did she clean and dress her own wounds. She stripped out of the stained tee-shirt and gargled mouthwash, spitting out of the window. After that, she retrieved a clean marl-gray tee-shirt from his duffel and put it on. They weren't twenty minutes from her place when she climbed between the seats to sit at his side again. Her body sagged, like she'd shed the tension of their experience. For comfort—his as much as hers—he dropped his hand to her thigh. Lacie took his sunglasses from the center console and slid them on.

Despite everything that had happened, things between them were easy. Being around Lacie was natural. None of his actions felt new, it was as if he was entitled to touch her like he did, like she almost expected it. He liked that she had helped herself into his bag, to his clothes, to his glasses.

Energy built and fizzled, but it didn't bounce back like it had. It merged, bred between them and settled in the air, holding them together with an invisible chemical bond. They were glued, a part of each other. How it had happened, or why, didn't matter. This was cosmic, meant to be, and he'd be the first to admit how crazy that sounded. If this had been a couple of days ago, he'd have laughed at anyone who suggested such a thing. But there he was, with her, and it was real.

He turned into her street, maneuvered into a space at her door, and turned off the engine. Neither said anything they just breathed together, taking stock.

"Quite an adventure," she said eventually.

"Yeah," he said. She unclicked her seatbelt. "Will I come in?"

"No," she said, taking her purse from the footwell where it had remained since before they got to the second address. "I'm going to take a bath, and then I'll have to phone Sorcha."

"What are you going to tell her?"

"I don't know. I'll think of something."

"Do you want me to come back later? I'll bring

food."

"I'm not really—"

"It's not about sex," he said, taking her hand from her lap. "We'll take our time."

"I know with everything that has happened—"

"We have to talk," he said, hyperaware of her misconception about his identity or rather his lie. He wanted her to trust him completely. After letting her down today, he had ground to gain. "There are things we have to talk about."

"You're talking about Sorcha," she said, sliding his sunglasses from her face though she didn't look at him.

The darkening bruise under her eye made him want to swing a U-turn to head directly back to where they'd come from.

"I—"

"I wasn't entirely honest. Bruce and I were never together, he was with Sorcha. When she and I spoke about it, she told me how badly you took the break-up. We didn't want you to feel awkward, and we didn't want to taint your view I suppose. I'm sorry," she said, squeezing his hand. "I know it can't be easy hearing about your lover's former lover."

"Lacie," he said, keeping her hand though she tried to withdraw. "What happened to starting fresh?"

"Thank you," she said. "For the last couple of days."

"Don't pull away from me. I want to see you again."

"She's my best friend, how can I—"

"Trust me, Lacie."

"Thank you, Seth," she said, using his hand to pull herself to him. She kissed his cheek and dropped his glasses in his lap. "Goodbye."

Every time she used that name, the bile churned

in his belly. The day had been tough for her. He let her go this time, watched her ascend her stairs, and get through the door. He'd let her have the bath, talk to her friend, and get a good night's sleep. This wasn't over, not by a long shot.

THIRTEEN

Lacie

LACIE HAD HER bath and phoned her friend. She'd told Sorcha everything minus what had happened between her and Shep… She'd omitted the details of what happened at Bruce's place too… so really nothing. She told Sorcha that their detective had found Bruce and that it seemed he was involved with something illegal. Sorcha had raved, cried, then asked Lacie to tell her again… which she did.

By going to bed early, her intention was to get a good night's sleep. Instead of drifting off, she lay awake watching the shadows on the wall. As darkness descended, Lacie grew more uneasy. Every time she closed her eyes, she relived the moment of hitting the floorboards. Tossed aside, pained through to her bones, unaware of her fate… Then the door closed and his voice had soothed her.

She didn't know where he was, where he lived, or whom he was with. That last thought festered, though she had no right to be preoccupied when she'd been so adamant.

But she'd craved him, damn her, but she had. Lacie wanted to bury herself against him like in that room. To breathe him in, embrace him, immerse herself in him. But it was done. Over.

When sleep eluded her, she lifted the bedroom rug and opened her trapdoor to the angled wide ladder. Her secret sanctuary, the reason she'd fallen in love with this place. The basement took the footprint of the rest of the abode. She turned on the florescent light and worked.

Despite working for hours, she was surprised to see the red bulb on the wall flashing. Someone had pressed the communal buzzer. Turning off the music with her elbow, she ran up the ladder wiping her hands on damp muslin. When she got to the bedroom, she kicked the trapdoor shut, and went through the living room. Someone was knocking on her door, eager for an audience with her though. She couldn't imagine why.

Tossing the muslin aside, she opened her front door. "I told you not to do that," he said.

He was in before she'd clicked her brain into gear. "What are you doing here, Seth?" she asked, closing her door.

When she turned, he was standing open-mouthed, staring at her legs.

Her arms were covered with clay. She'd tied her hair into a loose knot on the top of her head though it would be falling apart by now. Except she'd forgotten that all she wore was one of her thin painter's shirts, which skimmed her bare thighs.

"What's that look for?"

"I'm thinking about your legs," he said, still openly gawping at her pins.

"I figured that out," she said.

The smile in her voice was inappropriate, but so was his staring.

"How are you feeling today?"

"You're still staring. How is your head?"

"Which one?" he asked. "Can I come over there?"

"What for?"

As his eyes slid up, so did the corner of his mouth. She knew that look. "I'm here to talk," he said but that curl became a grin.

"That's not what your face says."

"I missed you."

"You saw me yesterday," Lacie said. "I didn't think we'd see each other again."

"We have to talk."

"You're grinning at me."

"Your legs," he said. "I'm thinking about your legs."

"We've done this," she said, knowing they were flirting again, and that she should stop. But her smile persisted. "I was thinking about you last night."

Something flickered over his expression, his grin became more intense. After a beat, he was bearing down upon her. Her feet were swept off the floor, and he pinned her to the pillar that separated her kitchen from the living space. Her head came up, his lips found hers, and once again, their mouths joined. The heat between them flared from her toes to her scalp. The fury of their union became slow, tender, overwhelming, but just as powerful in an entirely different way.

The pounding started again. It took Lacie a moment to realize it was the door. It took just as long for him to realize it too. So much so that he appeared genuinely confused to have her in his arms against the wall when he stopped kissing her. Did he wish she was someone else?

"Give me a minute," she said.

Pressuring his shoulders, he conceded and placed

her onto the floor with far more care than was required. She wasn't sure if it was the fog in their brains or if he was taking care of her again.

Her hand was on its way toward the handle when he spoke. "Check."

One word, but she lowered her hand and did as told, only to wish she hadn't. Flashing him a look of horror, she went for the handle again. Lacie had no choice, she had to answer the door. She couldn't imagine a worse scenario than this one, except if maybe this new guest had stormed straight in a few seconds earlier.

"I thought you were on holiday," Lacie said when she opened the door.

"After our talk last night, I got straight on a plane," Sorcha said, sailing past her friend.

Lacie closed the door and took a deep breath, steeling herself to face those facing each other behind her.

"Who's this?" Sorcha asked.

Lacie froze mid-exhale and replayed her friend's casual words. "What?" she asked, wearing a frown.

She turned to see beautiful Sorcha scrutinizing the man she'd been sucking face with moments ago.

Sorcha extended her hand and flicked her hair back over her shoulder. "Sorcha Reynolds."

He, whoever he was, looked to Lacie. Reluctance and contrition dwelled on his expression with a kind of mild panic mixed in.

"What do you mean who is he?" Lacie asked, moving toward her friend.

"I told you we had to talk," he said. "I wanted to tell you—"

"Tell me what?" Lacie demanded. "Oh my god." Her fingers touched her lips. "Oh my god!"

Sorcha looked from him to Lacie and back again. "I've been gone for like forty-eight hours. What's going on?"

Lacie couldn't answer her friend, and she was suddenly very aware of her sparse apparel. Walking behind Sorcha's back, she headed for her bedroom. Lacie wanted to change, but her clothes wouldn't be enough, right now she wanted to crawl out of her own skin.

He'd touched her, kissed her, made her feel safe. She'd trusted him, craved him—

"Dusty, I had to—"

He was in her bedroom at her back, closing the door as though this was normal behavior. Like they were a seasoned couple in the midst of a tiff, when technically this was their first fight. She wanted to scream, wanted to erase the memory of his hands, his mouth, his eyes, the heat. Except her body still tingled from their last encounter.

"Please leave," she said as firmly as possible, but she couldn't bring herself to look at him.

"I want you to listen to me. I didn't lie to you."

"You let me go on about Sorcha and you've never even met her! Who are you? I don't want to know! Get out of here!"

"No!" he exclaimed. "You're going to hear me out!"

"Why would I do that? You're a stranger! Leave!"

"Nothing was false. Everything was real. Baby, come on."

"Don't 'baby' me, get out of here!"

"Listen to me. Listen!" He got a hold of her and turned her to face him. "My name is Ryder Stone, okay? I'm an investigator just like I said. I was in Shep's office that day, I shouldn't have been. I saw you, I wanted to help. He's a vulture, Lace, you don't understand what he's like."

"You were looking after me?"

"Is that so hard to believe?" he asked.

The bedroom door opened. Lacie pulled out of his grip.

"You heard her," Sorcha snapped. "Get out or I'll call the cops!"

Sorcha stood with the phone in her hand; Lacie knew she'd do it. Sorcha was as protective of her as she was of Sorcha.

"Lacie," he breathed and reached out for her, but she moved away.

"Leave," she said.

Ryder considered his options but when Sorcha began dialing, he backed off, holding up his hands in surrender. Lacie couldn't look directly at him but could feel his gaze on her. He left the room. A few seconds later, her front door opened and closed.

"Well," Sorcha said. "I'm ready to hear what that was all about."

FOURTEEN

Lacie

LACIE DIDN'T EXPLAIN it. She set Sorcha to the task of making the coffee and grabbed a shower. When she was clean and they were both seated, Lacie was quizzed about her face, and about Bruce.

"Okay, so we know where he is, that's great," Sorcha said.

"You can't get involved," Lacie said. "Those people were… I don't think you should be anywhere near them. They'll hurt you."

Lacie pointed to her face.

Sorcha flinched. "I'm so sorry you got hurt, honey."

"It's over now."

"Okay, we'll start over together," Sorcha said.

"We're not going back."

"We'll get to the bottom of what's going on there. We'll go to Shep… for real this time."

Lacie squirmed. "He could get into trouble. I don't have all the specifics, I—"

"Get that guy on the phone."

"I'm not sure about—"

"I'll talk to him," Sorcha said. "Give me his number, and I'll get Bruce's address. You should cancel that check too."

Lacie wriggled some more, but she knew Sorcha would persist until she got the details of what Bruce was up to.

"I'll get the address," Lacie said.

"Great."

"Only if you'll promise not to go anywhere near it alone. Give the details to Sheppard and wait for him to find out what's going on."

Sorcha sighed. "Okay, fine. Get the details and I'll make an appointment with Shep. He'll see us today."

Sorcha was already dialing, so Lacie took her phone into the bedroom and closed the door. All she needed was the address. She didn't have to talk to him properly. She didn't need to ask him why. She didn't want to.

As hard as she tried, Lacie couldn't understand why he'd lied to her, why he had pretended to be someone he wasn't, why he had let her think he had been intimate with Sorcha. The only thing she could be sure of was that he wasn't who he'd claimed to be. Except he hadn't claimed to be, she had assumed, and he'd asked that there be no assumptions between them. His actions couldn't be excused for that reason alone.

The mistake could have been easily rectified with a straightforward introduction. If she'd had his name, things would've been different. Except if he was in Shep's office, and shouldn't have been, maybe he was up to something illegal. Maybe he wasn't an investigator at all, he could have made everything up. What would his motivation be? His assumed identity didn't get him into her underwear, in fact it kept him out. But she had given him that check, was the money motivation enough?

Sitting on her bed speculating wasn't getting her any answers. Sorcha would storm in within ten minutes ready to take over. Sorcha had been spared Lacie's experience in this matter; her best friend still had hope. The idea of going back to that place, of going anywhere those men would be, made Lacie ill.

Telling herself it was just a business call, she pressed the digits of his number from her cell memory to her home line. Pressing send, she closed her eyes and listened to it ring.

"Stone," he answered after ten rings.

His voice was hard, deep, chilling, yet a zap of painful pleasure shot from her throat to her thighs.

"It's Lacie," she said only to have her lips instantly parch.

"Baby," he said. She heard the relief in his smile. "Thank god, I was worried. I can come over—"

"No," she said, trying to hold him at a professional distance, hoping her tone would give him the message of what this call was about. "I need the information."

"What information?"

"The address, Bruce's address, I wasn't exactly paying attention to the street name or building number yesterday." Silence reigned for more than a few seconds. "Hello?"

"I'm waiting for the punch-line," he said.

"There's no punch-line," she responded. "I need the information."

"Not a chance."

"You can't withhold that information. I paid handsomely for it."

"I tore up the check, Dusty, you're not paying for anything, and I won't give you the address. I won't let you go near that place again."

"If you don't give me the address, I'll have to go back just to get it," Lacie said.

"Why would you want to go there again?" he asked.

"I don't," she said. "Sorcha needs to know what Bruce is up to. It's important."

"You think you can just walk up there—"

"We're going to Sheppard's office, me and Sorcha together, so I won't get it wrong this time."

"I don't think so, baby," Ryder said.

"You can't tell me—"

"No girl of mine is going anywhere near the competition."

"I'm not your girl," Lacie said. "And neither is Sorcha, we—"

"You want more information, I'll get it for you."

"You?"

"Yes, me," he said.

"Don't you have other cases? How do I know you're an investigator at all? You don't seem to have much—"

"I have a team," Ryder said. "My partner and I have six guys on payroll for investigations."

"So why would you give me so much time when—"

"You know why Dusty," he said. "Now, you tell me what's going on, what information do you need?"

"I'm not doing this," she said. "I don't know who you are."

"You know me better than you know Shep."

"Sorcha knows him, she trusts him—"

"Who do you trust? There was a reason Sorcha didn't go to Shep herself the first time around."

"She's sure that—"

"Who do you trust?" he asked again.

As angry, confused, and embarrassed as Lacie

was by whatever had, or hadn't, happened between them, she'd always spoken her thoughts to him. They didn't need any more secrets.

"Ryder," she said. "Is that your name?"

"Yeah," he answered.

"Can I call you Ryder?"

"Call me anything you like," he said. "Give me the information, and I'll get to work—"

"I don't want you going back," she spoke her thoughts. "I don't want you anywhere near that place."

"Baby—"

"I'm being honest. I don't understand it. I know I shouldn't care. I know you lied. I don't want you in that place, or anywhere near any of those people."

"It's my job."

"No, it's not. I'm not hiring you. I'm not paying you. This is nothing to do with you. All I need is the address."

"The chances that they are still there are slim," he said.

"I don't care about them," she replied. "It's Bruce we need the information on."

"What is it about this guy? What does your friend—?"

"It's not my place to answer that. We need the address—"

"You're not going back there," Ryder said.

"We just want to give the information to Shep—"

"He's a hack, baby. He won't do the job right for you. All he'll be interested in is getting your friend back into bed."

"Sorcha's not interested in that. It's Bruce she has to get to."

"Great," Ryder said. "Then it'll be your turn at bat."

"Excuse me?"

"If Sorcha turns him down, he'll move his attention to you. Hell, he'll probably aim for you first, he's had Sorcha, and you're more beautiful than—"

"Stop it," she said. "None of this has anything to do with sex, at least not sex and me."

"Say that after you've been to see Shep."

"Don't make this more difficult, Sorcha—"

"What about you?" Ryder asked. "You don't have to run around after her, what about your happiness?"

"What does that have to do with anything? I want the address so that we can give it to Shep, and he can carry on the investigation."

"Let me come with you," he said.

"Where?" she asked.

"To Shep's office."

"Why? Do you need cover for further illegal activities?"

"I can explain everything if you let me. I was there for a case. I can show you everything. If you come to my place—"

"Just give me the address," she said.

"I won't."

"But—"

"I'll send it to Shep," Ryder said. "I'll send him an email. I want to let him know I have a vested interest in this, and I'll be keeping an eye on things."

"You can't."

"I can," he said. "I know Shep well, he worked for me briefly. I've known him for years. I know what he's capable of and what he's like. He knows what I'm capable of too. That should be enough for him to keep his eye on the ball and off you."

"Me?"

"Yeah," Ryder said. "If he knows you're my

girl—"

"I am not your girl," she said. "And he'll know that because surely if I was your girl, you would be helping us out—"

"I'll tell him the truth," Ryder said. "You don't want me to get hurt. You're looking out for me and I'm happy for him to take care of the details while I focus on taking care of you."

"What does that mean?"

Innuendo slid into his voice. "You know what it means."

"You're flirting with me? After everything?"

"Nothing's keeping us apart now," he said. "I didn't plan on you finding out the way you did but I did come to your place to tell you… I got distracted by your legs."

"Send the address to Shep," Lacie said into the phone at the same time her bedroom door opened to reveal Sorcha.

"Lacie—"

"Goodbye, Ryder," she said then hung up the phone. "Did you get us an appointment?"

"He'll see us right away," Sorcha said.

"You look nervous."

"You look disappointed. The men in our lives really know how to keep us on our toes."

"I only have one," Lacie said, looking at the phone in her hand. "Or had, it's over now."

"You met this guy while I was away?" Sorcha asked to which Lacie nodded. "Then it seems to me you're only just getting started. Throw caution to the wind. I would if I were you. If you take no risks, you'll get no rewards."

Sorcha's endorsement meant a lot to her. But throwing caution to the wind was what got Sorcha in her current bind. Still, Lacie had to admit to herself that her concern for Ryder was true. If she was invested in his safety, then maybe their association wasn't as over as she tried to tell herself it was.

FIFTEEN

Lacie

THE WOMEN GOT in Sorcha's car and traveled to Shep's office. Sorcha checked her hair and make-up in the rear-view mirror. There was no need because Sorcha looked as perfect as ever.

When Lacie walked into this office for the first time she had been antsy but knew that she was helping her friend. Yet there she was walking in next to that friend, now Lacie felt she'd let Sorcha down. Sorcha had never wanted to face Shep, though from the swing in her hips Lacie wouldn't know it to look at her.

A tiny blonde with a D-cup sat at the front desk that had been empty when Lacie had been there the first time. The blonde examined Sorcha as Sorcha did the same to her. Lacie stood shrouded in invisibility, as she always did at Sorcha's side. But she didn't mind. It gave her the chance to look at the gray industrial carpet on the floor and the drab beige walls. Her gaze traveled past the plastic chairs to the dusty fake ficus in the corner. She wondered if this was how Ryder's office was set up.

Shep's office door opened. When Lacie turned, a part of her expected to see Ryder, but the man that was there wasn't anything like him. Shep was at least four inches shorter, and not as solid. He wore a washed-out yellow shirt, which did nothing for his short blond hair and pale complexion. That said, his eyes were sharp, his jaw square, and with a little wardrobe advice, and some time working in the sun, Lacie could see how Sorcha had been attracted.

"Shep," Sorcha drawled, swaying her hips around the blonde's desk.

Shep took the hand Sorcha extended, but his focus remained on Lacie, which served to confuse her. Sorcha was the noticeable one.

"Ladies, come in," Shep said, dropping Sorcha's hand.

Shep moved out of the way to let Sorcha enter his office and still he watched Lacie's every move.

Something lingered behind the smile Shep bestowed on her when she passed him to enter behind Sorcha. And though the office appeared the same as it had on her first visit, the air was different. Maybe it was because she subconsciously relived her first encounter with Ryder, which had taken place in this space. Carrying on inside, despite her unease, they all found their seats. Shep still watched her, which had Sorcha looking at her with a healthy dollop of her own curiosity.

"What am I missing?" Sorcha asked.

Shep completely ignored her. "I got an email from Stone," he said with a smile dancing on his lips.

"I know," Lacie said, glancing to her friend in hope that she would take over, she didn't.

"I tell you…" Shep said. "I've known Stone a long time, too long. He's never given up business to me. But that's not the shocking thing."

"What's the shocking thing?" Sorcha asked.

"The way he warned me off, it was almost… insecure, tough as he was trying to make himself out to be. Tell me, little lady, is playing away your deal?" His eyes dragged down to her chest. "'Cause I tell you even if he does kill me, I have a feeling it would be worth it."

"Did he tell you about Bruce?" Lacie asked.

"He gave me the bare bones," Shep said to her. "The first thing to do would be to check out the address."

"We did," Lacie said. "You don't want a piece of that."

"We'll see. Stone and I have different methods."

From what Ryder had told her that was true.

"Just don't go alone," Lacie said.

"I don't plan to," he said, switching his attention to Sorcha. "You want to see this guy?"

"No," Lacie said. "You're not taking her there."

"I don't want a showdown," Sorcha said.

"Do you see my face?" Lacie asked. "They did this."

"You'll be safe with me, sweetheart. Like I said, Stone and I have different methods."

"What?" Lacie asked.

"You told me not to go alone," Shep said. "You want to help your friend, don't you?"

"You want me to go back there?"

"Sure," Shep said. "I'll look after you."

"No, I can't. Ryder said they won't be there anymore anyway," Lacie said.

"Then there's nothing to worry about, is there? We can check out the place see what they left behind. Think of it as an adventure."

"I've had all the adventures I want this week," Lacie said.

"You can ID this Bruce guy."

Lacie wasn't going to make the same mistake

twice. "Sorcha has a picture."

"I work well with a partner," Shep said. "I'll give you a break on the final bill if you help me out."

"Why do you want me involved?" Lacie asked. "You're trying to rile up Ryder, aren't you?"

He didn't answer but the mischief in his eyes told her that she was right.

"You're not taking Lacie, she's been through enough," Sorcha belatedly asserted.

"Couldn't agree more."

The women turned in their chairs as Shep looked to the door. Ryder stood leaning against the frame with one thumb tucked into his jeans pocket. He looked cool and tough, he needed a shave and he'd clearly only combed his hair with his fingers today. Her lips parted in expectation of his. There was a room between them, and he hadn't even looked at her. Why was her heart racing?

No one moved for a minute, then Ryder began to swagger across the room one long, slow stride at a time.

"Lacie's going nowhere, neither is Sorcha. They're paying you to do a job. If you can't do it, I'll get one of my boys on it."

"Don't think it's you that the ladies want," Shep said.

"You had a personal relationship with the principal which is the only reason you're getting a crack at this at all," Ryder answered.

"You took the girl with you," Shep said.

"She's not the girl," Ryder said, stopping between their seats, widening his stance. "She's my girl and you know it."

"Would you excuse us for a moment?" Lacie asked, bouncing to her feet, and taking Ryder's arm to drag him to the corner. "What are you doing here? How did you know we were here?"

"I called Tiffany."

"Tiffany?"

"The girl out front. And Sorcha's car is outside."

"How do you know her car? Forget it, I don't want to know," she said, swiping an eyelash from his cheek and realizing for the first time how intimately close they stood. "I told you not to come."

"I'm glad I did, he was trying to strong-arm you. I told you, I know what he's like."

"I was saying no. I was handling it."

His hand went to the wall far above her head and he leaned in. "I know. But I'm here to back you up."

"Why are you here?" she asked. "He was only pressuring me to go in an effort to rile you up. With you showing up, he'll know it's working."

"We're having a private conference in the corner," Ryder said. "I'm riled up for reasons that are nothing to do with him."

Ryder's eyes traveled down her body. Instead of feeling violated as she had when Shep looked at her that way, the crackling of the air between them got almost audible. Touching his sternum with her index finger, she pushed up to her tiptoes and kissed the stubble on his jaw. His eyes flared as that corner of his mouth tilted up.

Parting her lips, she tipped her chin upwards and he took her cue, lowering his mouth to hers for a kiss. Though it was chaste in comparison to their last union, the kiss was certainly more than friendly.

"Are you okay?" he asked, any delight replaced with concern.

"He keeps staring," she whispered. "I don't like the way he looks at me. I'm angry at you and confused by this whole thing, but…"

"But?"

"I like the way you look at me. I like how it makes me feel," she said, stalling her examination of his tee-shirt to look up at him.

"I love your mind," he said. "And how you speak it."

"I'm not usually this… verbal."

"Then I count myself lucky."

"I'm angry," she said, sounding anything but.

"I'll grovel."

"Isn't that beneath you?"

"Not if it gets me beneath you," he muttered, leaning in again.

Lacie retreated. "I'm confused. I don't understand."

"I'll explain everything, anything you want to know."

"Why?" she asked. "Why me?"

"You feel it too," he said. "Can you explain it?"

She couldn't but knew what he was talking about. That undeniable, indestructible, invisible bond that drew them to each other, and had since their very first shared moment.

"Excuse me," Sorcha chirped. "Sorry to interrupt, but we have to get going."

"What?" Lacie said in unison with Ryder who hooked her under his arm as they turned.

Sorcha was closing in on them. "We're all going, together."

"Sorcha," Lacie said with warning, knowing that tickle in her friend's voice.

"Come on," Sorcha said. "Shep assures me it will be an adventure."

"You're not going," Lacie said. "It's dangerous."

"You're not going either," Ryder said to her.

Lacie completely ignored him and slid her hand into his back pocket. "Sorcha, you don't know what you're getting yourself into."

"Would you rather the boys went alone?" Sorcha

asked.

Shep was out from behind the desk and approaching. "Stone's chicken, he's already fucked this up."

"Watch your language in front of the ladies," Ryder said. "And you're not going to goad me into it."

"Just me and the girls then," Shep said, taking Sorcha's arm and eyeing Lacie.

"Keep looking at her like that and I'll make sure you lose the ability to look at anything," Ryder said.

"I'm going," Sorcha said. "I think I deserve this."

Lacie read between the lines, it might be her last chance for excitement and adventure. But Sorcha didn't know what lay out there.

Lacie couldn't let her go alone especially in her current condition. "Sorch, let's talk about this."

"My father doesn't know I'm back, if they see me—"

"Please, let's sleep on it," Lacie said.

"It's lunchtime," Sorcha said. "You know how important this is."

"Nothing will change between now and then," Lacie said.

"Actually it might," Ryder said. "Toby's following the money."

"Can't have much of a trail," Shep said.

"Got us there in the first place," Ryder responded.

"Turned out well didn't it," Shep said. "Hence why you're here."

"The guy is careless."

"If he was, you've scared him into hiding now."

"Bruce is not running from anything," Sorcha said.

"Why did he leave town?" Shep asked.

"We don't know what's going on," Ryder said.

"But he's mixed up with something, and from experience, I can tell you it stinks."

Lacie's phone started to ring. Her purse was on the back of her chair, so she dashed away from Ryder to get it. As she fished it out, she saw that Sorcha had separated herself from the men.

"Is it him?" Sorcha asked.

The phone screen held one word and when Lacie looked up at Sorcha she didn't have to say it, Sorcha read her expression and held up two hands of crossed fingers.

"Darwin," Lacie answered turning her back on the group and sticking her finger in her ear to block everyone else out. "You called. I wasn't expecting to hear from you so quickly."

Lacie listened to Darwin's pitch but was crucially aware of the prickle on the back of her neck, which signified the three sets of eyes on her. Somehow, dealing with business now seemed surreal even though this was her life.

"Yes, I promise… of course, thank you."

Lacie hung up and dropped her phone into her bag.

"Well?" Sorcha asked as she turned.

"Forty-five," Lacie said.

The men remained in the background while Sorcha bounded closer. "Have you heard from Briggs?"

"No, and I don't expect to. Not yet."

"Did you tell him about Spencer's offer?"

"No," Lacie said. "I'm not playing them off each other."

"You're terrible. Was he trying to get you onto his yacht again? Did you tell him about Elijah?"

"That's none of his business, and I still don't believe Elijah's offer was real."

"I think it was," Sorcha said. "I think that's how much he wants you."

"What's your other job?" Shep asked, moseying up beside Sorcha. "Are you a hooker?"

"Watch your mouth," Ryder said, smacking the back of Shep's head while passing him to reach Lacie.

"He wanted to host a reception?" Sorcha asked. "He's trying to court you. You have to play the game."

"I don't."

"So much for your girl," Shep laughed. "She's got them lined up."

Ryder propped himself on Shep's desk behind her but didn't touch her. Lacie didn't like Shep's attitude or Ryder's reticence.

"Shut up," Sorcha said, taking her turn to chide Shep.

"I have to go to dinner next week with a know-it-all millionaire," Lacie said then spun on the spot to fix Ryder in her sights. "Will you come with me?"

The brooding man's arms had been folded the width of his chest; he'd been examining his boots. But when she spoke, he seemed to snap out of his distraction.

"What?" Ryder asked.

"Their pursuit of her is relentless," Sorcha said, putting an arm around Lacie's waist to squeeze. "Everyone wants to commission her. It's worse since the MoMA exhibition. But she's so bad at this. She's got a reputation as a recluse because she hates to be the center of attention."

"I'm not social. I'm better in small groups," Lacie said.

"You're eccentric," Sorcha said. "Are you going to look after her, or am I going to have to set her up with another of my trust fund suitors?"

"MoMA," Shep said somewhere in the background.

Lacie couldn't help but notice that Ryder hadn't said anything, though he watched her intently.

"I think he only wants into your underwear," Sorcha said in judgment.

Lacie didn't think that Ryder heard her friend. His expression didn't change. There was an intensity in his attention that made her ears buzz and drowned out all other sounds.

Ryder's stance loosened, he reached for her. Lacie went willingly into the cradle of his arms, nestled in the vee of his thighs. He brushed her nose with his and kissed her again. A long, slow, deep plundering of her mouth as though they had all the time in the world. Like they were all alone with the night stretched out in front of them.

"…She needs someone alert, assertive, and focused," Sorcha said.

No doubt her words were in continuation of something she'd been saying for a while, but Lacie's body was Jell-O against Ryder's. His form held hers up and she had no desire to move and knew without asking that he'd fight to keep her in place. He wanted her right there in his arms.

"You will pay attention, won't you?" Sorcha insisted. "You know, the exact opposite of what you're doing now? She's terrible, she can't say no, and often fazes out… like now."

"I'll look after her," Ryder said to Sorcha as he stroked Lacie's face.

"Forty-five," Shep said, snapping back into the conversation. "Are you talking tens? Hundreds?"

"Thousand," Sorcha said.

"Now I know what the besotted look is for," Shep said.

"What?" Sorcha asked.

"This guy doesn't go gooey eyed over a woman, never seen it. She's an artist, she's raking it in."

Sorcha's outrage was audible. "Lacie is a

beautiful, smart, funny, sensitive—"

"He's not short of a few doubloons himself," Shep said. "Course you can never have too much."

"Are you listening to his babbling?" Ryder asked her.

"Is someone talking?" Lacie asked. His smile tasted hers. "I want to see your office."

"I want to see your bedroom," Ryder teased.

"You've seen my bedroom," she said.

"Not for long enough."

"This is all wonderful, and I couldn't be happier for you, Lace," Sorcha said. "It's about time you got a break after the whole Matt Rhys debacle. If you like this one, keep him. I know how nuts you are for loyalty, and this will tick a box but…"

Lacie kissed Ryder, then turned in his arms, not letting their bodies part for a moment.

"You're right," Lacie said, resting her hands on Ryder's arms that held her flush against him. "We have to get you sorted out. We'll all pack a bag and meet somewhere in an hour. We'll do it together and get it done."

"Really?" Sorcha gushed.

"We know what we're walking into or at least we're better prepared now."

"Pack a bag," Shep said. "Why do I need—?"

"Always be prepared," Lacie said, quoting Ryder.

"This is so exciting," Sorcha said.

"There are more of us this time," Lacie said to Ryder's unspoken reservations. "And we have to work as a team."

"Come on then, quickly," Sorcha said. "I have to drive you home first."

"I'll take her," Ryder said.

"But you'll have to—"

"He's already packed," Lacie said, linking their

fingers. "Everyone meet at mine in an hour."

"At yours?" Shep objected. "Why?"

"Because they're the couple who will need some alone time, duh!" Sorcha exclaimed.

"I could take you home," Shep said to Sorcha.

"Been there, done that," Sorcha said, sashaying those hips out of the office. "No thanks."

"And we all know why," Ryder said to Lacie's crown, but she elbowed him.

"Privacy, loyalty," she murmured. "What we discuss goes no further."

"You got it, baby," Ryder said and pushed away from the desk. "Better get moving to make the most of our alone time."

"Heard that part didn't you?" Lacie teased.

"I heard the word 'couple,'" he said. "It made me want to drag you back to my cave."

It was flattering that he didn't even look at the spritely Tiffany, despite her desperate attempt to get his attention. They got to the street and once again headed to his familiar truck.

SIXTEEN

Lacie

SORCHA HONKED AND waved as she passed. Ryder boosted Lacie into the truck and got to his own seat. He cranked the engine and handed her his aviators.

"You left these," Ryder said.

Happy to oblige him, she slid them on. "This is weird."

"What?"

"How normal this is," she said. "It is, isn't it? I'm mad and confused and we're practically strangers but—"

"It's normal," he said. "I know."

During the journey back to hers, his hand remained on her thigh, but it didn't stay still. He drummed his fingers upward, playing it coy, while they chatted about Shep's history both with Ryder and with Sorcha.

Not far from her place, his palm inched up further toward her crotch. Playing him at his own game, she slid down in the seat bringing his hand into direct contact with her heat. He swerved the truck like he had when she'd smiled on the first night of their road trip. The way he scrambled to get both hands on the wheel and back in lane made her laugh.

"You did that on purpose," he said, grinning at her.

"You were being coy."

"Do you want me to be direct?" he asked. "Let me find a place to park."

"I'm sorry," she said, bringing her feet up under her to lean over the console and drape her arms around his neck. "I won't play with you."

Kissing his cheek, she rested her head on his shoulder. He appreciated her proximity, and they rode for a moment. Curiosity ate at her. Coy was usually her color, but she'd gotten away with speaking her mind, it had got them this far.

Tilting her head, the tip of her tongue touched his earlobe, she breathed it into her mouth sucking gently as her hand fell away from his shoulder.

"Now, baby, we're almost—"

She cupped the length of him through his jeans though the length of her hand wasn't sufficient. Hissing in the end of his sentence, he swerved again.

"Baby!" he chided. She took her hand back to his shoulder. "No, put it back."

With the car back on track, he snatched her hand and pressed it to his groin.

"You're always hard," she said, kissing the side of his neck.

"I'm always hard for you," he said. "I'm in agony, baby."

"I should tell you," she said, nuzzling closer. "I'm not very… experienced. But I want to touch you, it excites me."

"I can tell from the way you're wriggling there. I love that wriggle."

"I won't be able to do anything for you, you know… if we get to it."

"If?" he asked and took her palm to his mouth. "We don't know what this is, but it's definitely headed in that direction."

"I wouldn't want to disappoint you. I'm being up front."

"Let's just keep doing what we're doing. It's worked out so far."

"Except for the part where you lied to me."

"I didn't want to scare you and I didn't know how or when to say it, to tell you."

"We haven't not known each other long," she said. "Can we just promise no more secrets? No more lies."

"You got it, baby."

Ryder pulled the truck over outside her building and pulled on the brake. The quicker she could pack, the faster they'd get on the road. An hour wasn't much time.

"You stay here," she said, unclicking her seatbelt.

"That's my order," he said, catching her wrist. "Why do you want me to stay here?"

"Because if you come in, I won't get anything done."

"I'll keep my hands to myself," he said. "I promise."

"And your mouth?"

"That I can't promise," he said but unclicked and opened his door. "Stay."

Without giving her time to answer, he got out, rounded the vehicle, and opened her door. "You're a gentleman on top of everything else?"

"It's easier to be a gentleman when we're in public."

The moment the front door of her apartment closed behind them, he kissed the top of her head. "Get packed," he said. "Then we'll get busy."

Her eye was drawn to that bulge in his jeans, now that she was aware of it, part of her was fascinated. It was like her birthday gift was right there in front of her but frustratingly wrapped and out of her reach.

"Who is this guy we're meeting next week?" he asked.

It was a subject changer from what had been in her mind and her body language.

"I've been commissioned before," she said. "But I'm not a huge fan of private projects."

"Is that who all the men were? Darwin, Briggs, Spencer, and Elijah?"

"You remembered all those names," she said to herself. "Yes. They've all shown interest, and I think they're trying to outdo each other. I haven't even decided if I'll do it yet."

Lacie headed into her bedroom to throw some things in a bag but left the bedroom door open to continue talking.

"Do you go to a lot of meetings with men like that?"

"Sometimes," she called. "I hate going alone, which is why I asked you to join me. Usually, I drag Sorcha along."

"I'll join you for all of them from now on."

"Planning to never let me out of your sight," she teased, throwing her toiletries to the bottom of her bag and piling clothes on top.

"I plan to be supportive," he said. "Whatever you need."

She took the bag to her bedroom door and dumped it at her feet. "What are we doing here, Ryder? You and me, what is it?"

"What do you want it to be?" he asked, putting down the snow-globe he'd just shaken.

"I don't know," she said. "This is new for me. I told you that."

"Whatever this is it's new for me too. Sex is easy, this is… different."

"I suppose it's probably moot anyway. If these guys are still at that place, we'll all end up—"

"What?" he barked, marching from the center of her living room to face her in the doorway. "What do you think will happen?"

"Do you see my face?" she asked. "That pain in the back of your head came from somewhere. You've probably got a concussion, that's what the gooey eyes are for."

"We weren't prepared. It was my fault. I was distracted. You will never be in that kind of danger again. Look at me, Dusty," he said, taking her shoulder. "I promise you."

"This isn't about guilt, is it?"

"I've wanted you since the minute I saw you, I'm not going anywhere. This is important, Dusty. Do you trust me?"

"Why do you call me Dusty?"

He lifted her hands. "I saw the dust on your hands in Shep's office."

"It's clay," she said.

"I know that now. Do you work downstairs?"

Curiosity nipped her. "How do you know that?"

"I saw the trapdoor under your rug earlier."

"It was closed," she said, impressed by his keen eye. "You don't miss a thing, do you?"

"I want to know everything about you," he said. "I notice you."

"That's a good quality in your line of work," she said. "How can I support you?"

"What?"

"If you want to support my work, how can I

support yours?"

"We'll get this case dealt with," he said, skimming his fingers down her face. "Then worry about us."

"Is there an us?"

"Oh yeah," he said, resting his hands on her waist to guide her backward.

Looping her arms around his neck, she hopped up when he lifted her from the floor. His mouth smothered hers, but he was careful about laying her down on her bed. Other things played round in her mind; things that should be dealt with because none of them could say how long the case would take.

The only thing Lacie could be sure of was that Sorcha needed her, she needed all of them. Whatever it took to support Sorcha, Lacie would get her through it. But it was unsettling, not knowing how this would all turn out. Sorcha wouldn't like that either, though she'd never admit it. Sorcha was shiny happy… on the surface at least.

Ryder's body was incredible. Her hands, of their own accord, shoved his tee-shirt up out of the way so her fingertips could dance over the ridges of his abdomen. She wanted more. On a mew, she turned her mouth away from his and tugged his shirt higher. The long fingers of his hands were flat on the bed at each side of her head in a half push up. When she whimpered again, her unspoken request was granted. He grabbed his tee-shirt at the back of his neck and pulled it off to toss it away.

Once it was gone, she sat up and whipped off her own top. The grin he'd worn over her request vanished when he realized her bra was on show. When Ryder's mouth opened, Lacie was sure he was about to drool into her cleavage. She'd never thought of her breasts as particularly magnificent, but no one would know that from Ryder's expression. Except when his hand came toward her, it was her shoulder he touched.

"Your skin," he muttered. "It's like silk."

Still lying on the bed, she expected his mouth to join hers, but his hand skimmed over her breast to her abdomen.

"Are you okay?" she whispered, taking her hands to his face when his desire cooled to torment.

"I'm sorry I wasn't there," he said, tracing the red welts on her stomach.

"They'll fade," she said. "Bruises heal, Ryder."

"I let you down."

"You wouldn't have been there at all if it wasn't for me. I should apologize to you."

His gaze sprang from her torso to her eyes. "Stay," he said.

His hands stroked her belly, her hips, her waist, then came to settle cupping her breasts. His eyes remained fixed on hers.

"Where?"

"Here," Ryder said. "Stay home, out of harm's way. I'll deal with this."

"I can't abandon Sorcha," she said, sliding her own hands up his perpendicular torso. "You have incredible form."

"I'll look after Sorcha. I still don't understand why this is so important, and without knowing why—"

"She's pregnant," Lacie said, scrutinizing the grooves and ridges her fingers were learning.

"What?"

"That's in strict confidence," she said. "No one can know I've told you, not even Sorcha. Her parents don't even know."

"And Bruce is…?

"Yeah," Lacie said, sliding the leather of his belt from its buckle.

"Your friend sure can pick 'em. I suppose that's why she sent you to Shep in the first place."

"He can't know, you can't tell him."

"We're not exactly bosom buddies," he said, pinching her nipples through the satin of her bra. "Can I take this off?"

She whipped his belt from the loops on his jeans. "I'm not asking permission to undress you, am I?"

Arching up, she lifted her brows, daring him to do his worst, and of course he didn't shy away from the challenge. His fingers forged forward until his palms covered her ribs, eventually his thumbs slid under the bra catch. The release made her moan, even though he hadn't touched her yet. Bliss was here, under him, all alone.

Shivering in anticipation of his hands, her eyes hadn't opened. But it was her lips that got his attention. Extending her arms upward, she hung them around his neck. His hair tickled her forehead, sending the cascade of vibration through each nerve ending. Her nipples were hard and sore, and the contact of his chest hair rasping over them made her squeak. He groaned; she took the chance to suck his lower lip.

When she released him, his tongue salved her top one, then he went on an excruciatingly slow stroll down her neck. His hands held her breasts, rolling, teasing her nipples in preparation for his mouth. She couldn't get closer. She needed to be closer. Forcing her body upward, her voice begged for more on the wisps of breath that escaped her lips.

"Ryder," she begged, rocking herself against the perpetual ridge in his jeans.

With superior strength and weight, his hips pinned hers. He lifted his head to look at her. His fingertips slid up her ribs, under her arms, making her flinch; he enjoyed noting that she was ticklish. When their fingers locked together above her head, his eyes became darker, his palms held her in place. She had no chance of going anywhere, and she wouldn't even if she could. His gaze gobbled up the feast of her body, her breasts free, bra gone, on show for him.

"Ryder," she said when he didn't move.

"Shh," he said, freeing one of her hands to palm one breast then the other. "You're gorgeous. I want to remember this."

"Remember what? We haven't done anything yet."

"Oh yes, we have," Ryder said. "I want to remember everything about the first time I see you."

"Okay," she said, walking her fingers down his chest to the line of hair that snuck down into his jeans. "Can I see you?"

"We're topless," he grinned. "We're doing this a little at a time."

"Are we now?" she asked, rolling her head to see the nightstand clock. "We better get a move on. Time's ticking away."

"We have all the time in the world," he said.

"Our friends will be here soon, and if we don't get—"

"I'm not rushing this, when we're intimate—"

"Everybody ready?"

Lacie hadn't heard the front door open. Her living, kitchen area was the size of a postage stamp. With the bedroom door open, there would be a clear view from the front door Shep and Sorcha must now be entering.

She didn't have to worry about decency. Ryder was off the bed in a flash, body-blocking her while swinging her bedroom door closed. Pushing up onto her elbow, she enjoyed the novelty of having such a perfect specimen of maleness topless, in her bedroom. A man who was enjoying her as much as she was him.

"I'm glad you didn't have your jeans off," she

said.

"Wouldn't have mattered," he shrugged, hooking his thumbs into his belt loops.

"It would have to me," she said. "I wouldn't want to be the one closing the door and giving Shep an eyeful."

Slowly, he shook his head. "Wouldn't have happened. From here on in, no male gets to see what I'm looking at."

"My breasts aren't that great," she said reluctantly leaving the bed to head for the wardrobe.

Pondering her outfit, Lacie didn't have time to make a selection. His reflection joined hers, moving in close from behind. Propping his chin on her head, his hands crept around to cup her breasts.

He rolled her nipples between his fingers. "I beg to differ," he said.

Both examined the simple action of those long, tan fingers kneading her pale flesh then resting and holding her in such a tender way. While he remained engrossed, her eyes wouldn't stay open. She pushed herself back into the column in his jeans that had become her favorite companion, but he moved his hips away.

"Don't encourage me," he said.

From the usual pant in his voice, she had a feeling he was encouraging himself.

Opening her eyes, she witnessed his hands all over her so slow, so tender... so tormenting.

"Come on, you two!" Sorcha's voice called from through the wall. "Get your clothes on!"

Sorcha's giggle was as loud as her voice. Lacie reluctantly left his hold to retrieve a short-sleeved smock top, which she pulled on.

"That's it?" he asked.

She tied her hair on top of her head again. "What do you mean?"

"No bra?" he asked, unable to take his eyes from her chest.

"I've got some packed. I don't know where the other one went. Does it bother you?"

"Yes," he groaned. "But only in the same way everything about you does."

"I wasn't wearing a bra in the car when we… when you…"

"You take pleasure in tormenting me," he said.

She smiled. "I don't."

Part of her did enjoy his torment just a little. It was an incredible power to wield with such a man. It couldn't be common for him to be so easily distracted.

He hooked his arm around her and snagged his own tee-shirt from the bed as they headed to the bedroom door. Mentally, she checked everything she needed was packed. Ryder had packed without knowing that they were going somewhere. She couldn't imagine why he would be so readily equipped. She feared it meant that situations like the one they'd been in weren't unusual for him. He may get himself hurt with some regularity.

"Oh," she said, ducking away from his arm when he opened the door to the living room an inch.

"What?" he asked, watching her skirt the bed to open the top drawer of the nightstand.

"Nothing," she said. "Go on. I'm right behind you."

He didn't carry on, he waited for her. When she reached the bedroom door, he opened her hand to see what she'd retrieved from the drawer, then he groaned again.

"Sorry, but I take them to give myself a break." Her birth control pills kept her regular and light. But she knew from the look in his eye just what they meant to him, and the tingling within her started again.

"We have guests," she murmured, sliding the

pills into Ryder's back pocket.

Her bag was already in the living room where Shep and Sorcha were. Lacie didn't want to reveal any more of their private life to Shep than was absolutely necessary. With a quick peck on a bounce upward, Lacie opened the door to join their guests. Apparently, they all had an adventure to get to.

SEVENTEEN

Ryder

"CASSETTES," SORCHA GRUMBLED, slamming the glove box of Shep's five-door, electric-blue Ford circa nineteen ninety something. "This thing is a relic."

Sorcha kicked at the fast-food wrappers around her feet.

Maybe under other circumstances Ryder would agree with her, but right then, he had a completely different focus. The car was a mess. It was rusted, old, and had more than a few suspect stains on the upholstery. The woman nestled under his arm, her head on his chest, kept hot blood rushing through his veins, so he only absorbed pieces of what was being said up front. Just enough to monitor what was going on, and that the environment remained safe.

Lacie's hair caught on his stubble. The inadvertent fortuity bred affection; he wasn't used to such intimate fondness. In his line of work, he was usually getting between people and trouble. His urge to protect Lacie was more intrinsic. She sighed in her sleep, muttered something then turned her face against his throat. Her hand slid further up his thigh.

"Hello! Hello!"

Ryder snapped out of whatever he'd been languishing in and saw Sorcha hanging over the shoulder of her seat.

"She talks in her sleep you know," Sorcha said.

"Doubt he hangs around long enough to find that out for himself," Shep offered.

"You're not looking at him looking at her." Sorcha fluttered her eyelashes. "She's so cute when she sleeps. She's always like this when she's preoccupied with something."

Concern zapped through him. "Preoccupied with what?" he snapped. "Are the rich boys giving her trouble?"

"You're cute. Oh, you're so cute… I mean you're rough and tough, not at all whom I would've thought Lace would end up with… Of course, she's never had luck with men. I don't know why… they don't get her, don't understand her. Not that many of them would be inclined to put in the effort to learn. Men are lazy when it comes to things like that… I don't know what—that's a girl talk thing, I guess. Sorry, but we've had no time for specifics, Lace and me. I'll get the skinny on you, and on what's going on—"

"You could just ask me," Ryder said.

"Why would I do that?" Sorcha asked with knowing satisfaction. "I'm not interested in what you think of yourself."

"You've been Lacie's best friend since college. You mean a lot to each other. You and I will be a big part of each other's lives from here on in."

"Is that so," she said, examining him and the slumbering woman in his arms. "Lacie's a life girl you know. She experiences things in a way no one else does.

She's unique. There's absolutely no one like her."

"An artist," Shep said from the driver's seat. "Nothing they won't do. Kinky as hell."

"Uh, that's my friend you're talking about."

"Yeah," Shep said. "So?"

"You're using a stereotype."

"Always pans out," he said. "Like you, Little Miss Aristocrat, never got you out the missionary."

"Why are you begging for more then, Slob?"

Shep didn't answer back. Ryder assumed he had no comeback and didn't have to think long about why.

"Did you hear from your friend?" Sorcha asked.

"What friend?"

"Toby, you said he was—"

"Following the money," Ryder said. "I've missed a couple of calls."

"I didn't hear it ring."

"Vibrate," he said.

"You don't want to disturb Lacie?" Sorcha asked like he was a teddy bear.

"That and Shep's in the car."

"Still don't trust me?" Shep asked.

"No," Ryder said.

"Will doesn't need your bunch to fight his battles."

"Will is the last in a long line of grievances and you know it."

"Just because I wouldn't sell out to the corporate overlord."

Ryder laughed, which made Lacie whimper again. "You can't use that one forever."

"What do you mean corporate overlord?" Sorcha asked.

"I'm the little guy," Shep said.

"You're corrupt," Ryder said. "I don't want you on my payroll. I told you that when you came begging for your job back."

"I didn't know you very well then," Shep said. "I'm over it now."

"I'm lost," Sorcha said.

"StoneWall," Shep said. "StoneWall Security and Investigations, that's him."

"Well, but I…" Sorcha said and trailed off as clarity struck. "Oh my God. I know you! Your company does all my father's work. You do all the high-profile personal protection details within a thousand mile radius. You're the only one anyone with money wants or will trust. Oh my God! Does Lacie know?"

"We haven't spent time on it," he said.

"His elite team works at the house," Shep said. "The whole lot of them think they're superheroes."

"Careful, Shep, you sound bitter," Ryder said.

"Who's the Wall?" Sorcha asked.

"Jamie Wallace," Shep said. "His high school buddy."

"What is your problem?" Ryder asked. "You've got a chip on your shoulder. You made your own decisions, I didn't make them for you."

"You and your smarmy friends think you know it all, think you're better than—"

"I'm sick of this fight," Ryder said.

"We're supposed to be a team," Sorcha said. "You need to find out what this Toby guy is trying to tell you. I'm hungry, and we need a strategy."

"You didn't think about that before we left?" Ryder asked.

"I like to act now and ask questions later," Sorcha said. "Which explains Shep."

Ryder snickered. Lacie muttered, her stretch suggested she was wakening.

"Let's find somewhere to eat," Sorcha said.

"There's a steakhouse a few miles up," Ryder

said. "We'll stop there to regroup."

"Is it business this time?" Lacie murmured. "Or personal?"

"I'm off the clock, baby," he said kissing the top of her head.

"Glad to hear it, or what we did earlier was highly inappropriate."

Even half-asleep, she could make him smile. Ryder didn't need Sorcha to point out how unique Lacie was. His instinct had figured that out while his obsession was still lost in a fog of desire. He desired the body, but he craved the woman. He just had to make sure she would never get over her urge to be this close to him.

EIGHTEEN

Ryder

"PLEASE, PLEASE, please," Sorcha begged, reaching over the steakhouse table to steal her friend's hands.

"I haven't drunk enough for those antics," Lacie said.

Ryder enjoyed the meal. Surprising given Seth Sheppard had been at the table. Relaxing his arm along the back of the booth, he liked that Lacie stayed close. They didn't have to be touching for people to know they were together. The sight of them would be enough to tell people that they were attuned to each other.

Petite Lacie nestled close, intimately close. For most of the meal, she and Sorcha monopolized the conversation. The men had been ignored, which was just fine by him. He liked the sound of Lacie's voice, the change in intonation with her varied meaning and emotion. Most of the people they discussed were strangers to him. He'd listened to Sorcha's minute-by-minute account of her short-lived vacation, though not as intently as Lacie. Sorcha sure knew how to drag out a story.

By comparison, Lacie was far more concise in her explanations and narrative. She knew her mind and was honest without once being negative or malicious. Lacie spoke more softly than the vibrant, animated, Sorcha who gestured wildly at every opportunity.

"I thought we were here to come up with a plan," Shep grumbled. "I've got places I could have been tonight."

"Your money will be as good to the poor girl tomorrow as it would be tonight," Sorcha said without looking at Shep, then switched to continue pleading with her friend. "Lace, when was the last time we had a night on the town?"

The question had been rhetorical, but Lacie answered it anyway. "Your birthday two months ago," she said. "You puked all over my bedroom floor."

"I did," Sorcha said, proud of the badge of honor. "But I haven't been drinking tonight, have I? And there's a motel right next door. We don't have to go to anyone's place."

"What about Bruce?" Lacie asked.

"He'll keep."

"Sorch, I don't know if this is a good idea."

"You have nothing to worry about. Your date is a bodyguard."

"He is?" Lacie asked, turning to him though Sorcha still held her hands.

"In addition to being a PI," he said, scratching the top of her head with his splayed fingertips. "If you want to dance, go on. I can see the floor from here. I'll keep an eye on you."

The large double doors at the back of the restaurant had been closed when they were there alone. Tonight, they were open, revealing a wide bar and dark dancefloor with scattered colored lights whooshing around. A DJ booth stood at the back of the room, though the tunes were more mobile disco than hard-core nightclub.

"I thought we were going to get this over with today," Lacie said.

"We can get moving," he said. "But Sorcha's right, it will keep."

Lacie sighed. "Okay."

"My rate's double after midnight," Shep said, moving out of the booth so Sorcha could get past.

As she did, he took the chance to squeeze Sorcha's behind, which earned him a glare.

"There's a fire door on the far wall and a janitor's closet in the south corner. Any trouble go for the fire door and I'll find you," Ryder said to Lacie as he too left the booth for her to slide out.

"Trouble?" she said, stopping mid-slide. "Will there be trouble?"

"Not for you while I'm around, baby," he said and kissed the top of her head.

"Kiss me here," she said, pointing to her lips.

"Happy to oblige," he said, doing as asked.

"She hates it when men talk to her," Sorcha said in explanation. "Hates it. It makes her uncomfortable."

"Okay," he said, taking Lacie's hand.

Sorcha stole the other in an attempt to drag Lacie to the dancefloor, but she didn't get far. "What?" Sorcha snapped at him.

Guiding Lacie close, Ryder stepped in and cupped her skull to angle her mouth up against his as he crouched to consume her. Any man who saw their encounter would know to steer well clear. Maybe kissing her with such devotion, or so much tongue, wasn't appropriate for the environment. But he'd forgo decency to ensure her comfort and safety.

"If you need me, just holler," he said, kissing

each corner of her mouth. "I'll have my eyes on you."

The way her body shifted told him she was thinking about their time in her bedroom that afternoon. The same memory hadn't been far from his head all day.

Sliding her hands up his chest, they glided over his shoulders and all the way around as far as they could go until she was teetering on her tiptoes. But this wasn't a move of seduction, she was holding him. When his arms locked around her, something in his heart clicked. His entire life had been about holding this woman, being a part of her. She was an extension of him.

"You don't mind staying over?" she murmured, tracing her lips against the crook of his neck.

"Do you?"

Her body melted down his. "No," she said, caressing his stubble.

No further words escaped her; the drowsiness in her air was nothing to do with exhaustion. Their visceral spark was tangible, yet all around them were oblivious.

Sorcha succeeded in dragging Lacie across the room and through the bar. Once they were safely ensconced in their pursuit, Ryder took his seat at the edge of the booth and continued to watch. Shep, in the center of the bench opposite, slurped his beer.

"If she's so rich, why does she live in a box?"

"What?" Ryder asked, swiveling his glass of ice-water by its base.

"Lacie," Shep said. "Some guy is supposed to be offering her tens of thousands for whatever it is she does, but she lives in a hole."

"Why don't you keep your opinions to yourself," Ryder said.

"I'm a detective. It's in my nature to speculate."

"Did you read that in a book somewhere?"

"Didn't get the details on how you got mixed up with this. How long have you been screwing her?"

"How many times have you or I called each other voluntarily to catch up?" Ryder asked.

Shep considered the question for a second. "Never."

"Which should give you a hint about how much I want to be involved in your personal life."

"We aren't talking about mine, we're talking about yours."

"Don't feel you have to fill the silence. I have no problem sitting here saying nothing," Ryder stated.

"I can see you're hooked," Shep said. "I'm not sure I get it."

"What?"

"She's hot, but I've seen some beauties on your arm, ones that can sit still, unlike Lacie. Is that the charm? She like that in the sack too? I can get how that tasty little tail squirming around on your cock could—"

"Enough! If you want to walk out of here with all your teeth, you'll shut your mouth and keep it that way," Ryder said, maintaining his focus on the dancing women.

Shep swilled his beer. Lacie laughed at Sorcha's spinning move and caught her when she stumbled.

"What happened to Tammy?" Shep asked.

"What?" Ryder snapped, gritting his teeth, trying to draw joy from the woman in his view.

"That stacked leggy blonde you hung about with, you were fucking her for months. Her I understood, she flamed in every room she walked into… she's single now?"

"Could be," Ryder said. "Wouldn't like your chances."

"Still got your finger in her pie too? Nice. Keep them all on a slow burn. No promises. No commitment. I like your style."

"Chasing after my cast offs?" Ryder said. "Maybe

you should get your own style."

"Are you kidding me? I'm counting the minutes 'til I get my greedy hands on the tits of that little wriggler."

Shep smacked his lips.

Ryder balled his fists. "Try it," he growled through gritted teeth. "I'd take great pleasure in ripping your body to pieces."

"Relax," Shep said, still drinking his beer. "Sorcha's good for another couple of trips. You can help yourself to her when I'm done. What she lacks in ingenuity, she more than makes up for in volume."

"Wouldn't be too sure about your chances there either," Ryder said.

"You planning to take them both on? Get enough liquor into Sorcha, doubt she'd say no. I might take a shot at that myself."

"You're full of hot air," Ryder said. "Why don't you sit here and think about that? It's the closest you'll ever get."

Ryder wasn't listening to anymore. He left Shep at the table and moved through to the bar, tipping his drink to Lacie to let her know his position. Lacie started to make her way toward him, but Sorcha got hold of her and the dancing continued. He'd like the chance to do a little dancing with Lacie himself. Of a different kind, an up close, all alone, slow sharing of each other kind of dance. For now, he'd enjoy the unfamiliar role of voyeur.

He wouldn't have thought it of himself before, but he was content to sit there watching her. He liked witnessing her rapturous laughter, enjoying herself, and her friend. She was happy and safe. His male pride swelled; his contentment came from hers.

They might not have much of a history, but he was sure their future would be secure. Even if there were bumps, or she had doubts, it wouldn't matter. He hadn't got to where he was by giving up. As he sat there watching her, there hadn't been a more crucial time in his life to be unforgivingly tenacious.

NINETEEN

Lacie

THE SUGAR FROM their lemonades kept them on the dancefloor for hours. Sorcha had been flirting on and off with a guy and his friends. Now Sorcha was in the guy's arms. Lacie herself had been approached half a dozen times too. Each time she would apologize and explain that she was with someone, pointing out exactly who that someone was if the pursuer pushed harder. Ryder didn't shy from giving them a wave and backing up her story.

Having him there gave her freedom and security. Without fear of harassment from other patrons, Lacie could suit herself. Ryder gave her an out no man could argue with. Lacie whispered to the slow-dancing Sorcha to get the nod that finally granted her the green light to leave the dancefloor.

Ryder hadn't moved from the stool at the bar since he'd sat on it. More than a couple of women had approached him, but his attention remained on her. Once or twice, Lacie tried to join him at the bar, but Sorcha pulled her back.

Now she'd put Sorcha on the clock with her new dance partner, Lacie was free to wind down her evening, and get to Ryder. The corner of his mouth curled upward as she got nearer. Quite a few females snarled at her, of that she was certain.

"You come here often?" she asked, taking herself into his arms.

"Recently?" he asked as she nuzzled closer. "Yeah."

Despite how their original night there had ended up, the reminder warmed her. "I'm tired. Do you think we'll get a room here? It's busy."

"We?" he asked.

Her body squeezed closer. When she put her mouth on his, his familiar bulge persisted in its attempt to probe her.

Purring, she wriggled against him and stole another kiss. "I told Sorcha we were leaving after this song."

"She's cozy with that guy," Ryder said.

"She enjoys the attention," Lacie said. "She's the first one to admit it. They'll have the dance then she'll blow him off. She's tired too. Is Shep still around?"

"He was messing around with some girl a while back. I'm not interested in what he's doing."

"Our things are in his car."

"I'll get them," Ryder said.

If he could break into his own modern vehicle, she didn't doubt he could get into Shep's ancient one.

"Should we find him, make sure he's okay?" Lacie asked. "Will he need a room?"

"I'll get us set in the motel and get our things," Ryder said. "We'll worry about him in the morning."

She nodded and rested her head on his shoulder. "Okay."

"Do you want to dance?" he asked.

"I didn't think you did."

"I enjoyed watching you. Now we've got the slow numbers…"

"Do you want to make out?" she asked, wrapping her arms around his waist.

"You're tired?"

"I slept in the car," she said, taking her head from its pillow. "I don't sleep well at night."

"You don't?"

"Stick around and you'll find out."

"You know there's no rush for us," he said.

"You don't want to spend the night with me?" she asked.

His arms were like a vice around her, they wouldn't let her withdraw. "There's something you should…" Ryder trailed off and then tried again. "I need to be clear with you."

"About what?" she asked. Acid began to chew at her guts. "What else haven't you told me?"

"No more secrets or lies," he said, kissing her into submission, which gave the acid a break; her body turned to Jell-O.

"So be clear…" she said.

"I want to spend the night with you."

"But?"

"But once I do, that's it," he said.

"I don't understand," she said.

"Once we spend the night together, there's no going back. You're in, we're in. You won't spend the night alone again."

"Ryder, this has all happened so fast, and—"

"You're backing out?"

"No," she said. "I don't want you to make promises that you'll feel guilty about breaking later."

"I won't break them."

"Just… no promises," she said. "I'm in, okay?

We're in now, neither of us know where this will end. But we're in it now."

He pushed her hair from her face to tilt her chin up. He took advantage of the position of her mouth for a while before he spoke again.

"My room or Sorcha's?"

"Yours," she said without hesitation. "Sorcha will want to talk all night. I'll get no sleep."

"Don't expect any in my room either."

"What did I say about promises?" she flirted.

"That's not a promise. It's an airtight guarantee," he said and kissed her again.

TWENTY

Lacie

SORCHA LEFT THE man she'd been dancing with begging for more and swept Lacie and Ryder into her wake. They got all the way outside, across the parking lot, and into the motel office with Sorcha talking the whole way. Ryder kept her hand and Sorcha stayed on her other side, arm-in-arm, chattering on.

Sorcha kept talking in the office and was quite happy to let Ryder go to the desk to get their rooms. She was busy telling Lacie about the guy who'd been hitting on her in the steakhouse. The pair followed Ryder to Sorcha's room.

"Stay," he said to her then gave her a kiss and left them alone.

Lacie didn't know how long he would take to retrieve their things.

"He's yummy," Sorcha said, kicking off her shoes as she flopped down on the bed.

"Who?" Lacie asked. "Ryder or the guy at the bar?"

"Ryder," Sorcha hummed. "He's so… male."

"That's good," Lacie said, smiling. "Otherwise my attraction to him would be kicking up all sorts of questions."

"You're different with him," Sorcha said, unbuttoning her blouse then taking out her hairpins before discarding everything on the floor. "You feel it, don't you?"

When Lacie smirked, Sorcha squealed and tossed her skirt across the room. "Yeah."

"I told you, didn't I?"

"I don't want to get in too deep," Lacie said. "Maybe it's all a sex thing—"

"It's not for him," Sorcha said. "The guy looks at you like you're the most precious thing in the world. Yeah, he looks like he wants to gobble you up too, but he definitely wants to take you home to his momma. This could be it for you! Wouldn't that be cool? Both of us settling down at the same time?"

Lacie laughed. "I'm not sure I was ever wild like you, and I'm not sure you're the settling down type." Lacie had seen some of the specimens trotted out like high-pedigree prize studs in front of Sorcha by her parents. But Sorcha had never been satisfied, she had a boldness and a confidence Lacie envied. There had been many times, like tonight, Lacie had been whirled along for the ride.

"How can I be here, Lace?" Sorcha grumbled and grabbed her friend down onto the bed beside her. "I have a thing in me… a human thing."

Sorcha plastered Lacie's hand onto her belly.

"Are you okay?" Lacie asked.

"I don't know what to do. I don't feel pregnant, and I don't know if I want to settle down."

"You know it will be okay. We'll all help you."

"I know," Sorcha sighed, sounding anything but

convinced.

"What about Bruce?" Lacie asked. "How do you feel about him?"

"I have no idea. My family will go crazy if I'm not marrying the father of my child. I'll be disinherited… but they won't be much happier about me bringing a felon into the fold."

"You can't make assumptions. We don't know how involved he is yet."

"Do you think we're going to find out? Will we find out what he's up to?"

"Yes."

"How can you be so sure?"

"Ryder won't let it go until we know," Lacie answered.

"You're so lucky," Sorcha said. "He's great."

"You're just finished telling me you don't want your fun to be over."

"It's not," Sorcha exclaimed. "My fun is not over yet."

"No," Lacie agreed. Sorcha crawled to the top of the bed and yawned. "We'll get back to the adventure tomorrow."

"Yeah," Sorcha said, closing her eyes. "Adventure."

Lacie pulled the blanket up over her friend and kissed her forehead. "Night, sleep tight."

TWENTY-ONE

Lacie

AFTER WATCHING SORCHA sleep for an age, Lacie began to tire too. Just as she pondered lying down with her friend, there was a light knock at the door then it opened.

"Trouble?" she asked.

Ryder stepped inside and put Sorcha's bag at the foot of the bed. "No," he said. "Sorry."

"I thought you'd forgotten about me."

"Not a chance," he said, taking her hands and drawing her to her feet. "You can stay here if you want. Remember, there's no pressure."

"I'm getting the feeling you want to talk me out of this."

With a smile, he twisted a strand of her hair around his forefinger. "Do you remember what I said earlier about remembering everything about our first time?" She nodded. "Usually, these things are done with so much desperation to get into bed that the whole thing's over before you have time to think about it. It's not like that with you. I want to remember this."

"Aren't I the lucky little undesirable one," she said.

"Hey now, that's not what I said," he said, gathering her close and pushing himself against her. "If I walk around like this for much longer I'm going to do myself permanent damage, and who knows one day we might want kids."

To take them away from Sorcha's room, Ryder linked his fingers between hers. At the mention of kids Lacie reeled, they'd only known each other a few days. Her attraction to him had already forgiven his deception. Usually, any lie would put her off a man, but she made all the excuses required. He didn't lie. She assumed. None of it occurred with malice. No actual harm had been caused other than her feeling silly. She had no reason to think badly of him; he'd gained nothing from the mistake.

Their room wasn't next door to Sorcha's, but it was close. As she waited for Ryder to unlock the room, Lacie tried to picture herself as a mother. Conjuring Ryder into the father role was easy. He'd be physical, lots of running around and sports, rolling around in mud and trips to the seaside to swim and hike. The trouble she had was imagining if she was capable of the complementary role.

When he opened the door, he placed a hand on the small of her back to guide her inside. Lacie came up short when she absorbed the features of the room. Lit candles covered every surface. In the center of the stripped double bed was a single rose next to an ice bucket, which held champagne for the two flutes on the nightstand.

"Ryder," she breathed. To close and lock the door, he crowded in closer behind her. "How did you do this?"

"I wasn't pacing outside talking myself into it," he said, hooking a finger around her hair to drape it down her back, giving himself access to kiss the side of her neck. "I wanted you to know that this was special."

"Oh, Ryder," she said, spinning into his arms to grab him close.

In his embrace, the warmth she'd felt for him became an inferno. Lacie had never felt overwhelming desire in her life. She'd told him that. Whatever brewed inside her was unfamiliar, but it had nothing to do with sex.

"Are you okay?" he asked.

She nodded against him then made herself break her hold so she could find his eyes. "No one's ever… This is… I honestly don't know what to say."

"There's no pressure," he said. "This is just as special to me if all we do is make out."

She grinned. "Is that the minimum requirement?"

"Yeah," he said.

He guided her to sit on the bed then popped the champagne cork and filled their flutes. While he did, Lacie picked up the rose to smell it.

"I can't believe you did all this."

"I'm desperate to get you into bed," he said, giving her a glass then seating himself beside her.

"You are not," she said, hitting him with the rose.

To keep it from being forgotten or crushed, she reached past him to put the flower next to the bed.

"We're in a shabby motel," he said. "I didn't want it to be seedy. I didn't want you to think that… I wanted to let you know that the location isn't the best I can do. I'll do better for you. Circumstances just—"

"Ryder," she said, placing a hand on his thigh. "I don't care where we are. I care who we are and that we're together. Our first kiss happened here. It's somewhat poetic that we would be back here for… this.”

“If you like returning to the scene of the crime, our anniversaries will be damn cheap.”

“Ryder,” she said, clasping his hand.

“You keep saying my name like that and I’ll do something crazy.”

“Like what?”

Removing their glasses and the ice bucket from the equation, he set them next to her rose. Holding both of her hands in one of his, he gave himself the freedom to stroke her face.

“Like make you promise to stay with me forever,” he said. “I don’t know what this is, Lace, you were right about that, neither of us do. But… something about this is right, it’s permanent. I didn’t realize my life was missing anything until I found you and then… I’m wondering what took so long for me to find you.”

Pushing forward her mouth touched his. With that slight contact, his eyes flamed, his devotion became a hunger. Usually to see a man so caught up in desire would leave her with a nagging pain, a frustration, an impatience to get it over with. This time was different. When his eyes lit, hers reflected the same fire. She wanted every second of her time with this man to count and to never end.

Despite her reservations about being a novice, she didn’t hesitate to kiss him again, to pour into him the things she couldn’t say. The things that wouldn’t articulate themselves because they were ethereal, intangible, yet vibrant within her. She was ready to explode, ready to merge herself with him and never be parted again.

Lacie kicked off her shoes without breaking their kiss and pushed him onto his back. Though she sensed reluctance, she flattened her palms to his chest. Pressing all her weight onto him, she slid her leg over his lap to straddle her bulge buddy.

For days, she'd felt his insistence, yet she'd never been this close. This free to do what she wanted, to get this close and not worry about having to hold back. Her hips moved of their own accord, squirming against him, getting that rod tight against her aching nub.

While fumbling under his tee-shirt, her mouth remained on his. She hadn't even noticed that his hands were absent until he took hold of her hips and lifted her clear off him. For the first time, she felt the shame of inexperience. It hadn't occurred to her to worry about skill or finesse, but she'd never done this before. She'd never taken the lead and never allowed herself to explore her own pleasure.

"I'm sorry," she said.

From his rigid position sprawled underneath her on the mattress, Lacie worried she'd hurt him. His head stayed tipped back and his eyes remained closed, but he held her hips a clear ten inches above his.

"You're killing me," he ground out between his clenched teeth.

"I'm sorry," she said again. "I should have let you… I'm not very good at this, and I did tell you—"

Her body crashed down on his when he released her. In the same moment, he flipped her onto her back and tucked her body beneath his.

"You almost had me coming in my pants like some rookie teenager."

"I don't understand," she frowned, tilting her head. "I'm sorry. I didn't know I—I mean I don't know how to—"

"Dusty, you're better at this than you think. If you ever figure that out, I'll be in serious trouble."

"I just wanted to kiss you," she said.

"You're like det-cord," he said, wearing half a smile. "Curled in the corner all quiet and innocent ready to blow up anything that sparks in your direction."

"Do you want me to go to Sorcha's room?" she asked.

With such an abrupt halt to proceedings, she had to wonder if something was wrong. Although he smiled, there was something tortured in the way he looked at her. However, that ridge was still between them, still there, still eager for a resolution.

"No," he said. "You just have to give me a second to calm down."

"Okay," she said, looking past him to the dancing light reflected on the ceiling.

The candles were beautiful. Such a special touch. This seduction was one she'd never forget.

"Your body," he grumbled, skimming his hand from her hair to her hip.

"What about it?"

"I love how you move, how your emotions, your feelings, your desires plug straight into your tight little muscles and make you… move."

"Can I get up?" she asked.

"No," he said, frowning instantly. "You're not going anywhere. I'm bigger and stronger. You're staying put."

His response was one of a petulant child being deprived of his favorite toy, but she had to smile. "I'll be right back." Holding his face, she drew his lips down to hers for a brief kiss. "Please."

"I'm not usually so clumsy with this, I promise you," he said. "You're just so… I want you so much."

"Okay," she said, accepting his claim. The next time she pushed his shoulders, he relented and rolled away. "What is it you Americans say?" Skirting the bed to head for the bathroom, she glanced back at him. "We need a little timeout."

"You're putting me in a timeout?" he asked,

leaping up from the bed. "Get back here."

With a laugh and a wave, she slunk into the bathroom before he could catch up to her. There was no doubt in her mind that she wanted to do this, and she wanted to do it tonight. The clawing impatience inside her had nothing to do with nerves, and everything to do with the heat gathered between her thighs, the unquenched thirst for fulfillment she'd been denied.

Checking her appearance in the mirror, she ran her hands into her hair. Having already fumbled this, she didn't want to make any more mistakes that might delay their union. Somehow, this felt important, this night, this experience, this man.

Something told her that tonight was imperative. Though her inexperience could be masking her arousal as something more significant than it was. Still, her body wanted it. Her mind played the possibilities over and over. She wanted each and every one of them right now. She took off her top and tossed it into the corner. Then reaching for the button on her jeans she decided to go all the way. Tormenting barriers had existed between them keeping them apart. She'd broken any mental and emotional barriers down to welcome him. Now she'd get rid of the physical ones too.

Every relationship she'd ever had left her feeling like more of a prude. In the past, she would never have considered stripping naked and laying herself bare for anyone. But Ryder made it easy. Everything was comfortable with him. She would push her own boundaries to experience everything with him.

Running her hands through her hair again, she flipped it over, gave it a shake and tossed it back. He might laugh at her, but she doubted it. If he wore the expression she anticipated, she would combust under his scrutiny.

She unlocked the door and opened it slowly.

"Baby, I'm sorry that—"

When he saw her, he stopped. His words stopped. His body stopped and his mouth remained open. The only part of him that moved were his eyes, he visually nibbled then gobbled what she put on display.

"You were saying something?" she asked but he clearly didn't hear her. "Ryder."

At the sound of his name, he groaned then he literally vaulted the bed to get to her. When he swept her into his arms, her laughter became a squeal. He took her from her feet, and spun her toward the bed, his mouth devouring hers.

"I want more," he growled when he tossed her down onto the bed.

Her womb contracted at that blank, primal film that settled over him. This was a man with one thing on his mind, and he would get it, he would do whatever it took. He yanked his tee-shirt over his head and was out of his jeans a flash later.

Her mouth parched when she saw the reality of his probe bobbing between his legs. He took himself in one hand as he came down on top of her, nibbling her lips, her chin, her throat. His hands were on her breasts followed by his mouth and his thickness prodded her entrance.

One of his arms came around her waist and he sucked her tongue into his mouth. Lifting her from the bed, he moved his arm from her waist to her hips, tilting her, opening her for maximum penetration potential. She'd forgotten how to breathe. Her eyes welled just looking at the girth of him, and now that girth was jabbing its way inside her. Yet the pulse of him became the pulse of her.

His body stilled. When she blinked, he was there with her, looking down into her eyes with a dedication that had her tearing up for a different reason.

"Ryder?" she whispered, sliding her hand to the side of his neck. "What's the matter?"

"You're my heaven. You're it, Lacie." A swelling of emotion released her tears. "I didn't mean to upset you, baby," he said, stroking her hair with engulfing affection.

"You haven't," she said, lifting her head to kiss him. "This is… it's better than I would have ever imagined."

"It's about to get a whole lot better," he said and kissed her again.

This was the point she readied herself to be impaled by his colossal insistence, but it didn't come. His kiss lost some of its hunger as he kissed his way down to her chest. Her eyes rolled back when his mouth found her nipple. The wave crashed to the shore when his hand moved down her belly to the slush between her thighs. One finger slid inside, she hissed at the unexpected invasion. The knuckle of his thumb pressed against her clit and her whole body bucked up toward his. A second finger joined the first. Of their own volition, her legs moved higher coiling themselves around his waist, trying desperately to bring him down into her.

"Wait, baby," he whispered. "You're tight. I don't want to hurt you."

His words bred her whimper. She wanted him. The fear was gone. Her hips undulated against his fingers until he didn't move at all. Sliding up and down his digits, she wriggled against his thumb. Her short little pants were punctuated by his kisses.

"My god," he sighed.

It wasn't for her, but she pushed hard up against him as a blast of pleasure burst inside her. On a gasp, she said his name and pushed up. He stroked her over the edge again, doing the work for her spent body.

Flopping back against the mattress, she didn't

want to open her eyes, didn't want this divine moment to end. Remaining beneath him, she wriggled down but his hands clamped her hips in place.

Opening her eyes, she saw that brutal intensity again. His next kiss was harsh, punishing, but so complete he reached down inside of her and stole her soul. His hands massaged her breasts like they were his, like it was his god given right to have his hands on her anywhere he pleased, anytime. But that was what she wanted. On another whimper, she breathed into his mouth. He slid down her, sampling her, licking, sucking, nibbling every part of her, learning the routes and stops he'd need from here on in.

The sharp drag of his teeth on her nipple drew a yelp. Her body spasmed up again in desperation to have him have her, but still he did not. His mouth moved lower and lower and when his hands gripped her inner thighs, the sting of his strength was salved with his tongue. He circled her entrance, lapping the juice of her previous release, and tasted his way to her center.

He kissed and licked her. She struggled to stay still; she wanted to move against him, to use him to pleasure her. Except he was doing it, taking all control by holding her firmly in place for his consumption. Her body fought against his hands now, not out of displeasure but in a desire to get closer, to mate, to be one, to move each moment on to the next. When he sucked her into his mouth, she screeched. He salved her briefly only to pinch at her with his teeth.

As his tongue dragged around her, again she screamed out his name. "Ryder! Oh god!"

The pounding in her chest was matched by that in her head and loins. Pleasure like this should be illegal. The experience was so heady that stars flashed in front of her. Her whole body tingled with the endorphins he'd poured into her and stirred up into a frenzy.

"You okay?" he asked.

Only now did she realize that he was at her side again. He stroked her hair and kissed her shoulder and her neck.

"I've never..." she panted. "I mean this is..."

"Hey, it's okay."

He rose above her again, but the agony in his eyes had her coming up short. Her hands leaped to his chest.

When he brushed her cheek, she realized she was crying again. "I'm sorry," she said, swiping at her cheeks. "I'm ruining it and it's perfect, Ryder. You're perfect, everything's so..."

"Perfect?" he asked. She nodded appreciating his joke. "I want you to be happy. I want you to have pleasure and I want to be the one delivering it."

"I've never... Like this, with someone I... not like this, nothing has been like this, but—"

"You've never had an orgasm with a man," he said. She shook her head. Stroking her again, he kissed her hair. "You won't have to worry about that anymore now, will you?" She shook her head again. "I'm doing okay?"

Her laugh was half sob, but she nodded. "You're doing more than okay."

"I know," he said with a cheeky glint. "You're the hottest thing I've ever... you're just the hottest thing."

Though he lay on his side next to her as naked as she was, despite all they'd just done, when his eyes slid down her body, she suppressed an internal shiver.

"You're big," she said, speaking her mind with him as had become their custom.

The statement didn't garner a response. His hand slid down from under her breast to her abdomen. She knew where it was headed so grabbed it to stop its journey.

"You've played with me enough tonight," she said. "You'll ruin me."

"I plan to," he said. "Over and over again."

He tried to take his hand from her grip but when she held fast, he desisted. "What's wrong?"

"I want your dick in me."

"That's about as straight talking as it comes."

"It's what I want," she said, letting her fingers curl around his length, gauging his size with a squeeze. His breathing grew shallow, and his hand moved back to her breast, testing her flesh, it seemed, as an anchor to combat the motion of her hand. "You're big."

"I'm not going to hurt you," he said.

The elbow he'd been propped on gave out so he could nestle her closer. When she squeezed tighter, he hissed out a breath.

Lacie released him and urged him to his back so she could roll on top of him. Her shoulders were narrower than his chest, but she'd always been little. Her breasts pillowed her ribs from his. The crush had her rubbing them against him enjoying the rasp of his hair against her engorged nipples.

His blunt head nudged her when her legs slid down on either side of his. Sitting up, she sandwiched him between her folds and undulated back and forth. His solidity gave resistance against her nub that encouraged her own panting. Holding her hair up, away from her neck, she ground up and down, back and forth, rolling her clit, squeezing it between her pubic bone and his erection. Her juices coated him reducing the friction but increasing her speed.

In the melee of her gratification, she'd almost forgotten what her pleasure was attached to until two huge hands closed over her breasts and pinched her nipples. Instantly she shattered. The cascade hit her again and she clawed at his hands, begging him closer before she collapsed over him and let out a long sigh.

"Now that was something," he said moments later, stroking her hair.

Shame flooded her. Lacie pushed her hands to his chest, keeping them apart to look him in the eye. "I didn't mean to do that. I'm sorry, I—"

"Would you stop apologizing," he said, testing the weight of her breasts that hung between them. "That was one of the hottest things I've ever seen in my life. I want to be your sex toy, day and night, whatever you need, baby, I'm there."

"One of the hottest things?" she asked, dropping down, trapping his hands between her breasts and his chest.

"Right on a par with you walking out of that bathroom buck naked. That's the image I'll replay on my deathbed."

Nudging him, she laughed at his mischief, and kissed him one more time. "Should we use a condom?"

"I'm clean," he said. "Last physical was just two weeks ago. But if you're more comfortable—"

"I'm on the Pill," she said.

"I know. They're in my jeans somewhere."

"So you don't mind if I…?"

"Ride me bareback? Not at all, baby, knock yourself out. I'm here for whatever you need."

With a show of aloof male pride, he stretched his arms out then linked his fingers behind his head.

"You're big, it might take me a minute to—"

"Hey," he said suddenly all serious. "We don't have to—"

She covered his mouth with her hand. "Shut up. I told you what I wanted."

Their eyes locked; they just watched each other. Her hand slipped away and her mouth dropped to his. They kissed for an age. Slow, fast, nibbling, passionate, from one extreme to the other, learning each lilt and crevice. He clasped her rear to roll them onto their sides, holding her against him, her arms looped around his neck.

The raw union of their naked bodies wanted more than the tangle of their tongues.

Her legs coiled around him, locking at the small of his back. He took control of her body and the mating of their mouths. Shifting one of his hands between them to rub her and test her opening, he stimulated her. Humidity built. When their eyes met again, the light had become shadow, and the moment so intimate, her heart opened to welcome his. When his finger slid free, the next occupier would stretch her; she throbbed with expectation.

With a fist around himself, he pressed into her. She hissed. He stilled with obvious panic on his face, and he wasn't one to panic. Lacie took the opportunity to caress him. With a smile, she kissed away his concern. When he relaxed, her body did too, which let him bob that first inch in and out to get her accustomed to the invader.

His intention wasn't veiled for long, he pushed in another inch. She swallowed her breath, pushing up to take him deeper. Never had she been stretched like this. Her limit was reached and surpassed, but she was determined to take all of him. They kissed and fondled, rocked together then his whole body went rigid. The glaze in his eyes wouldn't let him blink them from hers.

The impact of that intensity filled her; he was inside her, all of him. The sting of her tissues brought an ache that made her want to pull back. But the sheer gratification of being so completely pushed to the limit was hedonistic. He filled her, stretched her, made way inside her for his occupation.

He remained static, like his body was teaching

hers what was required. This was him and this was what she had to yield to accept him. His body wanted this space inside of her, and he'd take up residence to prove it.

Indulgence eased her tension; she pushed up at the moment he pushed down. Each and every stretched pore screamed for him in that climax of anticipation again. He growled and braced her down, but her muscles clamped around him.

All the while, she panted his name. "Ryder," she said. "Oh my god!"

"Baby," he murmured. "You're coming all over me and I haven't even moved yet."

Her apology never left her tongue when she saw the glee on his face; male pride and possession mixed with utter longing.

Lacie shuddered again. "You fit," she whispered. "Just."

"You're god damn right I do," he said and pulled back only to slide back in with delicious slowness.

Her insides gave to his will. He widened her as he extended himself within her. When he pulled out, she sucked him back in. With each tug he gave, each push, she yielded. Their synchronistic motion fused with the thrum of their simultaneous pleasure. The pace gathered, he was in her, out, in, her body wanted to explode, she couldn't breathe fast enough but wanted more now, all of him.

"Yes!" she hollered. "Oh god, Ryder!" She gasped and he hit her deep, making her scream. He slowed for a moment, but she dug her nails into his shoulder. "Don't stop!" she begged.

He hit hard again. That button pushed her over the edge, screaming for him as she clawed to take him within her. He growled and tensed, thrusting deep within her as she milked every drop of him, taking his seed inside of her, wanting every bit of him and then some more.

His weight came down on top of her; they lay together in the fog of their own humid panting. She stroked up and down wanting to soothe and care for the man who spoiled her. She kissed his shoulder. He rolled to his back keeping her in his arms, but slipped out of her body, which left her feeling oddly bereft. Now that he'd occupied her, she didn't want to be deprived of his habitation.

"Do you want me to get a blanket?" she asked, kissing his chest.

"What for?" he asked, burying his face in her hair.

"We might get cold when we're asleep."

"Sleep," he said. "What gave you the idea we were going to sleep?"

Lifting her head to witness the grin in his voice, she wasn't sure if he was serious or not. "We're done... aren't we?"

He swept her up into his arms, she clambered to keep hold of him when with one motion he pounced onto his feet to stand in the center of the bed.

"Done? That was the prologue. Now we do it in the shower... we've got a lot of bases to cover tonight, baby. I told you that you wouldn't get any sleep in my room."

He leaped off the bed with her still in his arms. She wasn't sure whether to scream or laugh, so she did a bit of both. Apparently, he was an ideas man, and she couldn't fault him for that. This had already been the ride of her life; she had a feeling it wouldn't end any time soon.

TWENTY-TWO

Lacie

"GIVE ME IT," Ryder said, reaching for her bag.

Lacie pulled it away. "I can carry my own bag," she said. "It weighs nothing."

"Neither do you and you can be difficult when you want to be."

"We were supposed to be out of here an hour ago," Lacie said. "Sorcha will be worried. She doesn't know where our room is."

"You were the one who insisted on having all that sex this morning."

Contrary to what he'd said, they had slept last night… for a couple of hours. "Uh, I woke up with your mouth…"

"My mouth, what?" he asked, mischief in his eyes.

"You know exactly what you were doing," she said, swinging her bag out of his reach again. "You started it."

"I did," he said. "But you didn't have to join me

in the shower this morning."

Heat suffused her cheeks. "I was saving water."

This behavior might bring a blush to her cheeks because she was still new to it, but she didn't shift her eyes from his. In fact, she let a smile touch her mouth, and it was just playful enough to have his smile fall to a smolder.

"No!" she asserted, rounding her eyes, but he was already upon her.

She couldn't refuse his mouth. Not when he was battling the same torment she'd struggled with knowing he was in the shower alone and naked. His tongue tangled with hers; she grabbed the back of his neck with one hand. He swept her bag from the other. Just as soon as he did that, he broke their kiss.

"Ha!" he said, triumphant, holding both bags up in one of his hands.

"That's cheating!" she cried, but he just opened the motel room door and gestured for her to exit. "That's cheating."

She passed with her nose in the air.

He hooked her under his arm and closed the door behind him with his bag hand. "I'll make it up to you," he mumbled into her hair, pressing a kiss to her head at the same time.

When they got to Sorcha's door, he knocked with the hand that was around her.

"It's sad," she said.

"What's sad?" he asked, leaning back.

Lacie assumed that he was trying to look in Sorcha's window. "It's all over."

"What's over?" he asked, glancing around.

"Our night, you know, us."

"Uh huh… What?" he snapped, having taken an extra second to process her words.

"It would have been nice to spend the morning

in bed, that's all."

"Right," he said, his concern evaporated. "I thought you meant… nothing."

"What?" she asked.

"Try the door."

Lacie didn't ask why, just opened her friend's bedroom door and swung it back on its hinges. The bed was a mess, it had been slept in, but no one was in it now. Lacie didn't have the time to panic, the sound of the bathroom door opening carried to them. Sorcha appeared wrapped in a towel.

"Lacie," she said, glancing back at the bathroom. "You're early."

"Actually, I'm late," Lacie said, stepping into the room only to freeze when someone emerged from the bathroom behind Sorcha.

Someone very naked… someone very Shep.

"Little lady!" Shep exclaimed.

Lacie held up a hand. "Spare me," she said then fixed on Sorcha who at least had the decency to appear ashamed.

"Am I getting my two for one," Shep asked, cozying up behind the rigid Sorcha.

Ryder cleared his throat, presumably to let Shep know that he was there. He hadn't ventured into the room and Lacie couldn't blame him.

"We'll leave you to it, I suppose," Lacie said. "Just let us know when you're ready to get this charade on the road again."

Lacie wasn't going to stand with them for longer than was necessary. She spun to leave, remembering only at the last minute to navigate around Ryder. Then she was glad that he had her bag because it didn't slow her down. She wanted out of there, away from the scene she'd just witnessed as fast as she could go. The coffee place set back between the motel and the steakhouse was open at this time. It never had been on any of the nights they'd rolled up. She marched on in and dumped herself at a window table.

"Do you want to tell me what that was about?" Ryder asked, sliding in opposite her.

"Not really," she said, taking the laminated menu from its holder at the top of the table. "Are you hungry? What do you like? My treat."

"She had sex with Shep."

"Looks that way," Lacie said. "Do you know what I love about America? Pancakes. You guys make great pancakes, and they're available everywhere… much more than at home."

He whipped the menu away from her hand. "Dusty, what is it?"

"Can I have my menu back please?" she asked.

He didn't relent and she didn't either, not until the waitress came over.

"What can I get you?"

"Two coffees," Lacie said. "And pancakes for me…" Ryder said nothing. "We'll share."

The waitress examined both of them but didn't crack her deadpan expression before moseying away.

"Tell me what's going on," Ryder said.

"No," Lacie said, glancing around the diner at the cracked-Formica tables and duct-tape- stitched static stools.

"Why not?"

"Because… she's my best friend."

"I'm your boyfriend." Lacie kept her attention on the coffee machine behind the counter and folded her arms. Distracting herself from the sting behind her eyes with her examination of the room. "Right?" he asked with authority. She nodded. "So tell me."

When Lacie looked at him, she caught sight of Sorcha through the window crossing the parking lot.

Lacie leaped up. "Wait here," she said.

Leaving the coffee place as quickly as she had entered it, she met Sorcha halfway. Though she could see the tears in her friend's eyes, it didn't quench any of her anger.

"I'm sorry," Sorcha sobbed.

Lacie got hold of her hand and pulled her to the back of the motel office. Although they were likely still visible from parts of the coffeeshop, she hoped neither of the men would see them.

"What were you thinking?" Lacie hissed.

"I'm sorry. I don't know."

"It's not me you have to apologize to," Lacie said. Normally she'd never take such a stern line with anyone, even her best friend, but that morning was different. "I don't even know what to say to you, Sorch."

"Please don't be angry with me," Sorcha said.

"How did it even happen? When I left you were sleeping."

"I don't know," Sorcha said. "I woke up and he was knocking on the door. He said there were no other rooms and I… I don't know, Lace. I'm sorry."

The difficulty with being angry at someone over something in the past was that it was finished. Often nothing could be done to change it.

"What if we find Bruce today? What are you going to tell him? Have you told Shep the truth?"

Sorch shook her head. "We didn't talk."

"Course not," Lacie said.

"What am I going to do? What am I going to do?"

"I can't get you out of this one either," Lacie said though Sorcha clung to her. "We could go home, forget about Bruce for a while, but that means facing your family."

"I can't do that," Sorcha said. "Bruce doesn't

need to know about last night, does he?"

"Ask Shep," Lacie said. "He doesn't know why we're looking for Bruce. He doesn't know about your condition."

"I'm pregnant not contagious," Sorcha snapped.

"I didn't mean that," Lacie said. "But were you careful?" Sorcha averted her eyes, the answer shone in their place. "If he has anything… you have to think about your child."

"Don't stand there being sanctimonious," Sorcha barked. "You couldn't keep your legs shut last night either, so don't look down your nose at me for something you did too."

Sorcha didn't snap at her, she just didn't… except she just had.

"Sorcha," Lacie muttered.

"I'm sorry. Oh, I'm sorry, Lace," she said, still clinging onto Lacie's arm. "I know it's a mess. I made a mess."

Like she had a penchant for doing.

Lacie sighed. "Tell me what you want to do."

"I don't know," Sorcha said. Lacie tried to turn away, but Sorcha pulled her back. "I'll tell Shep not to say anything. He'll keep his mouth shut. He's not interested in me, not for anything serious."

"You want to find Bruce?" Lacie asked. Sorcha nodded. "Are you sure? We don't have to do this. If you want to go home, we can."

"I can't do that," Sorcha said. "I have to find Bruce. He's not getting out of this one. I am not doing this alone."

"Don't be motivated by fear," Lacie said with a pang of sorrow for her friend. "I know you're scared. This is… it's unexpected and it's daunting, and…" Fat tears rolled over Sorcha's lashes, streaking down her perfect skin. "It'll be okay. You'll be okay."

Lacie gathered Sorcha into her arms. When Sorcha inhaled like that, Lacie recognized it as a prelude to the onslaught, and she was right. Sorcha sucked in long unattractive breaths and wailed in Lacie's arms like a child learning the truth of Santa Claus too young. Lacie stroked her hair and whispered words of comfort to her friend.

They stood for a while as Sorcha let out all her upset. Lacie damped her friend's tears with her sleeve, but let Sorcha wipe her nose on her own. Sorcha's lip still quivered so Lacie took her down onto the paving. Sitting propped against the rough concrete of the motel office back wall, Lacie held Sorcha in her arms.

She whispered into her hair, telling Sorcha the story of their first meeting. Lacie knew the best way to distract Sorcha was with a story. It didn't matter if it was new or one she already knew. Lacie kept it light, added the humor, and within ten minutes, Sorcha was laughing again.

"You're the best friend in the whole wide world," Sorcha said, sitting up straighter while keeping her head on Lacie's shoulder.

"You've been there for me," Lacie said. "I prop you up, you prop me."

"Ladies." Lacie wanted to swear when she saw Shep looming over them. "Unless this love-in's about to get intimate we should get a move on."

"You're a prick," Sorcha barked, clambering up to her feet.

"Didn't seem to bother you last night, sweetheart."

"You two should talk." Lacie rose from the ground. "I'll be in the coffeeshop if you need anything," she said to Sorcha, squeezing her hand.

In the coffeeshop, the table she'd occupied with Ryder was vacant. Before she could wonder where he was, a whistle drew her attention around to a table in the opposite direction.

"What are you doing over here?" she asked, joining him. He nodded out of the window, and she saw Sorcha and Shep talking… or some variation of that. "You were spying on me?"

"Keeping look out."

She tore a piece of pancake from the stack and dipped it in the syrup around the edge of the plate, then scooped it into her mouth.

"Sugar rush," she said, but took another piece in the same way.

"Mm hmm."

"What?" she asked, noticing him staring at her mouth, gripping his mug with white knuckles. "What's the matter?"

Sucking each finger in turn, she pushed the plate aside.

"I'm thinking about you," he said. "And maple syrup."

She smiled. "Are you?"

"That, and your mouth… and what else you could suck on."

Lacie leaned closer to quip, but in her peripheral vision Sorcha marched away from the coffeeshop, alone.

"Oh my god," she said.

Scrambling out of the booth, she charged right past Shep and out into the parking lot to chase her friend down.

"Sorch!" she called.

Her friend was running down a grass decline. "He's an idiot!" Sorcha shouted over her shoulder without stopping.

"Where are you going?"

"Home," Sorcha snapped. "Who needs him? No one, that's who."

"You're walking home?" Lacie said, catching up to Sorcha. "You can't walk home."

"I'm not getting in a car with him. I'll walk every step before I let him help me."

"Okay, Sorch," Lacie said. "Let me get my bag, and we'll…"

"No," Sorcha said. "I'm going now."

Her friend could be stubborn, but this was madness.

"Okay," Lacie said, falling into step with Sorcha.

"What?" Sorcha asked, drawing to a halt. "You can't walk with me."

"Why not?" Lacie asked. "If you are walking, why can't I?"

"You'll never make it," Sorcha said.

"You're talking to the girl who grew up with a bus pass. Your first car was a Bentley."

"Don't—don't do that! He did that! I'm not a spoiled little princess! I do not want my own way!"

"Forget about him," Lacie said. "What do you want to do? Do you want to go home, or do you want to find Bruce?"

"I'll find Bruce. I'll find him on my own."

"Just because Shep is a prick doesn't mean that you have to endanger yourself. Screw him. If he's being a bastard, let him go home alone. There are other ways to find Bruce."

"Ryder, you mean Ryder?"

"He'll help us," Lacie said.

"Only while you keep sleeping with him," Sorcha whinnied. "Men are pricks."

Lacie put her arm around Sorcha's waist and began to lead her back toward the hill they'd come down.

"I know," Lacie said, placating her friend.

"You did sleep with him, didn't you?"

"Yes," Lacie said.

"This is when he'll start losing interest."

As Sorcha rested her head on her friend's shoulder, Lacie looked up to see Ryder at the top of the hill looking down on them. He didn't look happy. Sorcha kept talking until they got up the hill and was then genuinely surprised to see Ryder waiting for them.

"What are you doing here?" Sorcha asked him.

Shep skulked in the background.

"Shep has something to say to you, Sorcha," Ryder said, taking Lacie's arm to draw her away from her friend.

Lacie watched Shep talk to Sorcha while the couple moved in the direction of the coffeeshop.

Ryder stopped, holding Lacie in place. "Don't do that to me," he commanded.

"What?" she asked, still watching the other couple though they were now ten yards away and out of earshot.

"Disappear from my line of sight without warning," he said. "I had to get all the way out of there while god knows what could have been happening to you. Wide perimeter security only works if both parties respect—"

Putting her fingers to his mouth, she smiled. "I'm not your client."

"I know that," he said though that furrow in his brow hadn't got the memo.

"I'm Lacie Hart. We spent the night together one time… do you remember?" Still he frowned, and she didn't think it was because she was losing her comedic touch. "What's the matter?"

"I don't know this area well enough," he said. "I'll have to start advancing our trips twenty-four hours ahead of time."

"This is the worst part," she said. "When I'm home, I hardly ever go out."

"Good," he said.

Tension radiated off him.

"Do you want to get a room and we can find a way to relax you?"

Pushing to her tiptoes, she kissed him until his hands unclenched. On the next kiss, he grasped her waist. A few seconds later, he had her toes off the ground. His arms were wrapped all the way around her, holding her against him.

"Sorcha tells me this is the part where you start to lose interest," she teased, kissing him again. "Didn't you get that memo?"

His anger had receded to an equally potent emotion. "Apparently not."

"She doesn't want anyone to know how she spent last night," Lacie said.

Ryder hadn't yet put her down, but he sauntered toward the coffeeshop again. "I don't blame her."

"I mean it," Lacie said, flattening her voice of any innuendo. "You won't—"

"You don't have to request my discretion," he said. "You told me what's important to you: privacy and loyalty. I heard you the first time. You don't have to tell me twice."

"Will Shep be as discreet when we find Sorcha's... you know?"

"Shep's not the settling down type," Ryder said. "He doesn't want to get mixed up with anyone and wouldn't get between anything for fear he might be the one left holding the baby. No pun intended."

She nodded. "You can put me down."

"Don't want to," he said. "You might run away again."

"Okay," Sorcha said.

Ryder let Lacie slide down his body to under his arm and kept her close when they approached Sorcha.

"Okay?" Lacie asked. "This is us now? Are we leaving?"

Shep was beside Sorcha though neither of them looked happy with the other.

"Yes," Sorcha said. "The boys will travel up front today."

"We will?" Ryder said.

"Yes," Sorcha said, reaching for Lacie. "You'll have to learn to share her if we're ever going to get along."

Lacie let herself be taken from Ryder's embrace, but she wasn't happy about it, not that she would tell her friend. Ryder had been a good sport about her friend's temperamental behavior. Lacie didn't want to push him too far. If he didn't tire of her, she'd be lucky, but he'd be more inclined to tire of Sorcha's moods if they carried on like this.

Still, they all went to the car and got in. From somewhere, Ryder produced a cardboard cup for her, and she grinned when their eyes met.

"You brought me coffee," she said.

"Yeah, what happened to your treat? That's two breakfasts you owe me now."

His static expression made her smile.

Sorcha tutted and took the cup from Lacie. "If the man can't afford breakfast, ditch him." She sipped the coffee and hummed. "Though, he gets big points for trying."

Ryder turned back to the windscreen. Lacie pushed her hands to her lap. He wasn't happy. Lacie wanted to silence her friend and to apologize to Ryder. Sorcha was clearly taking her foul mood with Shep out on Ryder. That wasn't fair when he'd been nothing but wonderful to her.

The journey carried on and no one was saying a word. Lacie eventually got her coffee back, but it was almost cold. In contradiction to her liquid consumption, Sorcha fell asleep promptly… Still, no one said a word.

TWENTY-THREE

NOTHING WAS SAID until they rolled up in the street Lacie and Ryder had fled days before. Sorcha hadn't been awake for long; her epic yawn was matched by a feline stretch.

"This is it?" Sorcha asked. "Doesn't strike me as Bruce's style."

"Right there," Lacie said, pointing to the communal entrance that she hadn't known would be recognizable until laying eyes on it.

It flooded back like a lucid nightmare she'd much rather forget.

Shep got out of the car to stretch his legs. Not to be outdone, Sorcha bounded out immediately after him. Lacie was in no rush to leave the vehicular sanctuary and was grateful that Ryder stayed in his seat too. After his own examination of the building, he turned to her.

"Do you want to make out?" she asked.

The joke was feeble even to her own ears.

"You can stay right here," Ryder said. "You don't

have to set foot inside. I'll lock the door and—"

"You're not going in there without me. If I stay here, you stay here."

"Do you want Sorcha upstairs with only Shep for protection?"

"Do you want me down here with no one?" Lacie asked.

Ryder looked around. "No, I don't. I don't like anything about this. I don't work like this."

"Ryder," she yelped, bouncing to the front of the seat when she saw Shep and Sorcha heading for the door.

"Wait here," he said and left the car.

Lacie wanted to follow but didn't want to add to the chaos. They'd all been so wrapped up in their own issues that no one had thought to discuss their non-existent plan. Except now, Ryder was taking obvious control. With a few words, he had Sorcha scurrying back to the car while he and Shep kept talking.

"We've to wait in here," Sorcha said, climbing back into the car at her side.

They sat for a moment while the men spoke then Shep stayed put and Ryder came back to the car. Sorcha rolled the window down as Ryder ducked to talk to them through the space.

"We're going to go up alone. You two stay here. If there's any trouble, hit the horn and we'll be back in a flash. Keep the doors locked and the windows up."

He spoke to both of them but looked more at her. Yet there was a detachment in his stature. When he turned away, Sorcha began rolling up the window, but Lacie wasn't placated.

Grabbing for the door, she popped it open. "Stay," she said to Sorcha while leaping from the car and slamming the door behind her.

The men paused to see her rush over.

"I'm coming," she insisted.

"No," Ryder said, taking her arm and guiding her round as though to take her back to the car, but she yanked her arm free from his grip.

"You don't trust him," she said, pointing to Shep who watched on. "He won't have your back. I won't let you walk in there alone."

"Baby—"

"No," she said, shrugging away from his reach. "I'm coming up."

"Do you remember what happened the last time you were up there, do you?" he argued. "I will not put you in that kind of danger!"

This argument shouldn't he held there when they may be ambushed at any time. So instead of vocalizing her concerns and wasting time, she skirted around Ryder and got as far as Shep when Ryder caught her up.

"I'm going up."

Whipping her off her feet, Ryder pinned her to the wall. Lacie struggled until he pushed closer.

"You're waiting here," he said. "You're staying here to be my back-up. My phone is in the duffel. If we're not back in five minutes, you phone the police and call the contact SW, okay?"

"I don't want you up there alone," she murmured, sliding her hands to his face.

"I'll come back to you, baby, every time," he said. "Trust me."

Clinging to him, she held him close, then released him enough to kiss the mouth so central to her pleasure last night. Hopefully it would do the same on some nights in the future.

"Come home," she murmured to which he nodded while setting her on her feet.

"Do I get one?" Shep asked.

Ryder shoved him up the stairs and glanced at her before continuing on up himself.

She listened to their footsteps until she couldn't hear anymore. Going back to the street, Sorcha sat eagerly staring out of the car. Lacie gave her a smile, but stayed on the asphalt, pacing, while craning her ear for sounds of aggression or distress.

Her heartbeat echoed in her ears with the reverberation of her footsteps on the sidewalk. Her watch beat each second on the clock, a foot closer, each step a moment in time longer than the rest, dragging out their time apart, their distance. A sound above made her pause. She tipped her head to see Ryder looking down at her.

"They've cleared out," he said. "Come on up."

Lacie made a stop at the car for Ryder's phone and for Sorcha. The pair went up the stairs. Sorcha seemed eager to get to the apartment, but the place gave Lacie chills. As if he had known of her anxiety, Ryder was in the doorway waiting for her. Sorcha bounded past him, exuberant that her adventure was progressing.

"Did they leave anything?" she asked him.

"I've looked through what's left in the trash, but the place is bare."

"Just like it was," she said.

The furniture was sparse when they'd been here the last time. The room they'd been in hadn't had a thing in it.

"Do you want to come in?" he asked. "You don't have to."

"We're a team," she said.

"Yes, we are," he said, giving her a kiss then taking her hand to guide her inside.

They spent almost half an hour looking for any hint of where the men had gone, or what they had been up to. But there was nothing of evidential value beneath the takeaway trays.

"What now?" Sorcha asked when they got back

to the street.

"Now we follow the money," Ryder said. "I spoke to Toby last night. There are a few leads though there are more than a few walls in the way."

"That means someone doesn't want to be snooped on," Shep said.

"Yes," Ryder said. "Which means when we break through the encryptions, we'll get answers."

"So we just wait?" Sorcha asked.

"We'll get answers," Lacie said. "But there's no point hanging around here."

"What an anti-climax," Sorcha huffed.

Shep and Ryder shared a look over the car when they held the doors for the women. Lacie caught it but said nothing.

The drive was as silent as it had been before they arrived. There was some chit-chat about the traffic. Shep put on the radio, and they chatted about some items on the news. After that, silence fell over them again.

"We have to find him before next Friday," Sorcha said.

"Your parents anniversary bash," Lacie said.

"Yes," Sorcha said. "Then it's Sadie's birthday the following week. Are you coming to the spa weekend?"

"I don't know," Lacie said, wishing the silence back.

"You can't leave me alone with my sister and her friends."

"Sadie and I don't get along at the best of times."

"She'll be thrilled to have you," Sorcha said. "It's all about her, remember?"

"Beth is over that week," Lacie said.

"Not until the Monday," Sorcha said. "And she's only coming for a few days."

"I'll wait and see. I have that meeting with

Darwin next weekend."

"Are you expecting to accept his offer?" Sorcha asked, shocked at the notion.

"I don't expect anything."

"You don't even like Darwin," Sorcha said. "He tried to feel you up at the opening."

"Which is why I don't like those things," Lacie said in jest. Sorcha didn't laugh and neither did Ryder who turned to her in the same moment. "What? You're coming with me."

"Did you tell him about Jimmy?" Sorcha asked, picking invisible lint from her skirt.

"Leave Jimmy out of this," Lacie said. "He's harmless."

"Who's Jimmy?" Ryder asked.

"An undergrad working with the gallery in town. He's like her puppy dog whenever she's in to see Monty, the curator. He's adorable… he probably won't like you though. You're getting access to the underwear he's been thinking about for months while jerking off," Sorcha said.

"Don't," Lacie said. "It makes me uncomfortable when you joke like that. He's a sweetheart."

Sorcha leaned forward toward Ryder. "She's so naive."

"What about you?" Lacie asked Ryder.

"What about me?"

"You're learning all about my life…" Lacie said.

"Good point," Sorcha said, following Lacie's lead just as she knew she could rely on her friend to do. "You can't expect to just move into our Lacie's life. We have a strict screening process."

"We do?" Lacie asked. "Has it ever been effective?"

"We stepped it up after Matt."

"Might have been a good idea to do it before

then," Lacie said.

"Who is Matt and what did he do to you?" Ryder demanded.

"Uh-uh," Sorcha said. "We're not answering any more questions about Lacie until we learn more about you. Are you sticking around or are you going to break her heart? Because if it's the latter you can get lost right now, and we can jet off to Cancun."

"Carlos," Lacie said, seeing through her friend's motive. "Is that where you went?"

"I love his casa," Sorcha said.

"How many men have you got on the go, sugar-hips? Shep asked.

"No one's talking to you," Sorcha sniped.

"Carlos is her cousin," Lacie explained.

"No more information," Sorcha said, taking Lacie's hand on the center seat. "He hasn't answered the question yet."

"He's not going to tell you that he's playing her," Shep said. "He'll just stop calling like every other man on the planet would."

"Actions speak louder than words," Lacie said.

"Ask him about Tammy," Shep said.

"Who is Tammy?" Sorcha asked Ryder.

"His ex-girlfriend," Shep answered for him. "Super-hot, supermodel type, smokin', I'm telling you."

"So?" Sorcha demanded at Shep's salacious suggestion.

Lacie wriggled deeper into her seat. A woman like that would know how to do things to a man that Lacie had never heard of.

"I'm telling you," Shep said. "She was every man's wet dream. He probably had to blackmail her into bed. How did you get her into bed? You were on the job, right? Did you drug her?"

"How many times did you meet Tammy?" Ryder

asked Shep. "Two or three times max."

"I didn't have to meet her. No guy cares what comes out of the mouth of a woman like that, unless it's his cock then pumping its way back in."

"Lovely," Sorcha said.

"True story," Shep said. "Ask him about his gang of eight. Ask him about their work off the books."

"Full of yourself now," Ryder warned. "But you'll have to stop this car eventually."

"What have you got yourself involved in, Lace?" Sorcha asked. "You thought my taste in men was risqué, you've got yourself a thug. Every woman loves a bad boy, how lucky are you? Maybe he could beat the crap out of Matt for you."

"This conversation is entirely inappropriate," Lacie said.

"That's Lacie's way of saying she's creeped out," Sorcha said. "How long will it take for you to find Bruce?"

"Who are you talking to?" Lacie asked.

The men looked at each other. Lacie would swear the scent of testosterone ratcheted up.

"I don't care who finds him so long as someone does."

"I'll find him for you, sweetheart," Shep said.

"You're doing such a great job so far," Ryder said.

"I'm working off your sketchy information," Shep said.

"You didn't consider getting any of your own?"

"You boys better play nice," Sorcha said. "There will be a very big check at the end of this for whoever gets the information about where he is and what he's up to."

"You want accurate information," Lacie said.

"Sure," Sorcha said. "But there's nothing wrong

with a little healthy competition."

They turned into Lacie's street. A moment later, Shep stopped the car and jumped out to rush them all out of his car, probably so he could get back to the investigation. When everyone had piled out and retrieved their bags, Sorcha lifted a hand.

"I want a meeting tomorrow," Sorcha said. "And I'll expect an answer. Shep's office at noon."

Shep jumped back into his car and sped away down her street.

Sorcha took Lacie's hand. "Girl's night! Only you can make me feel better."

Lacie knew what that meant. The rest of the day would be pedicures and cocktails… virgin.

"Okay," Lacie said. "Give me a minute."

Sorcha glanced at Ryder, then went into Lacie's place using her own key.

Ryder threw his bag into his truck. "Seems I'm not the one who is going to have the trouble sharing," he said. "I thought we could do dinner."

"She's going through a tough time. I know she isn't always easy, but she's scared. I don't envy her position. I would be terrified."

"You'll never be in that position," he said, gathering her into his arms.

"I envy your confidence."

"I'll never be mixed up in anything that could endanger you. And for sure you'll never be in her condition without me at your side."

"We haven't really had a chance to… talk about this."

"We could do that tonight," he said. "I've got a big bed and a great view… I can light a few candles…"

"I don't know how long Sorcha will want to stay. She might sleep over."

"I'd be a lot more fun," he said, teasing.

She didn't get the sense he was offended. He meant what he was saying yet didn't begrudge her Sorcha. That made Lacie like him even more.

"You're very patient," she said, lifting her elbows to his shoulders when he leaned against his truck, stooping lower. "Can I take a rain-check or is it a limited time offer?"

"Take whatever time you need," he said, gathering her hair in his hands and using it to pull her head back.

"We probably shouldn't make out on the street," she said.

"Probably not," he said, edging his mouth closer. "The truck's right here. Got time for a quickie?"

When she laughed, he closed the last of the space between their lips, tasting her so thoroughly that the idea of sneaking him in through her bedroom window seemed an appealing option.

"I'll call you tonight," he said.

She shook her head. "Let me call you."

"Uh-oh," he said then kissed her again.

"I'm not going to blow you off," she said.

"Sure, not out here on the street."

"Would you stop teasing me for a second," she said, smiling. "I'll phone you when I get a break from Sorcha. I know it seems silly, but…"

"But?"

"I'm not wild about flaunting any happiness I might have just now while her life is so… all over the place."

"Okay," he said. "I better get back to the office and work on locating this guy."

"You weren't tempted by the check," she said, watching him open the driver's door.

"No," he said. "But if we get her life in order, we can flaunt whenever the hell we want."

He got in the truck and started it up while buzzing the window down. "You be careful," she said, curling her fingers around the door over the slit the window had just disappeared into.

"I'm going to be sitting at a desk, baby," he said, but accepted her kiss.

"I've heard RSI can be a real pain."

"True," he said. "But I've got you now. All of those worries are in the past."

He winked and she took the leg of his aviators from her cleavage to slide them onto his face.

"I'll phone you later."

She kissed him again and backed off. With a wave, he disappeared out of her street. Lacie had an evening with Sorcha ahead, though she wished she'd been in that truck at his side. Telling herself that she would have time with him when this was over was a consolation, but not much of one. Still, she wasn't the type to turn her back on her truest friend. She certainly wouldn't just because she had a man of her own

TWENTY-FOUR

Lacie

AS IT HAPPENED, Sorcha did go home. After midnight. By the time Lacie got her friend into a taxi and on the road, she decided it wouldn't be fair to keep Ryder awake one night, then wake him up in the small hours the following night with a phone call. While getting ready for bed, she made up her mind to phone him in the morning, first thing, as soon as she woke up.

Sorcha had departed in a better mood, which at least meant Lacie's sacrifice of time with Ryder was worth it. Lacie recognized her own exhaustion and the aches in her body for what they were: overexertion. The reminder of their carnal antics warmed her; she treasured every twinge.

For once, she got to sleep relatively quickly, or she assumed she did. When she opened her eyes, the numbers on her alarm said three eighteen. Sometimes her insomnia struck that way. She could close her eyes and go to sleep but would wake up a couple of hours later and be wide awake. Except, she still felt tired and hadn't woken with the usual energy that told her sleep was history.

A creak came from somewhere within her apartment. She sat up in bed. Her insomnia hadn't woken her at all. Another sound drew her focus around, but that noise wasn't the same as the first. This was like a click and the slide of something metallic: her front door.

Instantly, Lacie was off the bed and on her feet but didn't know where to go. Her bedroom window was on the same wall as the living room one, and the communal entrance door. Going to that might alert whoever was breaking in to her being awake.

Her parent's house had been broken into when she was a teenager. She hadn't slept for months after that. Therapists that she spoke to now attributed her insomnia to that incident. Afterward, her family had moved, but it didn't matter. They'd been violated in their safe space and that didn't go away in a hurry.

Looking from one side of the room to the other, she recognized her options were slim… her gaze snagged on the floor. Without thinking again, she shifted the edge of the rug and got the trapdoor open just enough to squeeze through. Using a loose thread, she pulled the rug back into position as best she could.

Getting herself into the dark corner of the unlit, windowless room, her fears were confirmed. Heavy footsteps echoed from above. While she couldn't tell exactly how many people there were, there was more than one, more than two, and likely more than three. The footfalls stopped and there was some mumbling she couldn't make out.

Pulling her knees to her chest, Lacie cursed herself for never getting a phone line installed down there. With no exit, she could have just chosen her own tomb. If they found her down there, she could fight. She had a few tools that could inflict some damage, but if they had guns… or numbers.

"Lacie Louise!"

That was when her blood froze. Her mouth sealed itself over her arms, still holding her knees up.

"We're here for you! Where are you, Sweet-Cheeks?"

Her body locked itself in a spasm because she knew that voice. Her nightmare had invaded her home.

"Bruce told us we'd find you here! Where are you, Sweet-Cheeks? Boss doesn't want you out and about! You've seen us all now, little one! Why don't you come back to us, Sweet-Cheeks! We'll look after you! You're part of our gang now!"

More mumbling followed a laugh and then there was a crash like something being pushed over. Glass shattered. Mumbling. When they spoke to each other, the bass of their voices carried, but she wasn't sure of specifics. In a break-in, she would assume that burglars would try not to make noise. It was something of a contradiction that these guys weren't conscious of their voices. One of them had shouted, and from the sound of things the place we being trashed.

She hadn't moved in long ago, but she'd never be able to sleep here again. All she could hope was that the gang left some of her things intact. But when the mumbling stopped, the crashing carried on.

Closing her eyes, Lacie let her head fall back. Tactless, or inexperienced, whichever one it was, they must have assumed that she wasn't there. They hadn't spent much time looking for her and her place wasn't exactly a palace to get lost in. If you took the apartment at face-value, hiding places were scarce. Her love of her sanctuary had just saved her life. She was sure of it.

TWENTY-FIVE

Lacie

TIME PASSED, after the crashing and the mumbling stopped, the footsteps retreated, and there was a bang. Her front door closing. She waited. Lacie waited until she was convinced no one could be up there.

They may have left someone to wait for her. Though with the amount of noise they'd made, it was likely someone had called the police. As assumed, a while later, a siren wailed into her street. More footsteps followed. She didn't want to take a risk and leave her sanctuary, but she couldn't stay down there forever. More voices and footsteps that were less aggressive gave her the confidence to attempt an escape. She didn't have much choice.

Crawling up the ladder, she pushed the trapdoor only to have it open an inch and snap back on her. She yelped, grateful that her fingers hadn't been stuck in it. Weight on top of the trapdoor held it down, but her action had drawn attention. Within a second, there were half a dozen men in place dragging her furniture out of the way. They opened the door and she blinked up into the blinding light being shone on her.

"You got a panic room down there?" someone asked.

"Studio," she said. "Did they take anything?"

"You'll have to tell us, miss. I'm sorry to say, the place is pretty trashed."

"I know," she said, ignoring a hand that reached down to help. "I heard it."

"Do you want to tell us what happened?"

"That could take a while," she said, scanning the room and its disarray.

Her clothes were scattered. Her underwear drawer was empty. Her wardrobe was on its side. The bed was stripped, and the bedclothes and mattress were slashed.

"You must have a helluva enemy," the voice said.

She let herself turn to look at the tall, brown haired plainclothes cop. "You could put it that way," she said aware that the men in the room were looking at her legs, only to remember she was wearing another of her painter's shirts. "Let me put on some jeans, and I'll tell you the story."

"Sure thing," he said. "But try not to touch anything else in case of evidence."

"I'll do my best," she said, watching the men clear out.

Her purse had been on the floor next to her bed, it was gone. She needed to get dressed and tell the police what was going on. The trouble with that was that she didn't know herself.

TWENTY-SIX

Lacie

TALKING TO THE police had taken more than a while. First, she did a quick check of what was missing. That turned out to be anything of value, her underwear, and her purse with all her personal things in it.

The police had then taken her down to the station to give a statement. They'd asked her whom they could call. She couldn't tell her Aunt Elise, the older woman would only panic. Sorcha would be worse, and she didn't have Ryder's number.

By the time they'd logged the details, the sun was up. The cop in charge, Detective Deacon, loaned her a twenty. He'd tried to give her more, but she refused it.

Normally, she'd go straight to Aunt Elise's. From there, she could phone Sorcha. Except Ryder was likely to try to find her, and she wouldn't be able to call him without his number.

Lacie used the phonebook at the police front desk to find StoneWall. The only number listed went to a business voicemail. She didn't want to leave a message.

She tried the number three times, ten minutes apart, in case someone was on the line. Voicemail.

The clock read fifteen minutes to seven, it was unlikely that a receptionist would be in so early. Knowing there was little else for it, and little else on her day's schedule, Lacie scribbled the address onto the back of Deacon's business card and got in a taxi.

The twenty only just got her to the two-story white building set back from the sidewalk. Grass surrounded the building, and a high white brick wall swept the perimeter. The building itself was on a hill which allowed her to see it, she couldn't see what was beyond.

A single metal gate covered the only gap in the wall. Right beside it was a button attached to an intercom. Chances were if there was no one there to answer the phone, there would be no one to answer the buzzer either.

It wasn't a commercial area. In the cab, they'd passed a couple of industrial complexes. The rest of the area was almost all woodland or grass. There was a lake too, her aunt lived only a half a dozen miles from there and they often walked around the lake after dinner whenever she visited to eat.

Coming all this way and not attempting to get in would be ridiculous. The whole set up was intimidating, and nothing anywhere actually told her that this was StoneWall. If this was the right place, she'd made a major miscalculation. Ryder played with the big boys; Shep would barely ping on his radar. It was laughable to assume their offices were alike.

Moistening her lips, Lacie pressed the buzzer. No response. She waited and pressed it again. Still nothing. She'd happily walk six miles under normal circumstances, except she'd stuck her feet in leather boots without socks that morning. Why would anyone want to steal socks? It was nuts.

Finding the boots was a victory. Most of her shoes were trashed too, she'd almost ended up in flip-flops. The intruders had damaged her shoes, her clothes, her soft furnishings. No one could say the men weren't full of gusto, even if they were lacking in acumen. None of them had thought to look for her anywhere but in plain sight. Not that she would razz them for their ignorance, it had saved her life.

She pressed the buzzer one more time and bent to take her boots off. If she had to, she'd cut across the grass at the far end of the street. She'd rather walk over grass in bare feet than on concrete in shoes that chafed.

"Do you know what time it is, lady?"

Lacie stood bolt upright. The voice had suddenly come from nowhere. The intercom. The guy on the end had the gall to sound annoyed.

After what she'd been through, Lacie didn't have time for rudeness.

Stabbing the button with her index finger, she leaned in close. "You bet your ass I know exactly what time it is. If this wasn't an emergency, do you think I would be at your property at this time voluntarily? Do you think I go around pressing security buzzers on abandoned streets at the crack of dawn for kicks?"

A loud, scrapping buzz startled her. Recognizing it for what most buzzers did, she gave the gate a shove and it opened. Being on the other side of the gate gave nothing away about the property. Grass. White brick, large wrap around porch, a huge black front door after five stone stairs up to the porch.

The path was white shingle. The worse surface to walk on with no footwear. She skipped over it to the grass and continued to the house. Should she knock or just walk in? The question was answered when she got to the top of the stairs, the door was already open a few inches.

"I like her!" a male voice exclaimed.

"Where does, "I like her" fit in with your security training."

"She shouted at him, he's a masochist."

Pushing the door, Lacie peered around it to see a space the full width of the house with a solid wall at the back bearing only one door. Each end of the room was glazed floor to ceiling. A pool table stood at one end, while at the other was plush white leather seating around a mini kitchen that had a table in the center.

In between these extremes was a high white desk with a hutch over it. Three men stood around it: two on one side, one on the other. All of them stopped talking to scowl at her. The good-natured conversation of a few seconds before was forgotten.

They were huge. All of them. All over six feet. All in peak condition. One blond, two brunettes. Any of them could kill her with their bare hands, of that she was certain. But just in case, all of them were carrying weapons too.

"I don't know if I'm in the right place," she said, staying just inside the open door.

She'd learned her lesson about cutting off her exits. These men were far more capable than those who had lured her before. These guys wouldn't play with her first, it would be over before she got the chance to breathe.

"You're not," one of them said.

"Who gave you the black eye?" the second asked, hooking his elbows on the hutch behind him.

"None of your business," she said.

The bruises were fading. So much had happened she'd forgotten they were there, though the police had asked her about them too.

"What's with the shoes?" the first asked, nodding

to the boots in her hand.

"That's none of your business either," she said.

"No one gets in here without an appointment," the third, behind the desk, said.

"Funny, because I'm standing right here," she said.

Each of their harsh expressions changed with her sass. Usually she wasn't sassy, but it had been a hell of a week.

"Sweetheart, if you're looking for—"

"I'm not your sweetheart," she snapped. "What is it with men? Why do you do that? Do you think you can just pat me on the head and send me on my way? Do you think I want to be here? Do you honestly think in a million years that I would be here right now, like this, through choice?"

"So what is it we can do for you?" the second one asked.

"Nothing," the first one said. "No one gets in without an appointment. I don't care how cute or needy you are. Our business is through referrals only."

"At least I know I'm in the right place," she said, dropping her boots to the floor and shutting the door. She pointed to the kitchen. "Do you have coffee?"

"You can't walk in here and—"

"Watch me," she said, crossing to the kitchen.

"What the hell is this?" one of them asked the others.

"If she's a terrorist, I'd love to see where she's packing the bomb."

"I'm not even wearing underwear," she said over her shoulder. "I think I'd have prioritized that over C-4, don't you?"

"Is this a drill?" they said to each other.

"Usually people leave when we tell them to."

"Are you pranking me 'cause of that thing last

week with that librarian? Is this a hazing?" another of them said.

The conversation carried on as she discovered coffee already percolating. Almost squealing with delight, Lacie started to hunt for mugs.

"Should I throw her out?"

"Call the boss."

"Don't do that," another jumped in. "She's not going to do any damage, is she? There's three of us."

"Learn nothing from the librarian about underestimating your opponent?"

Lacie crouched and found the mugs under the counter. On the shelf below was a bag of ready-made pancakes.

"See," she murmured to herself and opened the bag. "There are always pancakes."

A door opened, introducing more voices. Lacie just continued trying to fish the pancake from the packet.

"What's the matter with you three?" another male voice.

"Uh… well…"

"What?"

"There's something of a… situation."

"I am not a situation," she said, straightening her legs to bring herself to full height, and tore off a piece of the pancake.

New in the room from the only door on the back wall were three men… one of whom she recognized: Ryder.

"Pancakes," she said to him, holding up the piece she'd torn off. "What did I tell you? Everywhere."

"They've probably been in there a while," Ryder said, separating himself from the group. "Come up to the house and I'll cook you something."

"The house," one of the men behind him stuttered.

"Can't," she said, pouring coffee into the mug she'd found.

"Why not?" Ryder asked.

"I don't have an appointment."

Ryder stopped to look back at his men. "You wouldn't let her in?"

"Didn't make an ounce of difference," the second one said. "She made herself at home anyway."

"She's not wearing underwear," the third, and visibly youngest, member said.

"How do you know that?" Ryder growled.

"She told us," he stuttered, probably fearing Ryder's wrath, not that she blamed him.

Swallowing the pancake, Lacie took a mouthful of the scorching liquid then hummed at the heat cascading through her. "Does anyone have the time?" she asked, putting the mug aside and laying the pancake beside it.

All the men except Ryder looked at their watches. "Seven twenty-seven," they all said in slightly different timing to each other.

"How adorable is that," Lacie said, brushing her hands together to rid them of crumbs. "I have to go."

"Go?" Ryder said, approaching her. "You came here just to leave again?"

"Something like that," she said, resting her hands on his chest when he wrapped her in his arms. "I wanted to let you know that I wasn't going to call."

"You didn't call," he said. "I know because I was waiting for it."

"I know," she said. "That's a different story. I'm sorry. I must go to Elise's and then I have to speak to Sorcha. I'll probably be at the twelve o'clock, but I'm waiting for the police to get back to me."

"The police?"

"Yes," she said. "They'll let me know when I can

go back into my place."

His expression hardened. "Do you want to go back to the beginning?"

The truth was she didn't. He would overreact… maybe it wasn't overreacting. He couldn't do anything to change what had happened. But she couldn't hide the truth from him, not when he could be in danger too.

"They came," she said. "They came to my place… they were looking for me."

The clarity turned his body to stone. "They were in your place?" he growled. The depth of his voice rumbled from his chest to hers. This was a man beyond angry. The coil in him tightened, she wouldn't want to be around when it wound too tight. "Did they touch you?"

"No," she said, smoothing her hands over his newly shaven face. "No, they broke in. I was in bed I… They trashed the place… I got downstairs, and they didn't look hard enough thankfully."

"You're sure it was them?" he asked.

His embrace tightened with each second that passed. "Yes," she said. "He was… he was shouting, taunting me, before they decided I wasn't there."

"What did he say?"

"I don't want to talk about it," she said and tried to back off, his embrace brought her back to his chest.

"You're going to tell me everything."

"I have to go to Elise. I have to go to Sorcha."

"Why?" he asked. "Are they in danger?"

"No," she said. "I can't stay at my place. I'd rather stay with Elise than with Sorcha. I'm not sure if Sorcha's at her place right now because she's avoiding her family."

"You're not leaving here," he said. "You're going nowhere until this is over."

"I didn't come here to ask you to look after me," she said. "They took my purse. I don't have my phone or your number. I don't have any money either, can you lend me cab fare…?"

"Come here," he said, taking her hand to lead her toward the internal door.

The men parted for Ryder and her in his wake. He took her through the door into a hall with a set of stairs running up one side. The other side had several doors. They didn't go up the stairs. Instead he took her through a door near the foot of the stairs and down another set. They descended to a space with three doors, he took the first one into a lounge with a big soft leather couch and recessed lighting.

Ryder sat on the couch and pulled her into his arms, covering her mouth with his own. She hadn't had a chance to breathe, but the shock quickly ebbed to the comfort of his kiss. Enveloping security coiled around her, easing the prickle at the back of her neck. The tension and awareness that had plagued her like paranoia all morning, departed.

Her toes stretched and her curled fingers held his body to hers. Pulling on him, she lay herself back trying to bring him with her. But they only got to forty-five degrees when he took his mouth away. He kept her close, stayed above her, teasing her with what she'd almost had.

The low lighting and dark coloring of the room made an artificial night conducive to comfort and intimacy.

"Do you have time to have sex with me right now?" she asked, uncurling her fingers from his tee-shirt to slide them up to the sides of his neck.

His pulse beat against her palms and trickled its way down to her center.

"Yes," he said, the corner of his mouth twisting upward.

"Here?" she asked, linking her fingers at the back of his neck.

"We have the time," he said. "And we can do it wherever you want."

Except he sat up, taking her with him, then gave her a shove to the opposite end of the couch.

"We're not touching," she said. "Is it possible to have—?"

"I want you to tell me what happened," he said. "I want the details."

"I came here to tell you so that you wouldn't panic if you came looking for me or heard that the police had been to my address in the middle of the night. I didn't have your number, and I was aware that you could be in danger too."

"Me?" he said.

"One of the things he said was that the boss didn't want me out and about. I can only assume he was referring to the man who came in with Bruce. The man who was unhappy with my presence."

"He probably wasn't happy that you were gone when he got back. The question is, how did they find you?"

"Bruce," she said. His chin rose. "He said that Bruce told them."

"If Bruce told them, they would have come for you straight away. He can't have been eager to tell them. Still, when I get my hands on him—"

"That's the father of my best friend's baby," Lacie said, sidling toward him.

"Was Sorcha there?" he asked, landing a hand on her thigh.

"No," Lacie said, moving in closer to touch his shoulder, his neck, his back. "She left after midnight. I didn't want to wake you up. I was going to phone you this morning but…"

His hand slid from one thigh to the other to pull her legs against him. "You're going to stay here," he said.

"I don't want to impose. Your friends don't like me."

"My friends are also my employees. They'll like you just fine now they realize we're together. We're an insular group; we don't let other people in. But you're part of the team now."

"I'm not part of the team just because I had sex with you."

"No," he said. "You're not. You've got skin in the game." He touched her face, tracing her bruise. "I never should've left you alone last night."

"We had no idea this was going to happen. None of us could have foreseen this."

"I'll be honest. I didn't see this as a legitimate case until what happened in that place. What happened to you…? Good luck got us out of there and…"

"You just supposed they were small time," she said. He nodded. "I did too. They didn't look for me last night, not really. The men we met, those were the men there last night. None of them is the sharpest tool. They're muscle, not brain."

"And certainly not trained," Ryder said. "Which means you'll be safe here. I won't take anything for granted. We'll give you full clearance for the house, and—"

"Wait a minute," she said. "We… you have to be sure about this."

"I'm sure," he said. "If you stay with Elise or with Sorcha, that could put them in harm's way. Here, we can keep you safe."

"I'll tell Elise to go stay with her sister for a couple of weeks," Lacie said. "Bruce doesn't know her, but I want her to be safe."

"I can send one of the boys with her."

"You don't have to… I'm sure this will all blow over."

"It's our top priority now. You're our top priority. We'll get you a phone and a panic button, and—"

"Stop punishing yourself," she said.

His anger became agony. "I let you down again."

"You haven't let me down once," she said. "No one touched me last night. Yes, I was scared but it's over now. We were broken into when I was a kid, and it was horrible. I can't go back to that apartment, I can't sleep there again. But I'll sleep in your bed for a week if you're sure—"

"A week," he said. "You'll be lucky if I let you go at all. Who's the detective?"

"Deacon," she answered.

"I'll get a copy of your statement, I'll brief the guys, and we'll coordinate." Ryder got off the couch, but she stayed put. He went to a panel on the wall and pressed a button. "I'll take you back to the house now."

"What happened to the sex?" she said.

The door opened and in walked the young guy from behind the front desk.

"Lacie, this is Sonny," Ryder said. "He's our resident grunt."

"Thanks, boss," Sonny muttered.

"You're welcome. Get Gabe on to Deacon for what they have on the incident at Lacie's last night. We want everything," Ryder said then turned to her. "Did you tell Deacon about who they were?" She nodded. "Did you use my name?" Lacie didn't have a chance to respond. "Course not, he would have called me."

"I didn't want to—"

"That's okay," Ryder said. "Privacy and loyalty, you told me already. Your morals are our morals too." He addressed Sonny again. "Find out when the scene will be cleared and tell Rocco he'll be going down there." Ryder was back to her. "We'll get your cards canceled and scramble your phone. Is there anything sensitive in your purse?"

"Your phone number was written on a receipt," she said.

"That's okay. We'll kill my line too. Anything else?"

"Not really. I only use my computer to shop, so—"

"We can scramble that too," Ryder said. "If you think of anything, let us know. We'll put in a few ghosts for them."

She didn't even know what that meant. "They took my underwear," she said.

"They stole your underwear?" Sonny repeated.

The same thing was written on Ryder's face, in much less discreet language.

"It beggars belief doesn't it," she said, liking the kid already.

Sonny didn't have the hardened, cynical edge of the others.

"Clothes aren't a problem," Ryder said. "We'll get you everything you need, baby."

"I know," she said, driving her fists into the lush leather to push up to her feet. "I'd kill for a bath."

"You got it," he said.

TWENTY-SEVEN

"OKAY, START TALKING," Ryder said, sitting down at the head of the oval boardroom table in HQ.

He'd left Lacie in the tub in his en-suite and told her to sleep when she was done. Rest was important, but he didn't know if she'd take his advice.

Sonny sat at the far end of the table next to Rocco with Gabe opposite them. But it was Toby who did the talking.

"There is certainly something corrupt at Lewis Investment," Toby said. "I told you about the accounts we pulled? It's obvious someone was skimming."

"We knew that days ago," Ryder said. "What else have you got?"

"Establishing who's getting that money is where it gets complicated. We've linked it to several offshore accounts. Under various aliases."

"But we assume it's the same person," Ryder said.

"Or a consortium," Rocco said. "But, yeah, the

signature of the activity was the same. It's being orchestrated by one group."

"And Bruce Booth was their inside man," Ryder said.

"Appears so."

The police information didn't amount to much. Lacie's statement revealed it had been a close call. She was lucky; they'd come close to losing her. His men had noticed his reaction, they were in no doubt about his depth of connection to this case, and this woman.

"If it's one group, it's small time," Gabe said. "They're skimming a serious amount of money but nothing like the big boys play with."

"The question is why did they pull Bruce Booth?" Ryder asked. "On the inside, he was useful. Lacie said he split three months ago. Told his girlfriend he'd been poached by a bigger fish out of town."

"Anyone else notice we're preoccupied with size today?" Rocco asked, easing some of the tension.

"How is your girl involved?" Gabe asked. "I read her statement. But where do you fit in?"

Ryder recounted the story minus the intimate parts; his men would read between the lines for those.

"So Seth Sheppard's involved," Rocco said. "He'll blunder in with his big feet and track mud over us all."

"I'm meeting him at noon," Ryder said, glancing at his watch. "I'll get him to back off."

"He's not going to find anything we wouldn't," Rocco said. "He has no value in this. It's—"

"You don't have to convince me," Ryder said. "He has history with Bruce's ex, otherwise he'd be nowhere near this at all."

Ryder had no way to know that for sure. Shep's name had come up because Sorcha knew him. If she hadn't, the women might have looked through the phone book or gone looking for Booth themselves.

"The most valuable advice you can give these women is to back off," Toby said. "There's no reason to pursue this guy… and he'll be no remedy to a broken heart."

"It's more than that," Ryder said. "I don't care as much about the original case as I do about Lacie right now. They've focused on her because of my initial blunder."

"You had no reason to believe there would be any danger. You found her in Shep's office," Rocco said. "This isn't his bag. She's lucky that you were in there and not him or…"

"Yeah," Ryder said. "They don't know me. They knew her. I didn't see the boss, but Lacie did. Keeping her safe is our primary mission."

"Keeping her safe is easy," Rocco said. "But the danger won't go away until we find out who is behind this."

"I know," Ryder said. "She won't like being penned in."

"This place is a palace, she'll be fine. We entertain ourselves here, she can too."

Their land was extensive. The HQ building, their center of operations, was closest to the street. Visitors didn't get beyond that. Most visitors. The land rose and then dropped, hiding the house from the street. The house itself was on a high plateau, a cliff edge, giving them a terrific view over the city below.

The view from his bedroom was the first thing Lacie noticed. His circular bedroom sat on top of the building. Three quarters of the walls were glazed. The part that wasn't blocked his and Jamie's rooms from looking in on each other.

Gabe was right that they had a lot of services covered. They had a gym, and a pool, and a library among other interests, but those weren't Lacie's loves. She'd need somewhere to work.

"Clear out tactical storage in the house," he said to Sonny.

"Me? Why?"

"Just do it," Ryder said.

"Have you spoken to Jamie?" Toby asked.

"Yeah," Ryder said. "I spoke to him last night. I'll let him know what's going on."

"What are you going to do about Shep?"

"I'll see if he's got anything worth looking at," Ryder said.

"Doubtful."

"I'll give him the chance. Meanwhile, we stay in touch with Deacon. We'll hand over what we've got about the Lewis Investments when we know where Booth is."

"Won't that information help them track him?" Sonny asked.

Gabe offered the answer. "If the police start poking around one of two things happen, either they'll go so far underground we'll never find them, and we have to just sit around waiting for the other shoe to drop…"

"Or?" Sonny asked.

Ryder knew the answer, but a wave of reluctance swept the room. No one wanted to answer or make eye contact with him.

"Or they go to any lengths to clear the board," Ryder said. "No witnesses, no testimony."

"They could have killed him," Gabe said.

"Booth? I thought of that."

"And?"

"It doesn't matter," Ryder said. "It'll matter to Sorcha, and I'd never wish the guy dead despite what's happened. But these guys think we're on to them. We've got them panicked. We just have to hope that leads to mistakes."

"Lacie can get into her place whenever she wants," Gabe said.

"Okay," Ryder said. "You and Rocco get over there and find anything the cops have missed. Then I want you to clear everything out."

"Everything?"

"Get our storage guys onto it. I want the place empty. I'll ask Lace if there's anything important but trash what's not salvageable."

When he left the table, the men did too. "I want everyone on amber until this is over," Ryder said. "We don't know if they'll come at us but if they do I want everyone ready. I'm going to phone Deacon now myself."

"We've got the Waverley Ball this weekend," Gabe said.

"I haven't forgotten," Ryder said. "We carry on with business as usual. But everyone stay on your toes."

"Boss," Rocco said when Ryder was about to leave the table.

"Yeah?"

"She's hot."

These were serious men, highly trained, precision workers, but it could always be left to Rocco to keep priorities straight. Right now that meant admiring the woman who'd stolen his heart.

"You keep your eyes front, soldier," Ryder said.

"You haven't had a woman up at the house since I've been here," Sonny said.

"It's rare," Toby said.

"She's special," Ryder said.

"We got that," Gabe said.

"We'll work hard for you, boss."

"You always do," Ryder said.

The room paused then went to work. This was their priority. Ryder just hoped that he could bring this to a resolution quickly for all their sakes.

TWENTY-EIGHT

LACIE HADN'T MEANT to fall asleep. When she came out of the bathroom, she'd sat on the bed to admire the view and suddenly her body became heavy. When she lay down, it was like bathing in his scent, which only made her face bury itself deeper. That must have been when slumber took her.

A slight noise startled her awake. She sat up looking around for the source. In the mist of sleep, she might not have remembered where she was, except Ryder was right there, the first thing she saw.

"What are you doing?" she asked him. He whirled around to find her examining him. "What are those?"

"Sonny went to the stores for you," Ryder said, abandoning the boxes and bags he'd been placing down. "You slept?"

Lacie stretched and yawned again. "A little."

"Lie down," he said. "Go back to sleep."

She shook her head. "If I sleep today, I'll never

be able to settle tonight."

"You're in my bedroom," he said, sitting on the bed, facing her. "You might not be entitled to any sleep tonight."

"Do you still have my pills?" she asked. He nodded. "I'll need to phone my doctor for a refill if I'm going to be staying here."

"Yeah," he said. "For the foreseeable future."

Closing her eyes, she rolled her neck on her shoulders, working out the kinks of a tense night. He pinched her nipple, on reflex, she slapped his hand away. The direct contact had taken her by surprise until she remembered she'd lay down wearing only her towel. It had fallen off her body and was in a crumpled mess beneath her.

"You're naked," he said. "That's an invitation."

"I did everything but send you an embossed invitation this morning and you didn't take advantage of it. What time is it?"

"I don't have time right now," he said. "But when I'm back, we'll spend the rest of the day in bed. How is that?"

"Why don't you have time now?"

"I have to go out," he said.

Glancing behind herself, she read the time on the nightstand clock. "It's eleven thirty. We'll be late."

"No, we won't," he said.

She scrambled off the bed to search the bags he'd dumped for something to wear. "You should've woken me."

"You're not coming," he said.

A top dropped from her fingertips. "Why do you say that?"

"You're staying here until this is over," he said. "Right here."

"You're going to leave me alone with a dozen

men who have the ability to kill me?"

"Don't be scared of the guys," Ryder said, leaving the bed to join her. "None of them will hurt you. Every single one of them would give their life for yours."

"What?" she asked. She'd never heard such… Ryder was so matter of fact, like what he'd said was no big deal. Their worlds were poles apart. "Why would you say that?"

"It's what we do, baby," he said. "We do investigations, but we work private security too. We have a lot of high-profile customers who pay us very well to make sure they remain safe. We do this all the time. You have nothing to worry about."

"Nothing to worry about," she said, clambering to her feet. "The last time I was alone in a room of strange men, they tried to force me into sexual acts. Do you really think—?"

"None of my men are like that," Ryder said. "You will be safe, trust me."

"I should go home," she said.

He hooked her hair and guided it back over her shoulder. "I'm having the place cleared for you. Is there anything of importance we should look out for?"

"My apartment?" she asked. "Everything important to me they took or is in the cellar."

"I'm happy to replace anything that they—"

"But I didn't mean there," she said.

"What did you—?"

"Home," she said. "I can take Sorcha and we'll—"

"Home? You mean over the pond?"

"I doubt they'll chase me that far."

"We don't know how far they'll chase you. Do you want to go back to your parents?"

"This whole situation is a mess," Lacie said. "They want to hurt me and none of this is anything to do with me. I can't walk away because Sorcha wants Bruce. But we don't know if Bruce can, or wants to, walk away from whatever he's mixed up in."

"I know you're scared. That's good. Means you won't take unnecessary risks. I will keep you safe."

"I don't want you to be hurt," she said. "There's every chance that their boss doesn't know you were there. He flipped out when he saw me, I doubt anyone wanted to tell him about you. Just being here, I could be putting you in danger."

He smiled. "Don't worry about that."

"I do worry about that."

"You shouldn't," he said. "They won't get in here. You were alone out there; that won't be a mistake I'll make again. Here, we have reinforcements, you'll never be alone."

"I have to go to Shep's with you," she said. "Sorcha will be there. If I'm not, she'll panic or take her own risks."

"I can't put you in that kind of danger."

"I won't be in danger," Lacie said. "I'll stay with you, I promise. We'll go straight in and come straight out again. I'll come back here with you, and I'll be a model housemate, I promise."

"You'll come back here with me?"

"Yes," she said, nodding. "I was serious when I said I didn't want to go back to my place. I would only have done what you have. I'd have the place cleared, throw everything out, and replace what had to be replaced. My work is the most important thing and that's in the basement. I suppose I can put my things into storage until I find something more permanent. I won't be able to do the commission. I suppose I should cancel my meeting with Darwin at the weekend."

"Leave it for now," he said. "Don't cancel anything. If this is still going on then, yes, I agree with you. But we have the next few days to figure this out. I'm hoping it will all be over by then."

"Ryder," she said, taking his hand. "Thank you."

"What for?" he asked.

"This week," she said. "I don't think I would be so… calm, if I didn't have you to help me through this."

"Don't thank me, baby," he said. "I've done nothing but make this worse."

"I'm sorry I mistook you for Shep," she said, easing the intensity of the moment.

"Yeah," he said on a nod. "You should be sorry for that."

Securing her neck in his arm, he dragged her to his chest.

She wrapped her arms all the way around him. "I'm still naked," she said.

"Yeah… I like that about you."

After she nipped his jaw with her teeth, he relented and let her return to the bags. "I just need five minutes," she said.

"Okay," he sauntered to the bed and sat down, leaning back on his hands.

"Are you going to sit there and watch?" she asked, reaching for the bags again.

"Yeah," he said. "That's exactly what I'm going to do."

"Okay," she said. Her lips stretched to a smile when she read the hunger in his eyes. "I'm putting my clothes on."

"I know," he said. "There's something sexy as hell about just watching you. I discovered that when you were dancing with Sorcha. Just watching you is…" He paused without finishing the thought. "Pretend I'm not here."

"That might be difficult," she said.

Lacie carried on searching through the bags.

Most of the items were low cut, or short, but there were a couple of pairs of jeans, and a bag of underwear… mostly rather lacy, or see-through.

She pulled on a matching set then stuck her legs in the jeans. "How did you get all my sizes right?"

"Gabe cut the labels out the things left in your place."

Smart. Lacie chose a top then used the band from her wrist to tie back her hair. When she looked down at her vest, her breasts seemed to be trying to liberate themselves.

"Do you have an internet hook-up?"

"Several," he said, coming to her and cupping her breasts.

She was sure that they grew a cup size with his pampering attention. Her nipples pebbled against his palms. He dipped his head to kiss each swell, then he kissed each nipple through the fabric.

"You could've done that when I was naked," she said, looking down to the top of his head when he nibbled at her again.

"Could I talk you into canceling this meeting?"

"No," she said, nudging his head away and stepping out of reach. "When we get back, I'm going online to order something a little more… me."

"Spoilsport," Ryder said, draping his arm around her to lead her from the room.

"You like enjoying me in clothes another man bought for me? Do you think he imagined what I'd look like in his choices?"

Ryder frowned. "When you put it like that…"

"Get your business head on. Stop thinking about my breasts. You'll have unlimited access tonight. But can we get through this meeting first?"

"Unlimited access," Ryder said. "I'll hold you to that."

From the snarl in his voice, she could tell he meant it. Whenever he touched her, she wanted to block out the world too, to pretend it was only them. That there was no danger lurking on their horizon.

Unfortunately, they had a meeting, which brought everything slamming back into focus. Still, every step forward was one in the right direction. If they worked hard together all this would be over soon… she hoped.

TWENTY-NINE

Lacie

WHEN RYDER LED her into an underground garage in the HQ building, Lacie was surprised by the number of vehicles. She still hadn't established how many people were there. Only the center section of the space lit up when they opened the stairwell door. What was in the shadows?

Ryder pressed a button and his truck flashed. Oddly warmed by the familiar sight, she realized just how much she liked entrenching herself in his life. Being in his presence had felt natural since the beginning, but her seat in his truck could be her seat, her place… maybe she belonged there.

"Will I get to meet Jamie?" she asked, putting on the aviators while Ryder drove.

"Hmm?"

"Jamie, you said he was your business partner. Was he one of the men I saw this morning?"

"Jamie's in Sweden," Ryder said.

"Not somewhere I would consider security a necessity."

"We work where our clients need us," he said, squeezing her thigh.

"You have a beautiful home."

"We work odd hours. It made sense to have something close to work."

"Do you think Shep will have found out anything useful?"

"We're about to find out," he said.

"Yesterday when we were getting in the car after the search you looked at him… that look you exchanged, what was that?"

"Nothing," he said. "It was nothing."

"It was something," she said, only to be met by silence. "I thought we weren't having secrets."

"It was nothing to do with the case."

"So what was it about?"

His evasiveness had bought him time to arrive at their destination and park. She hooked his sunglasses into her cleavage while Ryder rounded the truck to open her door. Shep's office was unchanged. They completely bypassed Tiffany. Ryder kept hold of her hand and led her straight into Shep's office. Shep and Sorcha were already seated at opposite sides of the desk.

"You're late," Sorcha said.

"It's been a busy morning," Ryder said.

"So busy that you forgot about my life?" Sorcha said.

She took a minute to look at Lacie, and then at Ryder. Lacie didn't have to look at him to know that he was scowling. Of course his iron grip on her hand gave Lacie a clue. He wasn't happy with Sorcha's show of petulance.

"What's wrong?" Sorcha asked Lacie.

As soon as Sorcha realized something wasn't right, her whole aura changed. Her sulk was forgotten in a flash. Just as quickly, she was at Lacie's side.

"I don't want you to worry," Lacie said. "I'm fine. Ryder will tell you what happened."

"Ryder?" Sorcha said with a tinge of disgust that would've existed in her tone whether he was in the room or not.

"Do you mind?" Lacie said, looking from Sorcha to Ryder. "I really don't want to go through it again myself."

"And you shouldn't have to," Ryder said and kissed the top of her head.

He carried on like a consummate professional, objective, reasoned, and utterly calm. The only nod to any sort of personal relationship was that she was perched on his knee. There were only two seats on the guest side of the desk and Sorcha was in one of them.

"I'm not holding my breath that you've found anything useful," Ryder said when he'd finished recounting the night's events.

"I have a few interesting leads," Shep said.

"The nature of this has changed," Ryder said.

"How so?" Sorcha asked.

"I appreciate that this started as an operation to locate Bruce Booth, and that's still an objective, but Lacie's safety has to be paramount to us all."

"That goes without saying," Sorcha said.

"What are you getting at?" Shep asked.

"You're in or you're not," Ryder said. "The games stop now. This isn't a competition and it's not about the money. You help or you don't."

"Are you going to share what you've learned?" Shep asked. Ryder said nothing, Lacie slid her hand to the back of his neck. "Yeah, that's what I thought. Why should I share with you?"

"You'll have to give all your findings to the police."

"Like you did?" Shep asked. "I know what I'm

doing."

"What are you doing?" Lacie asked. "So far you've done nothing."

"What has he done for you, sweetheart?" Shep asked. "Except clear the cobwebs out your panties."

Ryder took offense, "Hey, you just—"

"We have to talk" Sorcha shot to her feet and grabbed Lacie's hand, pulling her from Ryder to drag her across the room.

"Not out there," Ryder said. "We'll leave you two in here."

"We will?" Shep asked.

"Move," Ryder growled.

The men left the room. Lacie waited for Sorcha to say something… she took her time about it.

"I'm so sorry," Sorcha said, taking Lacie into her arms. "This is all because of me. You've been hurt twice now."

"None of this is your fault."

"Maybe, maybe not," Sorcha said. "But you're involved because of me. Are you staying with Elise? You should maybe think about going to your parents."

"I thought about that," Lacie said. "But what about you?"

"Me? I wasn't there. They're not coming after me. Ryder's right, we have to keep you safe."

"I'll be safe. We have to find Bruce. We have to find out what he's up to."

"No." Sorcha shook her head. "I had no idea… what is he mixed up in? What have I got myself mixed up in?"

"It might not be as bad as you think."

Sorcha led Lacie to the desk so they could sit. "Shep spoke to Alan."

"From Lewis Investment?"

"Yeah," Sorcha said. "Shep cornered him in the

coffee place down from Alan's house. He really put the legwork in."

"What did Alan say?"

Sorcha looked one way then the other. Although they were entirely alone, she lowered her voice. "Bruce and Alan were close."

"I knew that. I met Alan a few times."

"According to Alan, Bruce didn't get headhunted. He was fired."

"Why?"

"There were complaints by some of his clients about his behavior," Sorcha explained. "He was acting weird, stressed out, missing meetings, being all erratic."

"So they fired him?"

Sorcha shrugged. "That's what Alan said. Except after that Bruce skipped town… Alan said Lewis are in the middle of an internal audit and things are showing up… inconsistencies."

"Such as?" Lacie asked.

"He didn't elaborate, but…"

"So Bruce was skimming money, or laundering it, or—"

"I don't know," Sorcha said. "But it started at Lewis whatever it was."

"Do you think they've told the police," Lacie asked. "If something has happened at Lewis…?"

"I don't think they'd want to advertise that one of their employees has been stealing from their clients."

"Good point," Lacie said. "But where did the money go? I didn't think of Bruce as the greedy type."

"Neither did I."

"I think it's fair to say he's in over his head with something. The people he's associating with aren't his usual type of friends."

"Lacie," Sorcha started, from how she began to fidget, Lacie expected a bombshell. "I could make this go away… do you think I should?"

"This isn't about the baby," Lacie said, covering Sorcha's hand with hers. "The ball is rolling. The horse has bolted. We're in this now, don't do anything rash."

"How will I tell my parents?"

"They're not going to cast you out. They might be shocked, but they'll get over it."

"Do you think I should tell them?" Sorcha asked. "Now?"

"Your parents have the resources to keep you safe," Lacie said. "Their house is like Fort Knox."

"My safety isn't an issue, yours is. Will you at least consider going home to your parents?"

"I don't have to do that."

"You do," Sorcha said. "You have to be safe."

"I will be," Lacie said. "I'm not leaving while all this is going on. I won't let them scare me away."

"So you'll let yourself get killed?"

"I'm not going to get killed," Lacie said.

"How do you know?"

"Ryder won't let that happen."

Sorcha said nothing for a few seconds. "Do you really trust this guy? You've known him for five minutes. I know he's good looking, and he's tough, but… this is serious, Lacie. You can't be ruled by your… you know."

"My libido?" Lacie said, smiling because she'd said the same thing to Sorcha countless times. "It's not like that."

"How do you know?"

"I know," she said.

"You can't know," Sorcha said. "Has he said something?"

"Not exactly."

"Does he love you?"

"We've known each other a week," Lacie said. "Not even a week."

"So how can you trust him?"

"What choice do I have?" Lacie asked. "He's capable, and he cares about me."

"I know that but—"

Sorcha's purse began to vibrate, she bent to retrieve her phone.

"Who is it?" Lacie asked.

Sorcha only shrugged and answered the phone. "Hello?" Immediately her friend squeezed her hand, wide eyes betrayed her shock. "Where are you? What's going on with…? Well, yes of course but—okay… Okay… Yeah."

Sorcha hung up the phone. The call was over as quickly as it had begun.

"What was that about?"

"We have to go," Sorcha said, hooking her purse onto her shoulder, pulling Lacie to her feet.

"Go where?"

Sorcha hurried her to the door in the corner behind the desk. Inside it looked like any other closet. Her friend knew different and threw the hanging items aside to reveal a door at the opposite end. Why did Shep need a secret door? Ryder had explained the necessity of multiple exits. Maybe Shep was smarter than she'd given him credit for.

The door led outside. Concrete and light. Outside. Sorcha took Lacie out, across an alley, and then the street. Lacie was separated from the information about where they were going or what was going on by the length of her arm and Sorcha's. Her friend's tight grip on her hand didn't relent. They crossed another street and went into a park, up a steep incline to a residential area.

"Where are we going?" Lacie asked. Sorcha struggled to breathe as she soldiered on. "What's going on? Who was on the phone?"

Still Sorcha didn't answer. Lacie yanked her hand free and stayed put.

Sorcha came rushing back to her. "Come on, I don't want to be late."

"For what?" Lacie asked. "Who was on the phone?"

"Bruce," Sorcha said, her smile growing. Relief and joy were plastered all over her face. "It was Bruce. He's back in town and he wants to see me. Lacie, he wants to see me. Everything will work out now."

Sorcha squealed with delight and hugged her. Lacie couldn't be quite as exuberant. This was wrong. There was something odd about him calling. If he was in town, if he was truly back to his life, then any normal man would phone and make a date, not demand to see someone there and then.

Lacie hugged Sorcha back but couldn't put any effort into it. Ryder. Oh no. He wouldn't be happy that they'd just upped and left. Without a purse, or a phone, or anything, she had no way to contact him. She could only hope that when he realized they weren't in Shep's office that somehow, he'd find her before… just before.

THIRTY

Ryder

"THIS IS TAKING too long."

"Who knows what women talk about," Shep responded.

Ryder paced the outer office, trying to play this forward.

Shep was happy lounging around, drinking coffee and making eyes at his receptionist. Ryder wasn't. More than happy to be bawled at for interrupting them, he went to the office door. When he lowered the handle, a draft circled his ankles. Dread in his spine spread like ice through his bloodstream.

Throwing open the door, his worst fear was confirmed. The women were gone. An open door in the corner revealed the light of day. He got over there and shoved the obstacles aside to find himself on another street. Scanning the area, he didn't see either of the girls or any disruption of where they might be.

Shep sauntered up to his side, casually glancing around. "Looks like they made a break for it."

"Or were taken," Ryder said, but there hadn't been a sound or signs of a struggle.

"The door only opens from the inside," Shep said.

"How did they know the door was there?"

"Sorcha used to come visit," Shep said with a shrug.

"So they left by choice," Ryder said mentally sorting through the possibilities.

He couldn't believe that Lacie would abandon him to his distress. But he also knew that she wouldn't leave Sorcha alone. The question was, what would motivate Sorcha to leave so suddenly and through a back door?

Ryder hadn't intended to bring Lacie to the meeting. Damnit. He hadn't given her a phone and had no way to contact her. Desire to put his fist through something, or someone, pumped his blood. Regrouping, he retrieved his own phone and got in touch with the team to get the investigation up to speed.

Shep did a whole lot of nothing while he spoke to his guys. When Ryder went back inside, he noticed Shep and Tiffany exchanging whispers. The clandestine activity could mean nothing, the pair made no secret of their intimacy. Tiffany nodded in his direction drawing Shep's attention to Ryder's entrance.

The men met in the doorway. "Are you calling the cops?" Shep asked him.

"I'll call Deacon when Rocco gets here. Gabe's liaising with the cops now."

"It's crazy of them to just run off. Your girl could get herself in trouble."

"The thought had crossed my mind," Ryder said.

"She'll have gone after Sorcha," Shep said. "That woman can be an idiot."

"I witnessed that myself when I walked into her

motel room yesterday."

"Whoa, draw your claws in," Shep said instead of returning his usual quip. "They could be around the corner having coffee, or the mall is just up the street."

"Lacie knows I'll be worried," Ryder said. "I thought they would be safe in your office."

"They got out of there for a reason," Shep said. "Something got Sorcha riled enough to do a runner, and she didn't want anyone to know what it was."

"Booth," Ryder said.

"Could be," Shep said. "We won't know until they get back to us. There's a good chance they wanted to ditch us. Maybe Sorcha thinks daddy could do better."

"Except she doesn't want her father to know what's going on. Why don't you check that out?" he said, watching the black sedan pull up outside.

"What are you going to do?" Shep asked.

"We're tapping Sorcha's phone and keeping an eye out for credit transactions."

"You think we'll figure this out?"

"I think the stakes just got higher," Ryder said. "But, yeah, we're going to figure this out."

"You're confident."

"Damn right, I've got to get this woman back just so I can chain her to my wall," Ryder said, leaving the office to update Rocco.

He would get his woman back. When he did, he'd never let her go again.

THIRTY-ONE

Lacie

SORCHA LED Lacie through the streets. Now they were heading down a long road into a retail district.

"Where are we going, Sorch?" Lacie asked.

Sorcha changed direction to yank Lacie between two buildings, down an alley to a perpendicular street.

Turned out her panic was justified. There, a few feet down the street, was a car: a beige Toyota with out of state plates. As Sorcha picked up speed, Lacie pulled her weight back to slow her.

A car door opened. The moment Sorcha let her go, Lacie realized Bruce was emerging from the front passenger door. Lacie slowed but Sorcha ran, launching herself into his arms. Joining her friend was inevitable, but she dragged her heels wishing for a phone or even a passer-by.

Lacie stopped further from the car than normal. She wasn't ready to trust Bruce or cut off her exits.

"What is going on?" Sorcha asked Bruce. "I have no idea what to think. Are you in trouble?"

"I can't explain here," Bruce said. "Come with me, I'll explain everything."

Bruce reached for the rear passenger door handle.

"We're not going to get in a car with you, Bruce," Lacie said, stopping him in his tracks.

"Lacie," Bruce said. "I'm sorry, what… what happened was terrible."

"Why should we trust you, Bruce?" Lacie asked.

"You're in danger," Bruce said. "We're all in danger."

"Why are you here?" Lacie asked him.

"We found him," Sorcha said. "This is all over now."

The sun was low in the sky. The glare made it difficult to see who else might be in the car.

"It's not over," Lacie said. "Ask him what he was doing at Lewis."

"I'll explain everything," Bruce said. "But it's not safe here. We have to go."

"You sent them to me," Lacie said. "Last night, if they had found me, I'd probably be dead now. You gave me to them."

As Lacie spoke, Sorcha retreated a few steps from Bruce.

"No," Bruce said, trying to bring Sorcha back to his side. "You don't understand what they're like, what they're capable of."

"I'm the only one here with bruises courtesy of your friends," Lacie said.

"They're not my friends," he said, beseeching Sorcha. "You have to trust me. I'll explain everything."

"Why the clandestine meeting?" Lacie asked. "Why didn't you just go to Sorcha's?"

"I got away from them. I have to go now because they'll come after me."

"You should be safe at Sorcha's," Lacie said. "Or did you give them her address too?"

"Come with me, Sorch," Bruce said. "Come with me now."

Lacie didn't believe Bruce for a second. Her friend, on the other hand, would want to believe in him. It was written all over her face. Sorcha could be reckless, desperation could fuel her to make the wrong choice.

"We can help you," Lacie said, trying to come up with a compromise.

"What?" Bruce asked. "You mean the police? No. No, you don't understand these people."

"Not the police," Lacie said. "My friend, remember in that room, remember the man who was with me?"

Sorcha sighed. "You can't trust Ryder to—"

"I do," Lacie said. "You're asking me to trust Bruce for you. If you're wrong, we'll both end up with a lot more than a few bruises."

"What if he calls the cops?" Bruce asked.

"He won't," Lacie said. "You're not exactly selling me on the idea of trusting you. If you're worried about cops, you've confirmed that you're involved in something illegal."

"Sorcha, come with me," Bruce pleaded.

Sorcha took a deep breath and tossed Lacie her purse. "Tell him to come alone."

Lacie didn't hesitate. She retrieved Sorcha's phone and searched for Shep's number because she didn't have a number for Ryder. All she could hope was that Ryder was still at Sheppard Investigations. Tiffany wouldn't have a direct number.

Bruce was getting more antsy; she might not have much time.

"Sorcha?" Shep answered the cell number she'd come across.

"It's Lacie, where's Ryder?"

"You don't want to talk to me?"

"Cut the crap and put him on," Lacie said.

Wind touched the line, and a car passed, suggesting that Shep had gone from inside to out.

"Baby?" Ryder said with clear desperation in his voice.

"I need you to—"

Lacie stopped when Bruce reached for the back passenger door.

"What, baby?" he asked. "What do you need me to do?"

"Come here alone," she said. Sorcha moved away from Bruce but the two continued talking. "And fast."

"Where?" he asked steady, objective, and clear.

"He's here," she whispered unsure if Bruce would hear her or if he cared while he and Sorcha argued. "Bruce, he called Sorcha. He wants us to get in his car, to go with him."

"Do not get into that car, do you understand me?" Ryder said. "I don't care what it takes. Do not get in that vehicle."

"Okay."

"Where?"

Reading him the street name from a dusty sign nearby, Lacie reiterated that he shouldn't bring the police. He promised he would be there in minutes and told her to keep the line open.

Lacie kept the phone to her ear to buy some time, she didn't want there to be any developments that might change the situation. The line had long since gone silent. Presumably, he'd muted his end, so she put the phone back in Sorcha's purse.

Bruce was moving in closer. Lacie recognized Sorcha's hair toss. Sorcha backed away, taking Bruce from the side of the car. Nice style... Except, damnit,

Bruce swooped in for the kiss, taking hold of Sorcha, giving him just a little more control than Lacie liked. Bruce began to back up toward the car taking Sorcha with him. The pair remained lip locked. Somehow, it appeared to be more of a power struggle than a couple overcome with lust.

Lacie considered her options. If the situation went south, there weren't many. Ryder wanted her to stay put, but if Sorcha was forced into that car… The couple jarred apart when the truck raced up the street, skidding to a halt at Lacie's side.

Less than ten seconds later, she was in his arms. Ryder crushed her against his chest. Her eyes flooded when she took in his scent. Throwing her arms around him, she wanted to crawl up him, to be inside him, a part of him. He took her face in his hands and jammed his mouth to hers with bruising strength that fueled her desperation for him.

"I'm sorry," she said, tears were skidding down her face.

"You scared me," he asserted. "Get in the truck."

Immediately happy to follow this order, Lacie went to pass Ryder, but Bruce spoke up. "Hey now, wait a minute," he said, coming toward them.

"What's your game, Booth?" Ryder asked, subtly blocking Lacie's body with his own.

Ryder's words about giving his life for a client played through her mind. She didn't want him losing his life for anyone, or anything, least of all for her.

"No game," Bruce said. "But we've got a few things to clear up."

Lacie heard the quiver in his voice. Fear. Why would Bruce be afraid?

"How about we let the women get in the truck and we can talk about this," Ryder said. "We can deal with whatever's going on."

"I don't know you," Bruce said. "But I can't let Lacie go with you."

"What?" Lacie said, leaning back to see past Ryder.

Sorcha stepped away from Bruce. "What has Lacie got to do with anything?"

"I'm sorry," Bruce said with apparent apology in his eyes, but it hung for only a moment.

"For what?" Sorcha asked.

Bruce grabbed Sorcha's arm and yanked her body in front of his. He grabbed a gun from his back and shoved the barrel against Sorcha's temple.

"I have to ask you to come with me Lacie," Bruce said.

Sorcha struggled. "You bastard."

"You're not going to hurt Sorcha," Ryder said, holding his hands up in a calming gesture. "You're not going to hurt anyone. We can help you."

"No," Bruce said. "No, you can't help me."

"Why do you want Lacie?" Sorcha asked still struggling.

Bruce increased his grip. "The boss wants her," he said. "She saw him."

"I was there that day too," Ryder said.

"You didn't see him," Bruce said. "He doesn't know you were there. No one told him about you."

"So what am I doing here?" Ryder asked. "Why did you let Lacie phone me?"

"You have to stop investigating me. You have to leave it alone. Forget you heard my name."

Ryder crept closer but kept himself between Lacie and the man with the gun. "I'm not going to do that," he said. "You don't have it in you to hurt Sorcha. You know it and I know it."

"I never meant for any of this to happen," Bruce said.

His resolve was slipping, wasn't it? She willed Bruce to drop the gun.

Ryder spoke again. "Let her go. You're not going to hurt her."

Bruce's hand loosened. Yes, they had a chance. If he would just...

Another man stepped from the shadow of the building at their side, then another got out of the car.

"He might not, but I will," the shadow man said, cocking his own gun and pointing it at Sorcha.

The man from the car wrestled Bruce back into the vehicle, keeping hold of the screaming Sorcha all the time. When he turned his gun on Sorcha, the shadow man trained his on Ryder.

"Get in the car, Lacie."

"She's not going anywhere," Ryder asserted, moving closer still.

This was a show of protection or machismo. Someone was going to get hurt. The two most important people in her world were in danger. She was the only one who could get them out of it.

"You'll let them go," Lacie said.

Tension rippled through Ryder. He didn't turn and kept his focus on the gunmen.

"Yes," the shadow man said. "They have to call off the investigation."

"They'll call it off," Lacie said. "No more digging."

"Get in the car," the shadow man said.

Lacie deliberately walked away from Ryder, around the back of his truck and onto the road so he couldn't reach her.

"Do not get in that car," Ryder demanded.

"She has no choice," the shadow man said, strutting. "She doesn't want a bullet in her best friend or her boyfriend."

The goon kept manhandling Sorcha. They didn't know shew as pregnant, Lacie was hyperaware of the child and how it could be hurt.

Lacie stopped when she got near the Toyota and looked at Ryder. He couldn't move, there was a gun on him. He would give his life for hers, but if he was killed, the gunmen would pile her into the car and get their way anyway.

"I'm sorry," she mouthed to him.

Rage radiated from him. She wanted to ease his anger, both of them were helpless. He might not see it the same way, but just like he would give his life for hers, she would give hers for him.

"I'll find you," he mouthed back.

This was the end. He didn't think so, but there wouldn't be any other outcome. Her heart swelled with grief, tears blurred her vision.

The car door opened fast, catching her in the ribs. Winded, there was no time to register the pain. She was tugged inside and forced into the middle of the backseat, between the man pulling her in and Bruce.

Doors slammed.

The air around them was muggy, humid. Laced with the smell of dirty, lowlife men. Outside, Sorcha screamed. Lacie tried to see out, but the man who'd pulled her inside, yanked her head to his lap to hold her down, her hair coiled in his fist.

A gunshot beyond the car made her jump. The man who held her laughed, then there was another shot. She tried to scream, to struggle and get away, but he squashed her against his groin. With his grip in her hair, he jerked her head to the side and stuffed a dirty rag into her mouth.

Lacie tried to spit it out, but he kept it in place. "Don't you worry. You'll have something better in your mouth soon enough," he snarled, his erection growing against her cheek.

Once again, he turned her face downward, rubbing her over him. She gagged but couldn't vomit with the rag in her mouth. All she could do was suffer the abuse.

Two doors slammed, then the car sped away. No words were exchanged. After a while, the rocking of the car lessened. Had they slowed down? Was that good?

A podgy hand slithered over her behind; she was glad of the jeans she'd put on. Whoever it was grabbed her hip, pulling her to her knees on the floor between the seats to smack her rear a couple of times.

"Boss is going to be happy with us," a voice from the front said.

The man who still had a hold of her hair in the backseat adjusted himself, and her, to keep her face in his crotch.

"You did good work, Bruce," the man who held her hair said then fondled her breast. "She's perfect."

THIRTY-TWO

Ryder

"WHAT THE FUCK!" Ryder exclaimed when the car careened around the corner and disappeared.

The thugs had shot out his two front tires. He got on the phone to Rocco giving him a license plate and a heading. His colleague should catch up with the car… he better. If they lost them… he had no idea where they were going.

"Oh my god," Sorcha sobbed. "What do we do? What do we do?"

"What the hell were you thinking?" Ryder shouted. "Why did you bring her here? Lacie's safety is paramount, you agreed with me!"

"It is! I know! I'm sorry," Sorcha cried. "I thought… I thought… oh, what do we do? What are they going to do to her?"

"Use your imagination," Ryder snarled, stepping in closer. "She won't be the same when she gets back to us. She'll never be the same again. What you've…"

Another car screamed around the corner onto

the street. Yes. Fuck. Ryder recognized Gabe at the wheel. The car stopped, Ryder shoved Sorcha into the backseat, then he leaped into the front.

"Where did they go?" Gabe asked.

"North," Ryder said. "Best I can tell at least. If they're heading to their new lair, it will be further out than the last one. They won't come back this way."

Gabe was already speeding toward the interstate. "Why come all this way for her? What does she know?"

"She saw the boss. He's paranoid. Can only mean he has a reputation to protect."

"Fear of jail?"

"Maybe," Ryder said. "Doubt that's his sole motivation. This is a lot of effort for one witness. He made his men come back here, close to Lewis, back to the scene of the crime. Booth left Lewis for a reason."

"There's money missing," Sorcha piped up from the backseat, speaking through tears. "One of his friends told Shep that Lewis Fund and Investment are doing an audit and there's money missing."

"We knew that already," Ryder barked.

Gabe flashed a frown in his direction. Taking his anger out on Sorcha wasn't fair, but the memory of Lacie being hauled into that vehicle was too fresh for him to let it go.

"We have to phone the police," Sorcha said. "I have to phone my father, and—"

"You phone them now and they kill her," Gabe said.

"What?" Sorcha whispered.

"They don't want us sniffing around," Ryder said. "They told us to stop the investigation, they told us not to bring in the police. They have to be monitoring communication in some way. Even if they're not, I can't take that risk."

"They don't want us to investigate," Sorcha

sniffled. "They told us to stop too."

"What do you want to do?" Ryder asked. "Go home and forget this happened? They'll rape her, do you understand that? Lots and lots of dirty, depraved men will use her to fulfill their sordid wants, each trying to outdo the others. They'll rape her. They'll torture her. And then, they'll kill her. Do you want that to happen?"

"No!" Sorcha screeched. "I'm sorry. Oh, I'm sorry! I'm so sorry. What did I do! What will… oh, Lacie, I'm sorry!"

She continued to wail.

Ryder tried to tune her out. His adrenaline was too high to cope with her emotions.

"How long do you think we have?" Gabe asked quietly.

"Until they get her to wherever they're going," Ryder said, keeping his eyes trained on the road.

His jaw locked. He'd promised to keep Lacie safe and he'd failed. Blame belonged on his shoulders as much as it did on Sorcha's. More so because he knew what these people were capable of. Sorcha was naïve; that was her only crime.

"Who have we got on our tail?" Ryder asked.

"Will is driving, but Toby's with him."

"Will," Ryder said. "He's back from California?"

"Just," Gabe said. "Rocco's ahead. He might have them."

"Might not," Ryder said.

"He was a street away when you called," Gabe said. "He'll have them."

Ryder appreciated that Gabe was trying to be positive, but until he had Lacie in his arms again, he would work on the assumption that the worst would happen. That light of innocence in her had already dimmed after what she'd been subjected to at the hands of these men. If they got their hands on her again, he might never get her back. That innocence would be extinguished forever, and there wouldn't be a damn thing he could do about it.

THIRTY-THREE

Lacie

THEY'D DRIVEN FOR hours. The light outside was long gone. They'd been bumping and rocking for twenty minutes. They were off-road. Throughout the journey, Lacie had been groped, repeatedly, everywhere. So far, they'd stayed on top of her clothes.

When the car stopped and the engine was switched off, everyone sat in silence for a second. The rag was so far down her throat that breathing around it was difficult. She had to make a conscious, careful effort to keep her breathing steady. They had stopped. What would come next?

"Got to get you inside for the boss," someone said.

Using her hair, the guy wrenched her head back at a painful angle. Duct tape was stuck over the rag still in her mouth.

"Do we need to cover her mouth?" the man she'd been face down on asked. "Few things I wanna do with that tonight."

"Boss gets to see her first."

Her hair was yanked again so they could cover her eyes with cloth. The knot was pulled painfully tight in her hair. As it was tied and secured, her breasts were being fondled again.

Sticky breath fogged over her cleavage, and a slobbering tongue delved between her breasts. Holding onto her sickness was getting more difficult by the second.

"Take your time, man. We got her for as long as we need her, ain't that right, girl?"

Her nipples were pinched from behind while the tongue continued to lap.

A door opened and a rush of pine air assaulted her in a cleansing sweep. "You two cool it, will you?"

She was spanked before being hauled out of the car by her hair. Freedom from the vehicle was bittersweet. When she cleared it, she was dropped to the ground. Mud seeped between her fingers and through her jeans. She tried to clamber up, but a boot settled over her derriere and she was forced back down. The boot stayed there while the men spoke.

"Does the boss want her now?"

"He's coming back in the morning. He says he's got business."

"What we doing with him?"

"Booth? We keep him out the way."

"What about her?"

"Downstairs."

"Can we have fun with her?"

The man who'd been answering the questions chuckled. "He didn't say no."

They enjoyed that fact and jeered her with promises of what her night would hold. Turning her face into the mud, Lacie began to wish she hadn't been so careful with her breathing. Ryder would punish himself for this. None of it was his fault, but he would. Maybe if she was just dead, word would get back to Ryder. After that news, there would be no chance of him endangering himself for her.

Saving Ryder from a final fate was her objective. She'd put up with whatever these men wanted to do to her. She'd do what she was told and would do it to keep those she cared about safe.

"He didn't say yes either," a booming voice came from further away.

All the men stopped laughing immediately.

"Don't be a bastard," someone begged.

"Lock her up downstairs. You can have your fun tomorrow. Boss gives the instructions. You get the nod from him first."

Whoever had spoken had authority over the other men. Although it wasn't a full reprieve, Lacie might have one last night without fear… though that was probably a pipedream.

THIRTY-FOUR

Ryder

"I'VE GOT SOMETHING."

Ryder looked up from the desk he'd been staring for God only knew how long. Toby rushed in with Gabe at his side. They had tried to follow, none of them had found the car. Driving around without direction got them nowhere and prevented them from doing other things.

Sorcha was somewhere around, still in a puddle, crying and wailing. He didn't have time for apologies now. She was happy in her misery. He was not inclined to help her, so he left her to it. Evening was drawing in. As the light faded so did his hope that Lacie had been left untouched.

"What is it?" Ryder asked.

Toby slid the laptop onto the desk in front of him. "You know we got the pings from the cell towers while the call was still connected?"

"Yes," Ryder said. "But they only went ten miles out."

"Yeah," Toby said. "We've been trying all

afternoon, but the phone was out of range."

"Past tense?" Ryder asked, sitting up straighter.

Toby nodded. "It's not much, and I can't be sure, but I think we got a hit. The computer's been searching on an ever increasing radius and we got something."

"Show me," Ryder said, turning the screen toward himself.

"It's a big area," Gabe said. "We've got the cell tower triangulation."

"It gives us an area of around thirty square miles, cell coverage is sparse. But I've got a program looking for the GPS location. We'll get it eventually. We just have to hope that they don't destroy the phone… or move it too far."

"We only have the location of the phone. They might have ditched it."

"It's the best we've got," Ryder said. "Get together anything we need; we're moving the base of operations."

"Will's already on it with Rocco. We'll be ready to move in a few minutes."

"How far out?" Ryder asked, pushing away from the desk.

"A couple of hundred miles from here."

Ryder left the desk. "Which means they've not been there long."

"Where are you going?"

"To talk to Sorcha," Ryder said.

"She's pretty cut up," Gabe said.

"I know how she feels," Ryder said.

Leaving his men, Ryder went to the front room of HQ. Sorcha was lying on the couch looking out the west window. When he entered, she didn't register him at all, she didn't move. Given all the activity going on around her, people coming in and out, she'd probably blocked it out.

"We're moving out," he said, sitting in the matching armchair.

"Have you found her?" Sorcha asked, sitting up in an instant.

"We got a hit on your cellphone," he said. "We don't have an exact location, but it's better than nothing."

"I should come with you," Sorcha said, nodding. "I should come, and…"

"You don't have to come," he said, sensing that as much as Sorcha missed her friend, she knew she could be of little help. "I called Shep. He'll come and look after you."

"I don't need that," she said. "I'll go home to my parents."

"You can do that," Ryder said. "Their security system is top notch. I know because we installed it."

He managed a smile, which seemed to relax her.

"I am sorry about all of this. I had no idea that—"

"I should apologize too," he said. "I was rude earlier. There's no excuse for it."

"You're worried about her," Sorcha said. "She wouldn't have been there if it wasn't for me. She trusted you… I wasn't as confident."

"Turns out you were right," he said. "I haven't done much to help her."

"You'll get her back," Sorcha said. "Lacie's never had much luck with men… I can't really claim to have had much more luck myself… I'm such an idiot, I don't know what to do."

When her tears started again, he shifted over to the couch to hold her. "You care about Lacie, she knows that."

"Without her, I don't know what to do. I make bad decisions and she's always been there to bail me out.

Now she needs me and… I don't know what to do."

"She needs you to be here and she needs you to be safe," Ryder said, letting her go. "She got in that car to save me and to save you."

Sorcha nodded when he glanced at her abdomen. "She told you?" He nodded. "I told you I'm an idiot."

"You aren't an idiot. None of this is your fault. I was wrong to take my anger out on you."

"I did cause this," Sorcha said. "All of what has happened can be traced back to my decisions."

"They can be traced back to Booth's decisions. This is not your fault."

"I can't expect Bruce to marry me now, not after this. But if I go home to my parents without a father…"

"Their judgment won't be harsh."

"It will be," she said. "But it's what I deserve."

"Everyone makes mistakes."

"My friend is out there," she said, welling up again. "She's going through a nightmare and I'm sitting here with you talking about my problems. How can someone be so selfish?"

"I'm going to get her back," Ryder said.

"I know," Sorcha said. "Lacie has faith in you… and I do too."

Rocco entered and gave him the nod toward the front door. "Shep's outside."

Ryder helped Sorcha to her feet. "Rocco will take you out, Shep will take you where you want to go."

"Thank you," Sorcha said when Rocco came to them. "All of you for… thank you."

Ryder watched Rocco take Sorcha out of the building. Now he had to get his game head on. Every minute would be crucial. First, they had to get there, then they had to find her. As soon as they did, he'd get her out. Whatever it took.

Simple? Anything but. He'd never shied from a challenge in the past and wasn't about to start now.

THIRTY-FIVE

Lacie

WHEREVER LACIE WAS, it smelled awful. She assumed it was dark too; the blindfold prevented her from confirming that. They'd dragged her into a building, down some stairs, and left her there.

Footfalls echoed like on floorboards above. The bass of men talking came from overhead too. Sometimes there would be a shout or a laugh. The voices faded and returned but didn't broach the creaky door they'd opened to bring her down and closed after they left.

Now she lay in the corner on what felt like a mattress, her hands tied to something above her head. The sound of rodents scurrying and chewing shared her air. Would someone come back for her before she became their habitat?

Focusing on the sounds and smells only briefly took her mind from the people she'd left behind. No matter how hard she tried, she struggled to figure out how this would end. Either these men would finish her, and her fate would never be known, or someone would come after her…

Ryder.

He'd said he would find her before she got into the car, but she wasn't eager for him to keep his promise. He would go to any lengths. And being in his arms again would be a dream. But she didn't like the price that discovery may cost them.

If he found her there, Ryder would be outnumbered. Even if he brought all the StoneWall guys with him. The men she'd met at StoneWall had integrity. The men here did not. They would shoot first and ask questions later. Out there, civilization was a distant memory.

Sounds from outside weren't urban or even suburban. Their off-roading in the car gave her the idea that they were somewhere rural, far off the beaten track. No doubt so secluded that no one would hear any screams.

The smell of trees, the mud, and the rodents told her it was a wooded area. Somewhere with plenty of places to dispose of a person no longer needed or someone who got in the way.

Her temporary reprieve had come on the orders of one man. The other men wanted to play with her. Who was the boss they referred to? Would he give the order to let his men have their way? Why wouldn't he? If he had any respect for women, he wouldn't have hired the men in the first place, or he wouldn't have had them capture her at all.

On that sidewalk, there was no choice. Replaying the events of the last few days, the things she would change piled up. She wished she could make so many decisions differently. The only thing she wouldn't change was her time with Ryder. They'd been cheated out of any future, but at least they'd been together for a flicker of time.

Tonight, she could only breathe and hope that the "boss" wouldn't be back early or at all. A lot to hope for, but it was better than sitting torturing herself over what might, or might not, have been between her and Ryder. He was the first man, the only man, to provoke her in ways she'd always denied were possible.

Her experience with Ryder made her predicament easier. She couldn't explain the rationale. Ryder was out there somewhere. Out there angry. He'd be punishing himself, blaming himself for her choice. If she could make this easier for him, she would, but was helpless to console him.

THIRTY-SIX

Ryder

IT WAS TAKING too long. StoneWall had hired a cabin in the epicenter of their search area. They'd set up their equipment and worked until after midnight with most of them out combing the streets. The area was quiet with just a few homes in the commercial center. The town consisted of a general store, a fishing tackle store, a diner, and a hardware place that rented bicycles to tourists. There was only one resort for twenty miles around, so they'd set up base there.

Trying to be conspicuous in a group of six men wasn't easy when they rolled into town without a hint of recreational interests in mind. But the resort leased lodges, and when they paid twice the rate, the teen at the desk didn't ask any questions. Ryder didn't care about stirring up interest. Maybe if he did, the sloppy henchmen would get careless or come looking for him.

"You should get some sleep."

Ryder turned to see Gabe outside one of the three bedroom doors. "I was talking to Jamie," he said.

"Bet he told you to get some sleep," Gabe said, seating himself at the large kitchen table.

It dominated the back of the room, standing in front of the glazed doors that led to the rear deck. Right now, the surface was covered with computers, local maps, and other paperwork.

"We've been the best at what we do for so long," Ryder said, slipping his hands into his pockets. "Why am I no good when it counts?"

"It always counts," Gabe said. "It's just this time…"

"What?"

"You're the client," Gabe said. "We're hired by husbands and fathers concerned about people who mean something to them. You're the husband… so to speak."

"I've told clients to trust us… I told Lacie to trust me."

"She does."

"She shouldn't," Ryder said.

"I don't know Lacie, but a woman who has got your interest has to be something. Do you think she'd be impressed with your pity party?"

"I don't care about me," Ryder sniped. "I care about her. She's out there! She could be right under our noses. She needs me! And goddamnit, I'm standing here staring out the fucking window doing nothing!"

Ryder kicked a chair from the table, it shot across the room, splintering its leg on its sudden stop. All three bedroom doors opened and all his men appeared at once. Ryder held up his hands.

"Feel better?" Gabe asked.

"Go back to bed," Ryder said to the men on ready alert with eager trigger fingers.

They observed the scene then followed his orders. Once they were gone, Ryder began to pace.

"We're going to find her," Gabe said.

"And what happens in the meantime?" Ryder asked.

"She's tough," Gabe said. "She stood up to Rocco and Toby when she found HQ."

Ryder stopped pacing. "She's a fighter."

The message got through without any elaboration.

"You don't want her to fight?" Gabe asked.

"I don't want her to be in that position at all. But fighting could make things worse. What if they get angry at her? You weren't there the last time. All I can hear in my head is her screaming. It's deafening. It plays round and round, driving me crazy."

"You've got the scars to prove it," Gabe said, nodding at his wrists.

The scabs hadn't healed, but the pain they had caused him wasn't enough.

"Lacie's different," Ryder said, still looking at his wrists. "She's not a quick fumble."

"We know that," Gabe said.

"We?"

"I spoke to Jamie this afternoon. The guys know she's important to you. She's a part of the team and we never leave a man behind."

"We are going to find her," Ryder said. "But… what will this do to her?"

"She'll have physical wounds. She'll be scared, worried, traumatized by what they've put her through. Are you saying you won't take the time to get her through it? You won't be patient if she's not ready to jump straight back into bed with you?"

"No!" Ryder insisted.

"Right, so we concentrate on getting her back."

"How long will it take?" Ryder asked. "They'll get rid of her eventually. Could be a day or a week… how much time do we have?"

"We know Bruce Booth is working for them. We have to find out why. We have to find out what this is about and what they want with Lacie. What is this guy afraid of?"

"We'll only be able to find that out if we get to the guy. For that, we need to find Lacie."

"Get some sleep," Gabe said, leaving the table. "You've got to be at your peak. She's going to need you."

Ryder watched Gabe disappear back into the bedroom and turned back to the window. She was out there somewhere, all he had to do was find her.

THIRTY-SEVEN

Lacie

THE MORNING CAME too quickly. Lacie hadn't slept. It was impossible as she lay there listening to the men upstairs, drinking and shouting at the TV as well as each other. The activity slowed until she assumed they were asleep. Silence was interrupted only by creaks of the building, and nature, scurrying, squeaks, insects, predators, rain on the plant life outside. Trying to identify the sounds whittled some of the time away.

Still, she lay on the moldy mattress, blindfolded, gagged, restless but unable to move. The activity had begun again. Morning. Grumbling took the place of laughter and shouting. The footfalls were fewer. Most of her captors were morning people.

Time meandered on and she became aware of pressure in her bladder. She hadn't been offered food or water. Her inability to see, or move, made it difficult for her to relieve herself. As she worried about her options, the activity upstairs became more hurried. A car engine rumbled closer; the squelching of mud grew louder. In a final moment, both stopped. Her reckoning had drawn closer.

The men rushed around. Voices rose, more of them than before. Her bladder worries were forgotten as she tried to establish what was transpiring upstairs. Time went by and the car started up again. What was going on? A silence sparkled in the dew that seeped into her confines… then that creak, the door… Someone descended the stairs, but then… silence.

"Time to get up, girl," a voice sneered.

The mattress shifted and a hand covered her breast. She didn't move or give him the satisfaction of cowering away. A few seconds went before he just untethered her restraints from their anchor.

When he yanked her from the bed, her shoulders screamed in agony. Her arms were heavy, and hollow, without blood to warm them. He kept pulling her. With the quick, dizzying action, she stumbled up the stairs. The solidity of the floorboards under her feet echoed, she couldn't orient herself. A door was opened, and she was shoved into a room. In the same instant, her blindfold was ripped from her eyes. The overhead light wasn't on but the change in illumination left stars flickering in her eyes.

"You've got one minute," a voice behind her said. "Take a piss, wash your face, the boss wants to see you."

The door slammed. It was a washroom, with only a toilet and a sink in it. No window. A little light seeped under the door from the room beyond.

Her hands were still tied, but she managed to undo her jeans and relieve herself. Working quickly, she put herself back together and washed her hands. Bracing over the anticipated pain, she ripped the duct tape from her mouth and spat out the rag. Every second was crucial. Ducking her head under the cold water, she drank what she could. Her next drink wasn't assured.

Water dripped from her chin. She just breathed, trying to hold herself together.

The assault of sudden light brought her upright. The door was open. The man who stood before her was the same one from the car… maybe. She hadn't gotten a good look at him. He was definitely familiar; he'd been at the apartment. Try as she might, she'd never forget that.

The blindfold was put back over her eyes before being pulled from the room and taken up more wooden stairs. Following blindly, Lacie couldn't resist or run. Voices and movement along her journey were difficult to place. She hadn't been trained for this. The disorientation was nauseating. They stopped. She heard a single knock on a door, then one being opened.

Once again, she was shoved inside, and her blindfold plucked off. Light, much more light… it flooded through the large window to her left. Perpendicular to that, a desk with bookshelves behind it. To the right side was a broad couch and a four-poster bed. The sound of the door being closed startled her from her inspection. The chair at the desk turned. A broad sandy haired man sat staring at her. They were alone; all he did was look.

Trying to conceal her discomfort under his scrutiny was difficult, so Lacie shifted her attention to the window.

"You're not what I expected," he said after he was finished with his examination.

"I'm sorry?"

"Do you recognize me?" he asked.

"From the apartment," she said. "Isn't that why I'm here?"

"Something like that."

"How can I not be what you expected? You saw

me there too.”

“It’s unfortunate,” he said. “Really, it’s a shame.”

“You brought me here. You wanted me here.”

“You’re the kind of variable that’s almost impossible to predict. Those variables make men like me nervous.”

He gave very little away. He spoke in a measured tone and let no emotion register in his expression.

“Why are you telling me this?” she asked. “Your men were the ones that dragged me into this. They brought me into that apartment. They brought me here. I don’t care about you or what you’re doing. Your men did this.”

“My men have been reprimanded for their actions, but they’re not why you’re here.”

“No?” she asked. “They’re actions are why you’re afraid of exposure.”

“To whom?” he asked. “You couldn’t identify me to the police and my fingerprints are nowhere near the money.”

“Is this about getting rich?”

“The money is a motivator.”

“If you’re not worried about the police, and it’s not exposure you fear. Why am I here?”

“Who said I didn’t fear exposure?” he asked. “I’ve been doing this for a long time. I get away with it every time.”

“You fear exposure, but it’s not the reason I’m here,” Lacie asked, confused. Had the trauma of the last few days scrambled her brain or was he being particularly cryptic? “Why am I here?”

A slow smile crept to his lips. “Maybe I should introduce myself.”

“I don’t understand what—”

“I am pleased to meet you, Lacie,” he said. “I’m Jamie Wallace.”

For a minute, she couldn't breathe or think. "You're Jamie Wallace," she exhaled. "But you didn't know he was there. You didn't know he was—"

"Not until he told me," Jamie said.

Shock didn't begin to explain the implosion within her. "The men here don't know it, do they? They don't know that you know he was there."

"No," Jamie said. "I didn't know it until Ryder told me, that's why my men came to your apartment. As soon as Ryder told me, and I knew he wasn't with you, I got your address from Bruce."

"I'm here because of Ryder," she whispered, slotting everything together. "You fear exposure to Ryder. If he and I were seeing each other and you sauntered into HQ, I would have recognized you."

"Bingo."

"But you're in Sweden. Ryder said you were in Sweden."

"Easy to pull off that deception." He smiled. "He's worried about you by the way, seems to think you're in a lot of danger."

"Can you blame him? Your men are Neanderthals. Every one of them gropes me at every opportunity."

Jamie didn't respond to her words, he carried on of his own accord. "They're up here. The SW team. They got a ping off your friend's cellphone. We took care of that, and we'll be moving out tonight."

"We?"

"That's right," Jamie said. Gesturing to the seat at her side of the desk, he left his own seat to pour the coffee from a pot on a table next to the desk.

"How can you do this to him?" she asked. "How can you betray him like this? You have a successful business, what on earth could you need the money for?"

His easy manner vanished. He abandoned the

coffee to march back and slam his hands down on the desk.

"Betrayal? How about humiliation for fifteen years? Everything he touched turned to gold! He could never do anything wrong! At school he got straight A's and all the girls! He flew up through the ranks when we joined up at the same time! He made the money! He started the business! He got the clients! He got the jobs! Hired the men! Built up the company! Everything is his, for him, because of him! He dragged me along, expected me to be grateful, to worship him for the constant reminder that I was a fuck up! Not anymore! I'm a success! I have my own ideas! My own success! I am not his grunt!"

"It's illegal," she argued. "What you are doing is illegal. Why didn't you just walk away from StoneWall?"

"And get out of the easy life? I don't have family. I didn't have anything but my friends. He's not my friend! They all liked him better when he came along. He kept me down there just to show me how much better he was than me."

"You're wrong," she said. "He cares about you. He trusts you."

"I know," Jamie calmed and smiled again. "Which is how I plan to stay one step ahead."

"I thought you brought me here to kill me."

"I brought you here to silence you, to stop you from getting in the way of my operation. Turns out that there's another benefit I hadn't initially considered."

"What's that?" she asked, afraid she knew the answer.

"He's on self-destruct," Jamie smiled. "Sick with guilt. He'll never let this go and that's the beauty of it. All I have to do is keep you away from him. High achievers who are used to getting what they want, and being in complete control, don't cope with failure. They can't cope with being denied that control, with being helpless. He's useless, and he'll never solve this because I'll always be a step ahead. We're business partners, he believes we're best friends. He'll talk to me ten times a day if he has an operation going. He'll tell me everything he knows and all the plans before, during, and after. He'll fail again and again. This is a battle he can't win."

"Why not just kill me and get it over with?"

"I try to break as few laws as possible."

"So your men didn't shoot him yesterday?"

"Wheels," Jamie said. "We'll keep you around while this is fun. He'll move in or kill himself, one of the two."

Sickness churned in her anger and devastation. "This isn't a game," Lacie said. "You can't do this to him. I'm not a pawn there for your amusement."

"You're here for whatever I want," he said. "You should know, I'm not squeamish. If it comes to it, I will pull the trigger."

"But you want to play with me first?"

His gaze traveled down her body. "I'm not into Ryder's seconds, but we could be spending a lot of time together. Never say never."

"You're sick," Lacie said. "You plan to turn me out to your friends?"

"They're not my friends. They're the lowest level of scum, but they don't ask questions, and they do what my man tells them."

"I'm happy for you," she said.

"They're not going to touch you if you behave yourself. Rape is the lowest form of depravity. This is about money."

"And revenge," she said. "You're trying to destroy him."

His smile quirked in amusement. "The best part is I won't have to try; he'll do it all by himself. You'll be well looked after here. You've known Ryder a week, you can't care that much about my motives with him. I've known him for more than half of my life. You don't know him like I do. I'm sorry you've been pulled into this against your will, and I apologize that you've been taken from your life."

"Not sorry enough to let me go."

"No," Jamie said. "We'll make you comfortable."

"Until when?" she asked.

"Until I decide what to do with you or until you're of no use to me."

"Until Ryder realizes what you really are," she said. "That's it, isn't it? You'll wait until he figures you out and then you'll trot me out."

"Maybe."

"How long will that take?"

"I'd settle in," Jamie said. "You'll be our guest for quite a while. Behave yourself and we'll all get along."

"And if I don't?"

"Use your imagination."

THIRTY-EIGHT

Ryder

"YOU'VE DONE EVERYTHING you could," Sorcha said. "You've been running the length and breadth of the country for weeks. You couldn't have done more."

"When are her parents flying in?" Ryder asked.

"Later this afternoon," Sorcha said.

"Deacon just left. The missing person team has got bupkis."

The door to his office opened, Gabe came in with Rocco. "Jamie and Eric just got back in," Gabe said. "He'll be through in a minute."

"He's not been around much," Sorcha said. "I haven't met him."

"He's been working in Canada," Ryder said. "He's picking up the slack."

"Because of Lacie?" Sorcha asked.

"He's been in constant touch," Gabe said. "Jamie's with us on this."

"Hasn't helped, has it?" Sorcha asked.

Ryder didn't need to be told. For three weeks,

they'd followed every lead. They had split up, worked together, chased the ghosts of possibility. Every time, they came up short. For men, who apparently weren't professionals, they were remarkably skilled. Whoever was at the top, they knew what they were doing.

"When do her parents land?" Gabe asked.

"In a couple of hours," Sorcha said. "They're staying with Elise. I'm going over there for dinner. We're heading over to the police station after that. Her mother has spoken about a direct appeal. Do you think it would help?"

"We don't know what would help," Rocco said. "There's not been a whisper from Lacie or Booth since they disappeared from that street."

Sorcha took her attention from the men. Ryder didn't like her discomfort; Sorcha was never uncertain. She was about to ask the question they'd managed to avoid, even though it had been in all their minds.

"Are they dead?" Sorcha asked.

The four looked at each other but no one ventured to answer.

The door opened again, giving them a reprieve. Jamie entered wearing a smile but sobered when the tension in the air swamped him.

"This isn't a room of happy people," Jamie said. "Did something break?"

No one said anything for a moment.

Gabe stepped up. "Sorcha Reynolds meet Jamie Wallace. Jamie this is Sorcha."

"I've heard a lot about you," Jamie said and shook Sorcha's hand. "You're Lacie's best friend, Booth's other half."

Jamie's gazed dropped. Ryder hadn't told anyone about her condition. She still hadn't even told her parents. There couldn't be any correlation between Jamie's focus and Sorcha's pregnancy. A smile formed on his partner's face.

"You're quite something to look at," Jamie said.

"I'm not Booth's better half," Sorcha said. "He can rot in hell for all I care."

"I'm sure he'll be happy to hear that. Is that your way of telling me you're single?"

"I'm not your type," Sorcha said.

"How could you possibly know that?"

Ryder shouldn't be aggravated by the minor flirtation taking place in the middle of his office, but he was. Life managed to endure around him. People were continuing with their lives, yet nothing was normal. He'd found a woman that he wanted to make the center of his universe and he'd lost her. Three weeks after he'd told her he'd find her, she was still lost.

"Give us a minute would you guys?" Ryder asked.

"I need to get going," Sorcha said. "I'm going to the airport with Elise."

"Call me if you need me," Ryder said, rounding the desk to kiss her cheek.

Gabe and Rocco escorted her out and closed the door.

"You've frayed," Jamie said. "You look tired and stressed out… more than you did last week."

"I'm losing my mind," Ryder said, driving his fingers through his hair.

"People go missing all the time," Jamie said. "Some of them are never found. Some people don't want to be found."

"This isn't one of those," Ryder said. "I told her I would find her."

"You've told me this already," Jamie said. "And I told you that all our clients appreciate there's a risk. If there was no risk, we wouldn't be hired in the first place."

"How long are you in town?" Ryder asked.

"You're really mixed up in this," Jamie said. "You've let the business go."

"Gabe's keeping an eye on it."

"Sorcha's hot," Jamie said. "She could take your mind off things."

Ryder frowned at his partner. "You're kidding, right? Lacie's the only woman I'm interested in. Have you forgotten everything I told you?"

"You're not going to practice abstinence for the rest of your life. You have to get back on the horse."

"I'm not interested in the horse. It's only been three weeks."

"You've spent twenty minutes getting over relationships that you've been in for months. You knew this girl a week."

"She's missing because of me."

"She's missing because her friend's ex-boyfriend is an idiot. That's not your fault. How long are you going to stick on this?"

"As long as it takes," Ryder said.

"Okay, so we'll take you off the books here. You want to dedicate your life to finding your Dusty you can do that. But you have to realize that it might not happen. Are you willing to give up your life, your business, your future, for something that may not happen?"

Ryder didn't have to think too hard about his answer. "Yes."

"She means that much to you?"

"Yes, she does."

Jamie smiled again. "I thought as much. We need to get the guys back to work. But you'll have access to all our resources. We could hire a couple more guys, I guess. Are you sure she's alive?"

"I have to believe it."

"Is there anything else on the Booth guy? Are you still following that lead?"

"We've exhausted every avenue," Ryder said. "The guy has vanished. Everything we've traced has gone dark. It's as if none of it even happened."

"You're tearing yourself apart," Jamie said. "I hope this woman appreciates how you feel about her."

"You keep StoneWall going," Ryder said, heading for the door. "I'll find Lacie."

"Where are you going?" Jamie asked.

"The airport. I screwed this up. Her parents should know all the details."

"Be careful of backlash. They'll want to focus their anger on someone."

"You won't say it so I will: I'd deserve it. "

Ryder wanted to be in the thick of it. He wanted to hear her name and to talk about her. The longer she stayed in their minds, the longer they'd be aware, alert, on the lookout. Options might be thinning, but he'd said he would find her, and he'd meant it.

THIRTY-NINE

LACIE SIPPED WATER from the dirty cup she'd been using for almost a month. The gang had bumped from place to place for the first couple of weeks, but they'd hung steady at this house since then.

In that location, she hadn't been out of the basement like at previous sites. After some of the things she'd witnessed those men do to each other, or rather to Booth, she couldn't say she was sorry to be left alone.

There she spent a large portion of her time blindfolded. Her hands were bound, and a chain tethered her to the wall like an animal. She had just enough slack to reach the toilet and the sink she used to fill her cup.

They fed her when they remembered, sometimes several times a day, at other times she went without seeing anyone for days. In the initial weeks, she'd been jeered and groped frequently, but Jamie had kept his word. No one did anything more than that. After the Neanderthals got into their heads that she was off-limits, they lost interest.

She'd gotten used to her captivity with surprising speed. She hadn't changed clothes or bathed since her abduction, but she hadn't exercised either. She'd stopped crying, stopped screaming, she'd stopped trying to escape, or fighting to draw attention to herself.

Ryder would figure Jamie out eventually. It broke her heart to think of him betrayed. Privacy and loyalty. How would he feel when he found out his oldest friend had done this to both of them? It would tear him apart.

Jamie was the only person to speak to her. He came and went, and often didn't hang around long, but he always made time to speak to her. He would come to the basement and make fun of Ryder's latest plan to find her. He gave her updates on Ryder's mood, and he'd met Sorcha too. He'd also told her that her parents were in the country. It broke her heart to think of them missing her, possibly thinking the worst.

He probed her for information, just to increase the high he got at outdoing Ryder. The thought made her sick, but what could she do? There, she was at his mercy. At least she knew the game he was playing; Ryder wasn't so fortunate. She'd stay strong and exist for however long this charade took… there was no other option.

FORTY

Ryder

JAMIE TOLD him he needed down time and dragged him to the downstairs lounge at HQ. Even amid watching TV, Ryder was faced with his failure. A replay of the appeal for Lacie appeared in the break. She was always on his mind. Every second. Being on a couch he'd shared with her left him raw.

Jamie remained ignorant to his torment. "You didn't tell me she was famous," he said.

"She's not famous," Ryder said. "She hates the attention."

"Privacy and loyalty," Jamie said, taking another beer from the cooler at the end of the couch. "Doesn't look like she's getting either."

Ryder couldn't remember when he'd told Jamie about her values, but his head had been all over the place in the last month. There was a lot he couldn't remember. The thing he hadn't forgotten was the gut punch her smile delivered in his truck. He hadn't forgotten the meal they'd shared or their first kiss.

His life had been brought starkly into focus when he'd met her. With her, his future made sense. Everything had clicked into place almost as quickly as it had fallen apart immediately thereafter.

Gabe stuck his head in the door. "You've got a visitor upstairs."

"Who?" Jamie asked.

"For Ryder."

Gabe had been testy for the last week; Rocco had been off too. Ryder wasn't sure if the aggravation was aimed at him or Jamie, but something he didn't like had settled over the compound. He had enough on his plate without tearing apart their internal politics.

When Ryder got up the stairs, his thoughts had already trailed back to Lacie. All his mental pathways led back to her. Night had settled. He hadn't seen a clock but would put the time at around midnight, which made his visitor even more unexpected.

"Shep?" he said when he entered the reception to see the guy wandering.

"Ryder," Shep said.

The men shook hands. They'd never been the best of friends and they hadn't seen each other for weeks. After recent events, a tentative truce had formed.

"It's late," Ryder said. "What can I do for you?"

"I've been spending some time with Sorcha."

"She told me."

"Her mother's appeal yesterday was powerful."

Now he was talking about Lacie.

"Yeah," Ryder said.

"Lacie's disappearance has played on the news all day. You must be hopeful."

"I've had the cops on the phone. There are a few new leads."

"That's good," Shep said.

Ryder shrugged unable to be too optimistic

about unknown variables. It would take a major stroke of luck for anything to turn up valuable information. More often than not, exuberant apparent witnesses rarely panned out and actual leads got lost in the swamp of white noise created by nonsense factors.

"What can I do for you?" Ryder asked, not used to Seth Sheppard being so serious or cautious.

Reluctance shimmered around Shep. "We've not seen eye to eye for a long time," he said. "But what happened with Lacie, the whole thing, I… I'm really sorry."

"I appreciate that," Ryder said. "You came all the way over here at this time to tell me that?"

"No," Shep said, scanning their environment.

"So why did you come over here?"

"No offence man, but this place gives me the creeps."

"The lights aren't on," Ryder said.

"It's not the dark that makes me nervous," Shep said.

"So what is?"

"There's a blight on this place, you know that? It's in the air."

"Shep—"

"It's about Lacie," Shep said. "Or it might be. I don't know. Sorcha said… You're looking for her."

"That's not a secret."

"No, it's not. But I got something…"

"What?" Ryder asked, speared with hope.

"I'm not going to tell you that yet."

Rage flamed. "Like hell…" Ryder said, storming closer.

Shep held up his hands in surrender. "Did you ever wonder why you've got nowhere? You guys have been doing this for years, have you ever come up so empty handed? Have you ever had bad luck like you've had with this case? You have nothing, Stone. Almost five weeks since she vanished in front of your eyes, and you haven't even turned up the car that took her?" Shep said, shaking his head. "You found Booth in a few hours the first time around. Lacie came to you and a few hours later, she was in your car. The next day you were at Booth's door. Why is it so difficult? Where did the guy go? How did he get so good at hiding from you overnight?"

Maybe Shep was voicing what his men hadn't. He'd put their bad luck down to his own incompetence. Did Shep have a point?

"What do you have?" Ryder asked.

"I'm here because Sorcha trusts you," Shep said, looking left and right. "I think you care about Lacie, but I don't trust your men and I don't trust this room. Someone is listening to you. Whether it's a bug you don't know about, or a mole who has gained your trust, I don't know. But there's a reason all your leads have been brick walls. Sorcha's been telling me about your progress or lack of it. She won't be coming back here. This place isn't safe. You're not even willing to ask the obvious question."

"Which is?"

"The person, or persons, who have Lacie know your every move before you make it. You have to have realized that he knows."

"This is what you came to tell me?"

Shep moved in close. "I came to tell you that Booth's colleague Alan has left town. He was approached, spooked, the man is in fear for his life, or he was… now he's gone."

"Spooked?" Ryder asked. "Who approached him? What did they want?"

"I'm not interested in being a footnote to your investigation. I came here to warn you that someone is trying to erase the evidence. We spoke to Alan, Booth's colleague, the day Lacie disappeared and now he's gone too. Who is next?"

"When was he approached?" Ryder asked.

"Yesterday. He phoned me last night in a panic."

"It's taken you all day to tell me?"

"I spent the day trying to trace the guy."

"No luck?" Ryder asked.

"None."

"Did he tell you what was said?"

"Yeah," Shep said.

"Well?" Ryder asked when Shep didn't continue.

"I'm not giving you the details. I don't trust this place."

"How do you know this is related to Booth or to Lacie?"

"Booth is dead," Shep said.

"How do you know that?" Ryder asked, trying to maintain a bluster but the wind was seeping from his sails.

"Alan was told," Shep murmured, keeping their conversation as covert as possible.

"And you trust them?"

"Wishful thinking maybe," Shep said.

"You wish him dead?"

"Lacie's alive," Shep said. "That's why I'm here. He said Lacie was alive."

Torn by a desire to whoop in delight and another to wail over a possible missed opportunity, Ryder fought to keep himself in check.

"What did he say? I need to know exactly what was said."

"You're getting this information third hand now. I don't rely too much on Alan remembering specifics, the man was pissing his pants."

"How can you trust it's credible then?"

Shep went for the door. "Because he was pissing his pants and now, he's off the radar."

"What? That's it?" Ryder asked, experiencing a surge of tension.

"I thought you'd appreciate the news."

Ryder stepped toward him. "Thanks."

"Watch your six. Someone else sure is… for all the wrong reasons."

Shep left and Ryder loitered in the dark replaying their conversation. If he said he hadn't considered the possibility of surveillance, he'd be lying, but they were an insular group. No one from the outside got in. The HQ compound was as secure as an army base.

The only way anyone could be so far ahead of them every time was if they were bugging every room and every phone. That wouldn't be possible without the knowledge of at least one of the team members. That fact threw up the unthinkable.

"Everything okay?"

Ryder turned to see Jamie enter the room. "Yeah," he said. "Yeah, everything's fine."

"Who was it? What did they want?"

"Nothing," Ryder said with a foreign reflex to protect. "It was no one, nothing important."

"Sure?"

"Yeah," Ryder said. "Let's get back to the game."

FORTY-ONE

Ryder

TRUSTING NO ONE meant isolation. Ryder played his conversation with Shep round and round. He'd initially refused the premise… except if that was true, why had he stopped communicating with his team? His instincts were all he had left. Trusting them while paranoia infected his mind only churned him up more. Things had happened, he'd been close to Lacie, he'd known it, he'd felt it, but she'd been whipped away.

Nothing in the world was more important to Ryder than finding Lacie. He'd go to whatever lengths it took to complete his mission. His team had always been there for him, they provided a safety net, a sounding board, solidarity. But he was second guessing everything, including his own thoughts.

"I'll be out of here in ten minutes," Jamie said.

Eric tossed a bag into Jamie's truck, jarring Ryder from his thoughts. "How long are you gone?" he asked, trying to focus on the moment.

"Couple of days," Jamie said. "We'll be back by

the start of next week anyway… I've got a couple of things to grab from upstairs. Don't head out until we're back."

Ryder was meant to be on his way to the police station for an update meeting with Sorcha and Lacie's parents. Jamie and Eric were away on a job, the details were beyond him, he hadn't taken much to do with operations in recent weeks.

Jamie tossed his sunglasses on the passenger seat of his vehicle and headed to the stairwell with Eric. When the door closed, Ryder loitered alone in the parking garage. A flicker of reflected light caught his eye. Going closer to the open passenger door, Ryder frowned at the glasses. Jamie had just tossed aviators, reflective aviators, that he'd never seen his friend wear. The guys had enjoyed jeering him when he'd first worn his, but he hadn't worn them for a while… In fact, the last time he'd seen them…

The memory smacked him in the head like a two by four. Ryder staggered back. Lacie had been wearing them that day, she'd hooked the leg into her cleavage when they'd got to Shep's office. No, but… he couldn't be sure but would bet that they'd still been there when she got forced into that car… That would mean that…

Time was of the essence. Although Ryder tried to tell himself it couldn't be true, memories of the last few weeks conflicted. How Jamie had seemed to know of Sorcha's pregnancy. The time he'd referred to Lacie as Dusty though Ryder had been sure he'd never used the pet name in the presence of his business partner. Jamie had used Lacie's values of privacy and loyalty.

Too many things didn't quite add up. It had to be paranoia. Didn't it? Jamie had been his best friend for over decade and a half. Except how much concern had Jamie shown for Lacie's disappearance? Had he cared how it affected his best friend? But Jamie could be dry…

couldn't he?

Of its own volition, his body moved to the metal cabinet in the corner. He punched in the code to open it. On autopilot, he reached for a GPS tracker and closed the door. Returning to Jamie's truck, Ryder activated the tracker and attached it to the truck's underbelly. Moving away, he covered his mouth as the possibilities sank in. Still, he told himself that the evidence would prove Jamie's innocence and then he would have someone to trust.

"You okay, buddy?"

Jamie and Eric were back in the garage and piling into the truck.

"Great," Ryder managed to say. "Have a good trip."

"Sure," Jamie said. "Give me a call with the updates."

"Updates?"

"The police station, that is where you're going, remember?"

"Sure, yeah," Ryder said.

Jamie laughed and offered a wave then sped out the still opening garage door. Ryder stood static, his actions sickened him, yet something burned in his belly. A hope he hadn't felt during any part of the investigation.

He'd betrayed his best friend. A part of him had to believe that Jamie may be involved, or he wouldn't had done what he just did. Maybe his instincts hadn't completely deserted him. Except now he had to calculate his next step and he had to do it quickly and quietly.

Everyone thought he was going out, so that's what he would do, right now. Ryder leaped into his truck and moved the laptop he'd brought for the meeting from the floor to his duffel that was in the back seat.

Jamie and Eric had had enough time to get on the road, so Ryder wasted no more time. He got his truck into gear and drove through the open garage door. His life had become surreal. It was his instinct to go to the last place on earth he'd ever expect to want to go, especially for help. In that minute, he couldn't get there fast enough.

FORTY-TWO

Ryder

"I'M SURPRISED TO find you here," Ryder said, closing Shep's office door.

"Ditto," Shep said. "I just dropped Sorcha off at the police station. I thought you would be there too."

"I called and told them I wouldn't make it."

"Sorcha will be mad."

"Yeah," Ryder said, taking the seat that he'd once shared with Lacie.

"Clue me in."

Ryder examined Shep who appeared somehow more relaxed. His complexion was brighter, his eyes more aware, and he was wearing a tie that matched his shirt.

He narrowed an eye. "Where's Tiffany?"

Shep cleared his throat. "She and Sorcha weren't wild about each other."

"Things getting serious with you and Sorcha?"

"Could be," Shep said. The fact he said that with a smile instead of a scowl told Ryder more than the man was saying aloud. "What can I do for you? You wouldn't cancel a meeting about Lacie for no reason."

"What you said last week has been playing in my head."

"Good," Shep said. "Did it get you anywhere?"

"Paranoid," Ryder admitted, leaning forward to drive his fingers through his hair. "You've made me doubt my own men."

"You didn't blow off Lacie's meeting to come here and give me shit."

"I planted a tracker on Jamie's truck," Ryder blurted out.

A beat went by.

"Wow."

"I can't talk to my own guys because any of them could be in on it. If they're not, then they know I'm doubting them."

"So you came here?"

"I don't trust you," Ryder said. "But you came to me, and you care about Sorcha."

"Yes."

"I want Lacie back. I don't care what it takes. I'll sacrifice whatever I have to."

"Do you think Wallace is involved?"

"I don't want to," Ryder said. "He might not be, but there's… things that just don't quite add up. I want to be sure."

"Better to be sure than to live in wonder," Shep said.

"That's what I'm trying to tell myself."

"So where is it?" Shep asked. "The tracker."

"They left just before I did. Wherever they're going, they are not there yet."

"Do you have a plan?" Shep asked.

"It was impulse," Ryder said.

"Impulse that came from something."

"Sunglasses," Ryder admitted on a sigh. "The sunglasses that Jamie has look like the ones Lacie had."

"Is that it?" Shep asked. "I'll admit that's suspicious, but it's hardly ironclad."

"Maybe you're right," Ryder said. "Could be that I'm just paranoid, but you put it there."

"I might have helped it along but you're not an idiot."

"You've got me doubting my oldest friend!"

"If he's clean, then it's nothing and he never has to know. But if he's not…"

"He's my oldest friend. I can't believe that he—"

"Yes, you do," Shep said. "Because you wouldn't be here if you didn't. Check the tracker, what harm can it do? It's already on the truck. You've got an opportunity here to find out the truth either way."

Ryder considered his options, but Shep was right. The tracker was there. It would be a waste if he didn't check, and he'd kick himself for not checking later.

Reluctantly, he went back to his truck for the laptop and brought it to Shep's desk. That bubble in his gut returned. He wasn't reluctant to check because doubting Jamie was a betrayal of his friend. It was because somehow, he feared his betrayal was justified.

Ryder went through security and opened the software to triangulate the tracker. He expected the thing to be moving and steeled himself to be patient. There would be no instant results.

As the map zoomed in, it wasn't moving. The tracker had stopped somewhere a dozen miles south of the StoneWall compound.

"Do you recognize the street? Does he have family in town?"

"No," Ryder said. "He doesn't have family. He isn't seeing anyone. Eric's with him, he won't have stopped for a booty call. Anyway, he said he was late."

"It looks like a residential street. Not a great area but the houses are detached, spaced apart."

Ryder heard Shep. His mind was buzzing in confusion. Which was worse, that Jamie could be involved or that Lacie could have been this close the whole time?

"She can't be in there," Ryder said.

"Why not?" Shep asked. "Not all kidnap victims are kept in secluded mountain retreats."

"If she was that close to a public street, she could get away. She would have gotten away."

"Maybe that's the sicko's deal. Keeping her close to civilization and managing to keep her on a leash must give him a kick. He gets his high from knowing you're this close to her but can't find her."

"Sicko," Ryder said, looking at the roofs of the surrounding buildings displayed on Google Earth, wondering which one might house her.

"Do you think Wallace is being coerced?"

"We don't know it's him yet," Ryder snapped.

"Call him," Shep said. "Find out where he is. If he's lying, we'll know."

The suggestion was valid, but that didn't speed him taking his phone from his pocket. The possibility of what the call could reveal slowed him down. He got his phone, scrolled through the call list, and glanced at Shep before he pressed send.

It rang half a dozen times then Jamie answered. "Hey. What's up? We just left."

"Sorry man," Ryder said. "I'm waiting around for this meeting, and it occurred to me, I've got no clue where you're headed."

"You really are out of it, aren't you?" Jamie laughed. "Maine, risk assessment."

"Right, did you tell me that?"

"Yeah," Jamie laughed again.

"How long will it take you to get up there?"

"Eric's driving so I don't care."

"You're a terrible passenger," Ryder said. "Hasn't he driven off the road to strangle you yet?"

"Just started, there's a lot of road ahead."

"You going straight there?"

"Yeah," Jamie said. "Nothing but road up ahead... are you okay?"

"Yeah. Sorry, it's just... a lot going on you know."

"Sure, take it easy. Let me know of any developments."

Ryder signed off and lowered the phone to his lap.

Nothing was said until... "You're closer to her," Shep said.

"Hmm?"

"It's a kick in the sack, but you will get to slug it out with him. Don't focus on him. Focus on the girl you practically pissed on to stake a claim."

Shep jolted Ryder's thoughts into full reverse. Lacie!

He leaped from the chair. "We've got her!"

"Wait a minute," Shep said, chasing Ryder who was already halfway from the room. "You can't go charging in."

"Like hell I can't."

"Where?" Shep asked, smacking Ryder's chest to halt him. "You don't know what building she's in. You don't know the set-up. You don't know how many guys there are, or what weapons they're packing. You don't know where Lacie is, that could be a center of operations. She could be at a different location."

"You're the one who told me to call him, told me to confirm where they are."

"Yeah, and you did," Shep said. "But you need your head on. We don't know what this is. We don't know what his motives are. If all he wants to do is piss you off, he's done it. If you go racing in, you're giving him what he wants. If this is about money, we know he's already broken the law with Booth and I doubt he wants to go to jail. The possibility also exists that this is about something else entirely."

"Like what?"

"I don't know," Shep said, scratching the back of his head. "You know, I've never been one for hard work and perseverance. That's you... There's a reason you've been raking in the dough for years while I'm happy with my shitty storefront. You live for this. You know how to do it."

"Surveillance," Ryder said. "Patience."

"Two things I don't have time for."

"I can't leave her in there. We don't know what she's going through."

Shep softened a little. "She's been in there almost six weeks now. Whatever they're doing to her... they've done it already."

"Is that meant to make me feel better?" Ryder asked, sick at the thought.

"No," Shep said. "It's meant to remind you of your role. You do this properly because racing in and getting yourself shot and killed won't help her."

"A stakeout," Ryder said. "To sit and watch that house for activity, learn their routine, try to find out where she is and what's going on."

"Sounds like you're forming a plan," Shep said.

"A car on the street wouldn't work, it's too visible. Both Jamie and Eric would know my vehicles."

"What are you thinking?"

"We'll take a pass. Find a spot, a roof, or an abandoned building."

"Set up camp?"

"Camera or two," Ryder said. "Watch from a street nearby. We'll set up camp tonight."

"We?"

"It's never a good idea to watch alone. You don't have to come in with me. We watch tonight, find out what we can."

"Tonight?"

"I won't leave her in there," Ryder said. "She's been through enough."

"You could do more harm than good if you rush. If she's not there, you could drive them so far underground—"

"I know my opponent," Ryder said. "Wallace doesn't play well with others; he revolts against authority. Why do you think his name is above my door when he didn't have two cents to rub together?"

"Wallace?" Shep said. "You turned on him quick."

"He's holding my woman captive," Ryder snarled.

"You sure about that now?"

"You don't know him like I do."

"Couldn't the same be said for you, he knows you?"

"We have the element of surprise now, and he doesn't know me like this."

"He never saw you and Lacie together. Maybe he doesn't realize how you feel about her."

"Why hold her?" Ryder asked. "I can't see any reason why—"

"Are you going to tell Sorcha... or the police?"

"I'll call Deacon before I go in," Ryder said. "You stay on the outside. If I don't come out, you get the cops in to Lacie. Don't let Wallace move because if he does, we'll never see him or Lacie again."

"What happened to patience and procedure?"

"I'll be patient enough to find out where she is and how many men there are. I won't let the police go in first because I don't want Lacie caught in the crossfire. I'm going back to HQ to get some equipment. I'll meet you back here in two hours."

"Not here," Shep said. "We can't be sure it's him, and we can't be sure you're not being watched. I'll pick you up at the north park entrance, it's open but not covered by any cameras."

Ryder nodded. "Two hours."

FORTY-THREE

Ryder

EQUIPMENT FROM THE car was discreetly set up in an abandoned house at the top of the block. After two hours of watching, they'd seen Eric and three other men enter the house.

By five hours, they'd watched various lights go on and off. Five men entered only for eight, including Eric and Jamie, to leave again. Ryder sat up, watching them pile into cars and drive off.

"They're gone," Ryder said.

"There's at least one guy in there," Shep said.

"One guy is easy. We don't have the time to sit here for weeks. This could be our only chance; how often do they leave the place empty?"

"You want to go rushing in there?"

Ryder reached into the sports bag at his feet. They were sitting on an old, worn couch that had been abandoned in a neighboring room. It wasn't very comfortable, but it was better than the bare floorboards. Ryder pulled out a small plastic box from the bottom of the bag and held it up.

"Ears. I'll get these in," Ryder said. "That way if she's somewhere else we might find out where."

"The tracker's still active," Shep said. "We can keep watching that."

"You do that," Ryder said, pulling up the hood of his sweatshirt and sticking the box in his pocket. "I'll be in and out within ten minutes."

"I thought you were going to phone Deacon before you went in."

"I'm not going in. I mean I'm not going in after Lace. I'll put the listening devices in, and we'll be in a better position to find out what's going on."

"Are you telling me you're not going to look for her?"

Ryder didn't answer. Although he was being honest, his gut was desperate to know. If he thought about her in that place and him sitting out there doing nothing... It made him sick.

"We're on a clock," Ryder said. "Sit tight."

Ryder didn't wait for a response. He went down the stairs and out of the house to cut across the yard onto the parallel street. He walked around the block, carrying on to the back of Jamie's property.

The sensors on the back fence were a giveaway that more was going on than plain habitation. If he hadn't known what he was looking for, he'd have missed them, but it was a classic StoneWall signature. Ryder had given Jamie and Eric training on how to use and set up their security systems. Never did he imagine it would be used against him.

Observing the house, he took his time circumventing the security system. He crept over the yard, looking out for further security measures or movement in the house. He saw neither. A first floor window was open. He'd have to boost himself up to reach it and couldn't be sure it led to an empty room.

One of the basement windows was just visible through a broken wooden lattice that would've been part of a yard feature in the past. Ryder moved the lattice aside silently and spotted an alarm sensor on the basement window.

The window itself was about a foot and a half tall and maybe four across. He disabled the alarm and lifted the window while remaining on the lookout for more security features. There were none. There couldn't be anything to protect in the basement or the men weren't going to be absent for long. Could be that they were arrogant enough to believe they were at no risk of discovery.

Flattening on the ground, he slithered through the window and landed on the exposed dirt floor without a sound, closing the window at the same time. No light. The sky outside was dark. The window was in such an obscure place, only one slice of streetlight broke the abyss. Relying on his training, he took some time to adjust to the illumination.

"You're early."

The voice was small and unexpected. He whipped around expecting to see a specter or proof he'd imagined the sound. Shrouded in a shadow against the far wall was an outline, certainly darker than the rest of the gloom.

"Lacie," he whispered more in disbelief than relief.

"You're early."

"God, baby, tell me it's you. Is it—?"

"You're early," she said again in that same spaced, vacant voice.

Had she been drugged?

"What am I early for, baby? Tell me."

"There's no time," she muttered.

"Time for what, baby?" he asked, moving toward her.

The rattle of chains stopped him dead.

"Stay," she said, her voice a little stronger. "It hurts, the bars, they hurt."

Narrowing his eyes, he leaned closer. Bars rose from the floor in the alcove under the stairs, caging her in. A space of around seven-foot square with a doorway, minus the door, to a toilet and sink against the opposite wall. She was literally a prisoner. He'd heard the chains. How tethered was she?

"Leave," she whispered. The chain rattled again. "Leave."

"I won't leave you here," he said, forgetting about the bugs in his pocket. "Talk to me. Tell me how to get you out."

"He's angry," she whispered still spaced out. "He's so angry."

"Wallace," Ryder said. "You're talking about Jamie Wallace."

Silence. Had she passed out? His heart burst when she spoke.

A glittering, gut-wrenching smile tickled her tone. "You found out."

"Yeah, he's been playing me, and you got pulled into it. I'm so sorry, baby. I had no idea he would go this far to hurt me. I can't—"

"No," she said. "No, it's more than that."

"What, baby? Tell me."

"You're early."

Whatever they had her on, or whatever they had done to her, it was interfering with her mind. Keeping her on the same page would be tough. Getting her out became more urgent. He needed to get her away from there, to free her from the torture she'd been living in… because of him.

"I'm going to get you out, okay?"

"No," she said. "No, no."

"Calm down, it's okay."

"He's coming back. He'll be back. He'll—"

With one click, the game changed. Light flooded the space. Ryder stepped back to see the large space was clear of everything except her cage in the corner. The light dazzled. For a second, he couldn't pick out specifics.

Lacie hissed and clambered to the corner like a scared animal. Heavy footfalls started down the stairs. Ryder didn't have to see to know who those boots belonged to.

"Man, you're good," Jamie said, pausing halfway down the stairs with one hand on the exposed wood banister, a grin on his face. "I told you to call me with any updates."

"I thought this would be quicker."

"You got through security and everything."

"It's our security," Ryder said.

"You do insist on sharing everything."

"Now I know what you did with all that kit you've been taking on jobs."

"Are you going to tell me?" Jamie asked still smiling and continuing down the stairs to their level.

When he got to the bottom four other men appeared at the top of the stairs. A not-so-subtle show that rushing Jamie would be pointless.

"Tell you what?" Ryder asked.

"How you found us, has our guest been telling stories? She doesn't say much, perfect woman really, but I suppose you know that."

Jamie hit Ryder's shoulder and nodded at Lacie. Her knees were pulled to her chest, her head was turned down, but he could see the blindfold over her eyes.

Her clothes were the same he'd seen her in the

day he lost her, now they were dirty and torn. Her hair was limp and greasy, matted around the blindfold. But it was her figure… She'd been slight before but now her skin hung on her bones.

Pale and gaunt, she was confined and neglected. There he stood next to the man who'd orchestrated the whole thing. Her physical appearance slugged him a sucker punch, but it was the non-visible signs that scared him the most.

Balling a hand into a fist, he lashed out on impulse, smacking Jamie's jaw, knocking him to the floor. The men began to race down the stairs, but Jamie held up a hand to stop them.

"I'll give you that," Jamie said. "I probably deserved that."

"Probably? You fucking little bastard, what the hell—"

"This isn't my fault! You! You and your little girlfriend fucked up my operation! You want someone to blame? Blame yourself!"

"What the hell have you done to her? How the fuck—?"

"Not like you to swear in front of a female," Jamie said. "See how easy it is to forget about her?"

"What is wrong with you? How can you look at yourself? How could you look me in the eye? It's you! You stayed ahead of me because I trusted you!"

"You did me a favor," Jamie said, sneering. "I appreciate that."

"You're going to rot in hell. Let her out of there."

"Why would I do that?" Jamie asked. "I didn't want her fucking up my operation. Now you're here, you could fuck it up too. She's not allowed to leave, and neither are you."

"Do you think the guys aren't going to come looking for me?" Ryder asked.

"None of them know where you are. I spoke to Gabe. They think you're chasing ghosts. No one knows where you are. You've been acting crazy enough for these last few weeks. It won't take much to convince anyone that you couldn't live with yourself after what happened with Lacie."

"You're sick."

"Funny," Jamie said as eight of his men moved down to surround Ryder. "That's exactly what she said."

Jamie sauntered up the stairs while his men circled closer. Ryder floored the first two and the third was thrown back. The other five closed in and wrestled him to the floor, then their cuffs were on his wrists and his feet were tied.

The goons dragged him to the wall near the cage and attached him to the end bar. The guy he'd hit was covered in blood. Good. His nose was broken. That guy went to a control panel on the wall and keyed in a code. The bars could be electrified from that panel. Though, for the moment, Ryder was spared, Jamie would have a reason for that charity.

The men mumbled to each other. He was kicked by the second man he'd hit before they all piled up the stairs, turned off the light, and closed the door.

Movement on the floor that was their ceiling quickly ceased, and they were left to their waiting.

"What day is it?" she asked in a voice that was barely there.

"Tuesday," he answered. "You've been here for six weeks."

"No," she mumbled. "We traveled for a bit. We started in a forest in the middle of nowhere."

"Tell me, are you hurt? What have they done to you?"

"I'm sorry about Jamie."

"It's not your fault. None of this is your fault."

"He's angry with you. He blames you for…"

"I'm sorry. I'll do everything I can to make it up to you. He's hurting you to hurt me. It's the only reasoning I can imagine, though it makes no sense. I don't know what I could have done to—"

"He was in the apartment," Lacie said. "He was the one who came in with Booth that day. He didn't know about you until you told him what happened. He couldn't take the risk that I would recognize him elsewhere if you and I were seeing each other. Honestly, I think the fact that you cared for me only sweetened the deal for him. Otherwise, he probably would have killed me straight away."

Ryder processed. Jamie was protecting himself, his illegal interests, and he didn't care who got in the way. The man he'd considered his best friend all these years was nothing more than a selfish, common criminal. Ryder had given Jamie every respect and opportunity and this was how he'd been repaid.

"I'll never be able to make this up to you. Nothing can… nothing could… I'm sorry."

"How is Sorcha?"

"She misses you. We've all missed you."

"He told me… I mean it's good that you've…"

"I've what?" he asked, straining against the metal restraints.

Desperately, Ryder wanted to touch her, to soothe her, to convince himself that she was real, and to convince her that he would keep her sane. Everything would be okay. All they had to do was get out of this.

"I'm tired," she said.

"Have they given you anything?"

"Anything?"

"Drugs," he asked.

"They don't drug me," she said.

"They don't feed you either."

"They do," she said wistfully. "When they remember… so tired."

"Do they…? I mean have they—?"

"Ryder," she breathed.

"Yeah, baby?"

"You found me, just like you said you would. You're here. You figured him out."

"Yeah, baby," he said, overcome with guilt. "I figured him out."

"You're here."

"I'm here."

"I want to sleep now," she said. "He'll move us now we're together. Can I sleep?"

"You sleep, baby," he said. "I'll keep look out for them."

Ryder wanted to promise that he'd protect her, that he wouldn't let anyone hurt her, but he couldn't. While he was chained to the railings, there was nothing he could do for her. Any of the gang could come down those stairs and do anything they wanted to her, and all he would be able to do was watch.

Lacie hadn't wanted him to make promises that he would feel bad about breaking and he'd told her she'd be safe from danger. No actions he could undertake would be enough to earn her forgiveness, he'd carry this debt to her forever. Nothing could justify or excuse what had happened to her because of him.

FORTY-FOUR

Ryder

THEY WOULD GET out of this alive, Ryder hoped. When they did his life would be unrecognizable. The business was done, his friendships with Jamie and Eric were a fallacy. He couldn't know if there were other SW employees involved. He deserved all he got. He'd been an idiot, naive and idealistic. The woman he cared so much for had been tortured in a captivity of his making. He might not have been the one to turn the key in the lock, but he was as liable as the one who did.

Lacie didn't know how long she'd been there. He'd bet it felt like months, maybe years. She wouldn't have known her parents were there. She wouldn't have seen the televised appeal. Under normal circumstances, she had been an insomniac, this situation wouldn't have been conducive to rest and relaxation. Even after she was freed, the memories would plague every aspect of her life.

A shout came from above. A sound like a gunshot, then another. More shouting followed, and more shots. Yes, Shep. He better have called the damn cavalry. Chaos ensued above them, more shouting followed by hurried steps. A couple of men became a dozen more, one voice covered another. The door was flung open, and the light was turned on again. Lacie hissed away, but he couldn't see her with his back to the bars.

"Police!" someone shouted.

"We're down here!" Ryder shouted. "Just the two of us, there's no direct threat. Tell your men to be careful of security and possible traps."

A few whispers were exchanged then someone started down the stairs.

"Ryder?" another voice came from behind the SWAT guys surveying the basement. Deacon thundered down the stairs. "What the…? You could've given us a heads up about this. You could've got yourself killed!"

"I didn't know you cared," Ryder said. "Now quit with the chit-chat and get Lacie some medical attention."

"That's…" Deacon looked over Ryder's head and pity glazed his expression. "You found her."

"Yeah. Now get her out of here."

"You got it."

SWAT got working on the bars and Ryder was liberated quickly. Three of Jamie's men had been killed, two were shot and receiving medical attention. The rest had been taken into custody, including Jamie.

Deacon took Ryder upstairs introduced him to the agent in charge to give his statement. The men had been using the house for a while; the stink told him that that they hadn't been house-proud. But Lacie had said they would be moving out.

Drugs were found in an upstairs room, Jamie's activities stretched into dark areas. How had he missed it? What else hadn't he noticed? How long it had been going on?

Ryder was talking with Deacon and a couple of others when he saw two additional paramedics heading down the basement stairs. Ryder walked away from Deacon's boss toward the activity. People were on his heels, but he didn't pause to check who they were.

When he got to the bottom of the stairs, he saw three officers loitering and four paramedics crouching around Lacie who still cowered in the corner on the stained mattress. Her hand was over her eyes and the other extended holding the paramedics at bay.

"What's wrong?" Ryder asked the room.

"Nothing," one of the paramedics said. "It's common with captive victims."

"What?" Ryder asked.

"She won't let us examine her," the paramedic said.

"We got the blindfold off and she started yammering."

"Lace," Ryder said, crouching beside the paramedic who had spoken to him. "Baby, these guys want to help. We just want to know you're okay."

She started shaking her head, but still she covered her eyes and held her hand up toward them. "No, no, I have to behave," she said. "I'm not allowed to see."

"It's okay, baby. It's over," Ryder said. "It's over."

"No," she said. "No, I have to behave."

"Baby, it's over. I'm here now. You trust me, baby, don't you?"

"Lacie!"

Lacie jolted at the sound of the voice that just exploded. Someone roared down the stairs and soaked the room in the scent of expensive perfume.

"Sorcha?" Lacie asked, lifting her chin.

"Oh my God, Lacie!"

Sorcha wailed and fell to the floor, dragging Lacie into her embrace. Lacie's hands fell around her friend. Though her eyes remained closed, moisture gathered in them. Sorcha had broken through. The women cried and held each other. Sorcha sent everyone away except the female paramedic, then sat with Lacie through her physical assessment.

The next time Ryder saw Lacie was on the street. Shep approached and got the story. He expressed his gratitude to Shep for calling in the police and Sorcha. At that point, the women appeared in the doorway, both Sorcha and the female paramedic were holding Lacie up. The other three paramedics ran up the stairs, but Sorcha sent them away.

The women helped Lacie down the stairs. Her struggle was clear. All Ryder wanted was to go over there, gather her into his arms, and sweep her off her feet. Something in his manner conveyed that to Shep because his hand landed on Ryder's forearm.

"You don't know what she's been through. Give her some time."

Lacie and Sorcha got into the ambulance and the paramedics took off for the local hospital. It didn't matter that she was out of danger and in safe hands, he didn't like the distance. Physical and otherwise.

Ryder got his business at the scene over with, then Shep took him to the hospital. They rode in silence. Thoughts warred in his mind about Jamie and StoneWall. Thoughts of his men and what the future held. But none of that tempted him to change course, all those things could wait.

Getting to Lacie was his main objective, his only objective. Making sure she was okay was first. Then he had to convey to her his presence, to let her know he was there for her, for whatever she needed.

At main reception, they were directed to the fourth floor and a specific relatives' room. When they got up there, everyone was already present, Lacie's parents, Sorcha, and Gabe… No, Ryder didn't want to go there yet. Shep went to Sorcha, gave her a hug, and settled her down to listen. Ryder couldn't hear what was said from his position. Everyone else in the room just looked at him.

"You found her," Ann Hart sobbed and rushed over to hug him.

The welcome of the Hart family had been immediately warm. His guilt ballooned at this reaction. Yes, he'd found her, but it was his best friend who had put Lacie in peril.

"She's giving a statement," Martin Hart said. "They're giving her antibiotics and fluids, but they're saying she'll be okay."

Ann was still hugging him when Sorcha approached. "She's out of it, dazzled and spaced out," Sorcha said. "The doctor said that could just be the dehydration and malnutrition. But she's alive Ryder, she's alive."

Sorcha joined Ann in his arms. The women hugged each other and him at the same time. Martin went back to a seat. Shep was filling a paper cone from the water cooler, but Gabe stayed in the middle of the room as stoic as he'd ever been. Things weren't being said, questions hung in the air. The men faced off while the sobbing women were oblivious to the aggravation bouncing back and forth.

The door opened, breaking his stare, and drawing everyone's attention. Beth, Lacie's best friend from the UK, entered. She was closely followed by Monty, a local museum curator who doted on Lacie as he would a daughter. Jimmy, Lacie's good-hearted, mild-natured and harmless adorer entered too.

Monty held up his hands and took a seat next to Shep who filled him in. Ryder had gotten to know all these people in the last six weeks. He'd spent more time with them than he had with Lacie. Her motley group of family had become a part of his; he'd been accepted with unconditional love.

When the door opened again, Auntie Elise came in. "She's fine," Elise declared. "The police are finishing up with her. The doctor wants her to get some rest. They're hoping she'll be brighter and more with it tomorrow."

"She looks so… small," Beth said.

"She's always been a tiny thing," Monty said.

"Not like this," Sorcha agreed with Beth.

"She looks like a sneeze would kill her," Beth said.

They all considered that for a moment.

"Do we know what happened?" Monty asked. "Did they get the guy?"

"They got a lot of them," Martin said. "They're still interrogating them to get to the bottom of their motives."

Ryder knew his motives, his skin tightened across his body. "Excuse me."

Unable to get out of that room fast enough, he strode away. These people accepted him, they respected him, and they looked to him for guidance and action. But he'd been the cause of her torture. He wasn't sure he'd ever be able to look any of them in the eye again.

He paced down the corridor. The relatives' room door opened behind him, and he glanced back to see Gabe exiting.

"What are you doing here?" Ryder demanded of Gabe.

"I'm not here because you told me about tonight," Gabe said.

Ryder rounded the end of the corridor to take them out of direct line of sight of the relatives' room. "What are you doing here?" Ryder asked again.

"Sonny was on the scanner," Gabe said. "Jamie, did we hear right—"

"Yeah, what's it to you?"

"Are you crazy? This was Jamie's doing? We're all livid. Why the fuck didn't you—"

"When you find out your best friend has screwed you over, it makes it tough to believe the best of anyone else."

"You thought we were involved in this?"

Ryder shifted in close. "Jamie," he said. "If I didn't see this… If I didn't realize that he—"

"You're blaming yourself?" Gabe said. "You've got to have seen how Jamie has been recently. He's been… off."

"I didn't see it. I didn't see anything."

"You wanted to see the best in him, you two have been tight for a long time. But the boys and I—"

"So everyone's been hiding this from me?"

"You can't think we were involved," Gabe said.

"They're all in custody now," Ryder said. "I suppose we'll find out."

"Ryder?"

The female voice came from around the corner. Ryder left Gabe to head back toward the relatives' room. Elise was standing just outside with a doctor in a white coat.

"Are you okay?" Ryder asked Elise.

"They gave Lacie something to help her sleep," Elise said. "But she asked for you."

"For me?" Ryder asked.

"Follow me," the blonde doctor said and led him to a door at the other end of the corridor.

She pointed and gave him a nod, then left him

alone.

With one breath, he went inside. The lights were off, and the curtains drawn over the window. Her bed was against the far wall. He would never have seen her if he hadn't known she was there. Beth was right about her stature.

A bag of liquid hung at her side, the IV was connected to her left hand. He was almost sure she was asleep already, but when he got closer, she inhaled and rolled her head on the pillow.

"Hi," he said, reaching for her hand.

She lifted hers toward him granting permission for him to link his fingers in hers.

"Thank you," she whispered through dry lips.

"There's nothing to thank me for," he said, covering their joined hands with his free one.

"You found me, just like you said you would."

"Yeah," he said. "I found you."

"I want to sleep," she said, though her eyes hadn't been open since he entered. "Can I sleep now?"

"Yes, baby, you can sleep."

"I promise I'll behave," she whispered on one long, soft exhale.

"You sleep," he said, pulling the guest chair to the side of her bed without letting go of her hand. "Sleep."

Her breathing evened out, and he pulled himself closer. There, she'd be safe. Peace was what Lacie needed. He battled with his own demons. Those made him stay at her side, he needed to see her, to be there so that he could be sure that she really was back.

The lingering nightmare of being without her haunted him, so he'd stay with her. He'd remain at her side for as long as she let him. Whether it was a sixth sense, or an internal self-loathing, things weren't going to pan out perfectly for them. He just knew it. After what he'd caused, he had to admit that it would be in Lacie's best interest to get as far from him as fast as she possibly could.

He ached for her and fought his natural urge to crawl onto that bed beside her and hold her in his arms. He wanted her, now more than ever, but he'd given her nothing, and he wasn't sure he had anything to give her.

Truth was, she'd be safer and happier without him, but he couldn't let go of her hand, he wouldn't. Nothing made sense... nothing except Lacie.

FORTY-FIVE

Ryder

ALL OF THEM stayed the night at the hospital. The doctors told them that Lacie wouldn't be awake until the morning, but still, they stayed. Ryder supposed her family and friends didn't want to stray far just like he didn't.

He'd slept a little in her room, still holding her hand. Her mother and father had slept there too. At first light, Shep left, closely followed by Gabe. Beth got a ride from Monty who was also driving Jimmy home.

Everyone had promised to go home for a nap and to freshen up, then they would all return. He and Sorcha were left with Lacie's parents and her Aunt Elise. None of the core group were going anywhere.

Lacie slept through until ten a.m. She woke up with a mew and they'd all leaped to attention. Martin rushed off for the doctor. Lacie yawned then was startled into an upright position with her gaze darting around like a scared cat. She observed them and the room, and then let herself relax a little.

The tension didn't leave her entirely. For some

reason, her focus settled on him. He wouldn't sacrifice a second of her attention, this was the most alive he'd felt in six weeks.

When she'd been missing, he'd forgotten what contentment with her was like. Forgotten how her eyes burned fire and her lips plumped the second before she smiled. Then it was there, soft, sweet, and electric, that coy almost not there smile spread on her face and his dick tried to leap to her.

For six weeks, he hadn't experienced the simmer in his gut. In a flash, he relived the night she'd spent in his bed. In all the time he had been without her, he hadn't considered sex of any kind. He'd forgotten what it was, forgotten that it existed. His dick had spent six weeks limp and that hadn't bothered him at all.

Right then in one second, six weeks' worth of blood he'd saved only for her rushed into his groin with painfully torturous results. But he loved it almost as much as he loved her. The realization of his depth of feeling wasn't new. He'd known it for a while but wouldn't let himself admit it when she wasn't in his reach.

Her smile grew a little when the corner of his mouth tipped up. His intention to go to her side was thwarted when Martin came back in with a doctor and nurse. Everyone was herded out of the room for the doctor to complete an examination of Lacie.

They loitered outside Lacie's room waiting to be re-admitted. Less than a minute later, three men came around the corner, heading straight for them. The third man, at the back of the group, was Detective Deacon, which meant that whatever was coming, it was about Lacie.

"Is everything okay?" Martin Hart asked the three cops, placing an arm around his wife, and a hand on Sorcha's back.

Sorcha's grip on Elise's hand tightened.

"Yes," cop one said.

"Do you have information for us?" Elise asked.

"We're still investigating," cop two said. "But we have some questions. "

All three cops looked directly at Ryder. "Questions for me?" Ryder asked.

"Yeah," cop one said.

"Wallace has been talking," Deacon said. "I don't think you'll like what he's saying."

"I didn't need you to tell me that," Ryder said.

"What's going on?" Sorcha asked.

"We're going to have to ask you to come down to the precinct," cop two said.

"Wait a minute, you're arresting him?" Sorcha asked.

"We just have some questions at this stage," cop one said.

"You can't take him anywhere," Elise said.

"Yes, Lacie needs him," Ann said.

These women leaped to his defense, but they hadn't learned the truth of Lacie's torment in these last few weeks.

"I'll come," Ryder said.

"You can't," Sorcha exclaimed. "She needs you."

"I'll come back as soon as I'm done," Ryder said, leaning in to kiss Sorcha's cheek.

"There's no need for anyone to stay." Lacie's voice came from behind the group.

Ryder stepped back as everyone turned to see Lacie standing with her doctor and nurse just outside her room.

"Go back in there," Ann said. "Lie down."

"We tried to keep her lying down," the doctor said. "But she's not used her limbs much, so if she feels up to it, she can walk. The physical therapist will be in to see her in an hour."

"So go and lie down until then," Elise said.

"Mr. Stone?"

He'd almost forgotten about the police. Once again, they commanded the attention of everyone in the hall.

"What's going on?" Lacie asked.

Ryder didn't like the way she braced her hand on the wall. She was struggling and it was his fault.

"The police want to ask Ryder questions!" Sorcha said.

"About what?" Lacie asked.

Sorcha separated herself from the others to join Lacie. The women stood close. If it wasn't for Lacie's gaunt appearance, he could almost forget about the trauma of recent weeks and imagine them as friends exchanging gossip.

"About what happened," Sorcha said.

"Oh," Lacie said. "Okay then."

"No, it's not okay," Sorcha said. "He didn't do anything wrong."

"They asked me questions," Lacie said. "They're investigating. It's what they do."

The doctor adjusted Lacie's IV bag which hung on a stand just behind her.

"We need him here," Sorcha said.

"We don't," Lacie said. "You can all go home. I should get out tomorrow."

"Home?" her mother said. "We want to be here with you."

"I've been alone for six weeks. I can cope with another day," Lacie snapped, then went back into her room.

No one said a thing. Before her ordeal Lacie wasn't short-tempered, she wasn't the type to snap.

"We have to ask you to come with us," cop one

said. "Mr. Stone?"

"Yeah," he said, watching the door close behind Lacie.

"We'll talk to her," Sorcha said.

The nurse stepped forward. "It's not unusual for patients of severe mental or physical trauma to be psychologically disturbed. We'll have professionals speak to her later today."

"Mr. Stone?"

"Yes," he said, relenting to the police. "Yeah, let's get out of here."

Ryder didn't know what Jamie had been saying. He wanted to stay at Lacie's side and never leave. But as he followed the cops down the hall, he had to admit that a breath of fresh air might do him good. He needed to air out his body, and his mind, and try to figure out what the hell came next.

FORTY-SIX

Lacie

LACIE SPENT THE day talking to doctors and nurses, there had been physical therapists and psychologists, and her last guests had been the police. Her family and friends had been in and out all day, offering words of comfort and advice, telling her stories of what she'd missed during her captivity.

With the police gone and her family in the hospital cafeteria, she had a moment to herself, but it was short lived. There was a tap on the door, then it opened to reveal Ryder.

When she'd seen him this morning, she'd still been in a bit of a daze. Details of last night were still fuzzy. She couldn't really remember how she had been freed but remembered him. He'd found her.

He looked good, his dark brown hair curled over his ears, and his eyes were as sharp as ever. That night they'd spent together seemed so far away that she couldn't be sure she hadn't only dreamed the whole thing.

In that tee-shirt that strained over his broad chest, and the well-worn jeans that cupped him in all the right places, he seemed like a dream. All the way down to those heavy black boots, he was the epitome of male testosterone. Arrogance seeped from him and displayed in his gait, but there was something in his eyes. Something different. She couldn't put her finger on it.

"Sorry," was the first thing he said. "I've been with the police all day."

"I know," she said. "I'm more with it today than I was last night."

He took her hand from the bed. A sting of energy zipped through her, and him too, because he dropped her hand in that instant of electricity.

She smiled at his shock. "I figured that would've gone away by now."

"Never." Hooking a chair with his ankle, he pulled it under himself at her bedside and took her hand again. Guiding it to his mouth, he kissed the back of her fingers. "If you need space..." he said, his eyes trained to hers.

"Thank you," she said.

"I know that—"

"For yesterday I mean," she said. "You found me. You came through. Really, I'm—"

"You wouldn't have been there if it wasn't for me."

"You can't blame yourself," Lacie said. "I spent a lot of time talking to Jamie. I know whose fault it was."

"You talked to him?"

"He would come down and talk to me," she said.

"Why?"

"I don't know," she said. "Sometimes he would ask questions, other times he would just talk."

"What kind of questions?" Ryder asked.

Wriggling deeper into the bed, she loosened her

fingers from his. "I don't want to talk about this. I just went through it all with the police again."

"Sure," Ryder said. "I'm sorry."

"How's Sorcha?"

"Didn't you see her today?"

"I did but with people around. I don't know who knows about the baby."

"You didn't say anything?" he asked. "Jamie knew."

"Bruce told him," Lacie said. "Sorcha told Bruce on the street that day."

"We haven't found him yet, Bruce Booth."

"He's dead," she said. "It happened…"

The memory of that night blasted in front of her eyes. A desperate gasp vaulted from her throat in sync with the tears that flooded her. The clatter of Ryder's chair hitting the deck snapped her back to the present, but it took time for the fog to clear. She shook her head.

"I'm sorry, I didn't mean to take you back to—"

"No," she said, "it's not your fault."

"You didn't deserve any of it and I know it will take you time to work through it. I want to help you, baby. If you can forgive me—"

"It's not your fault. None of it is your fault. I don't want you to carry that guilt around with you."

"I'm sensing a but…" he said with a visible shudder.

"I'm going home, Ryder."

"Home to where?"

"I'm going back with my parents' tomorrow."

"Tomorrow? Isn't that too soon? What about your medical care?"

"It's free where I come from," she said.

He picked up his chair to sit again, without letting go of her hand. "If it's money you're worried about—"

"It's not money," she said. "Sorcha is coming

with us. She'll stay for a few weeks. The doctors say I'll be fine. If I need help, we have hospitals in the UK."

"How long are you staying?"

"Indefinitely," she said. His professional training kicked in; the openness of his expression hardened without a single muscle moving. "I'm not coming back, Ryder. There's nothing for me here."

"You've stayed here since college. Your life is here, it has been for a long time."

"It's a change of pace," she said. "It's what I need. I don't have a home here. I'm not working, but I can work from anywhere."

"So that's it? You're running away?"

"The psychologist thought it was a good idea." Having him angry or annoyed was better than the silence that followed. "I'll send Sorcha back," she said into the quiet. "I'll be okay at home. This will pass, for all of us. I'll keep in touch with the police, and I'll testify when the time comes. But it's time for me to go home. I don't belong here."

"You belong here," he said with complete conviction. "But I want you to do what you need to. I want you to feel safe. I want you to be happy. If going home is what you need to do, then do it."

"Thank you. You've been wonderful through all of this."

"We still have your things in storage, if you want anything sent over—"

"Thank you," she said. "Sorcha's arranging me some clothes and my parents are taking care of the plane tickets. Elise will be over to visit in a month or so."

"I could visit," he said. "If you want me to visit?"

Slipping her hand from his, she lifted it to his cheek. "You really are very sweet, Ryder. You've been so good through all this. I wouldn't have made it without you."

"You were in no imminent danger when I came in last night."

"He told me," she said. "After the first night, he told me who he was and why I was there. I knew you would figure it out because I knew you would come. All I had to do was stay alive long enough for you to find me and you did."

She caressed his face, his hand slid over her forearm. "I'm thinking about your mouth," he said, watching her lips.

The memory of their previous flirtations made her smile. The breadth of it was foreign to her face, she hadn't used those muscles in a while. "Are you now?"

Pushing up from his chair, he glided onto the bed at her side. "Yeah."

Despite knowing it was wrong, her heartbeat kicked up. During her low moments in captivity, she believed she'd never be close to a person again. Yet there she was.

"I missed you, baby," he said. "I missed you so damn much."

"I missed you too."

She knew when he leaned close what his intention was, but she didn't move away. He got so close that she could taste his breath. When the door opened, he backed off immediately. Lacie wanted to curse her own weakness.

"Am I interrupting?" Sorcha asked.

"No," Lacie said.

"Did you tell him?" Sorcha asked.

"I did," Lacie said. "I told him that you were coming to visit for a while, I hope that's okay?"

"Yeah, whatever," Sorcha said, dumping the bags she'd been carrying onto the end of Lacie's bed. "I got lots."

"So I see," Lacie said, reaching for the bags.

"I've still got that stuff Sonny bought for you at mine if you want it?" Ryder asked.

"At yours," Sorcha said. "If you won't go back there, why should she?"

"I can have it brought over," Ryder said. "No one has to go there."

"Why have you not been home?" Lacie asked him.

"Because we don't know who over there we can trust," Sorcha said. "Apparently he hires sociopaths."

"No one else was involved," Lacie said. "It was Eric, and it was Jamie. None of your other men were involved."

"You can't know that," Sorcha said. "None of us can."

"It doesn't matter now."

"Why not?" Lacie asked.

"I'm in the process of having the compound dismantled," he said.

"What?" Lacie and Sorcha said at the same time.

"They're taking it apart."

"Why? That's your home," Sorcha said.

"Not anymore," Ryder said. "Time for a change; keeps things simple."

"You don't trust them," Lacie said then took his hand again. "You don't trust me."

"You?" he asked, startled. "Yes, I trust you."

"None of them were involved," she said.

"Baby, you can't be sure about what went on behind the scenes."

"Ryder—"

"We got a flight at noon," Ann Hart said, entering. "Is that okay Sorcha, dear?"

"Yes," Sorcha said, embracing Ann. "We'll have to check in at ten. Will you be discharged before then?"

"It'll take about an hour to get to the airport,"

Martin Hart said.

"I'll talk to the doctor and make sure I'm discharged in time," Lacie said.

"Make sure you eat something," Ryder said, leaving her bed.

"We'll get breakfast on the plane," Sorcha said.

"Not pancakes," Ryder said. "She likes American pancakes."

"I do," Lacie smiled. "And American bacon…"

"Oh," Sorcha said, sweeping across the room to swing Lacie into her arms. "Nothing will be the same without you! What will I ever do without you?"

"You won't have time to miss me. You have your man to keep you entertained now," Lacie said.

Sorcha pulled back to show a frown. "You know about that?"

"Yes," Lacie said. "I think it's wonderful. You deserve to be very happy."

"Oh, Lace," Sorcha wailed again, pulling her back into a hug.

Lacie smiled at Ryder over Sorcha's shoulder and watched her parents smile at her. Everyone was happy to have her back. She liked seeing their faces, but something was missing. When she glanced at Ryder, she worried that she knew what it was.

FORTY-SEVEN

Lacie

LACIE HAD VISITED home for a couple of months at the start of the year. She visited every year. Sometimes for one week, sometimes for eight. Being home was nice. The place was modest but familiar, she'd grown up there, gone to school in the area. It was supposed to be home.

Sorcha had launched herself into local life and had embraced the "quaintness." Nothing could have prepared her friend for, as she referred to it, "the perpetual cold." Lacie got over her dehydration and was eating again, only what her mother put in front of her, and she struggled to eat more than a few bites, but it was something.

As and when she needed to, she'd visited doctors and kept in touch with the US police. Things were getting better. Except at night. She didn't sleep. The dark took her back to the basement. The black was the blindfold. Her life had been lived in unending darkness. The cocoon was a shroud, the sarcophagus she'd been tethered within. Her life at the mercy of another.

But there she was liberated and lost.

Her home country was foreign. Re-learning the customs of the place she'd grown up in seemed impossible.

"Hello!" Sorcha sang coming into Lacie's childhood bedroom. It looked the same and hadn't been decorated since she was a teenager.

"You're happy this morning," Lacie said, putting away the last of the clothes she and Sorcha had bought yesterday.

They'd been shopping every day in the week she'd been home. Her wardrobe was larger than it had been before the break-in.

"I just got off the phone," Sorcha said.

"Looks like love," Lacie said, sitting on the bed at the same time as Sorcha.

"I wouldn't go that far," Sorcha said. "Extremely intense circumstances, you know. I wouldn't trust him as far as I could throw him. He's screwing his brains out over there as we speak."

"You just got off the phone."

"Well, not right this second, you know what I meant."

"I think you're wrong," Lacie said. "He's not the type."

"He's exactly the type. He got me in a vulnerable moment."

"A vulnerable moment?" Lacie asked. "It's five a.m. on the east coast, if a man can make time for you at that hour…"

"He was just back from a drunken night out."

"And he called you?" Lacie said.

"I think he forgot I was out of the country, it was a booty call."

"Really?" Lacie asked, leaning back against the headboard. Sorcha did the same at the end of the bed.

"He didn't seem to be the type."

"Are you crazy? He's sex mad."

Lacie blushed and picked at a frayed edge of her crocheted bedspread. "You're a lucky woman."

"Not really. He hasn't got any better at it, despite my tuition."

Lacie considered that for a moment, then frowned at her friend. "You must be a difficult woman to satisfy."

"I'm not that high maintenance," Sorcha laughed.

"If he's calling you now, a whole week after you left town, he's still interested. You've been on the phone all week."

"I stayed with him when you were… I didn't want to face my parents."

"You still haven't told them, but you're going to start showing soon," Lacie said. "You're five months gone."

"I know but what do I do, Lace? He's… the father is…"

Lacie shifted down the bed and took Sorcha's hands. They'd already discussed Bruce. While Lacie knew that Sorcha hadn't been particularly in love with him, the knowledge that the father of her child would never meet their offspring was sobering.

"It will be okay," Lacie said.

"How can it be okay?" Sorcha asked. "I have no father for my child and my best friend is moving to the other side of the planet."

"I'll be on the end of the phone. Your parents will support you and you have a million friends over there as well as your man."

"He's not my man," Sorcha said. "He's messing around over there. I wouldn't ask much of a partner, but fidelity would be on the list."

"You have to tell your parents. Ryder will stand beside you. I know he will. He wouldn't keep in touch with you if he had no intention of being around."

"With everything so absolutely up in the air… Ryder?" Sorcha said, apparently just having processed Lacie's words. "I speak to Ryder every day and all he's interested in is you. Why won't you talk to him?"

"I don't want to get in the way of anything you two have going on. It's just not… right. I do appreciate all that he did for me."

"In the way… what are you talking about?"

"Ryder," Lacie said. "Your man."

"You think Ryder is *my* man?" she screeched, bolting upright. "My god! The man is insanely in love with you!"

"What? You were talking about sex with him, staying with him!"

"Shep!" Sorcha said, leaping up from the bed. "I was staying with Shep! He's the dog who's been screwing around! My god, that isn't…? Is that why you're here? Why you left the country?"

"No!" Lacie said. "He didn't want me after… I don't blame him for… It's difficult to go through something like that and the aftermath is no better. He didn't deserve to be pulled down by all my… It doesn't matter anyway I wouldn't be comfortable with a man who had been with my best friend."

"I've never been with Ryder. He's your man. He loves you. He was a shadow of himself without you. You are his world, even now when you're not in the country. He loves you. What would possess you to think he and I had been intimate?"

"Jamie said… it was Jamie Wallace, he…"

Sorcha came to her side. "Consider anything he told you to be false."

"He told me you were close and that you… that

you and he were…"

"Jamie wanted to hurt you, to hurt Ryder… he's doing it even after… They got him, he's locked up, they refused him bail. You have to put it behind you."

"Just like that?"

"Yeah," Sorcha said. "Is there any other way?"

A shout from downstairs had the women leaping from the bed to race down the stairs to find her mother on the couch. Martin frowned, arguing into the phone.

"What happened?" Sorcha asked.

Martin left the room, still talking on the phone. Lacie and Sorcha joined Ann on the floral pattern couch.

"Elise phoned," Ann said.

"What happened?" Lacie asked, gripped with the fear of possibilities.

"Ryder," Ann said.

"What about him?" Lacie demanded.

"They… they've arrested him."

"For what?" Sorcha asked.

"He was involved. They're saying he was involved."

"In what?" Sorcha asked.

"Lacie," Ann said, clutching at her child. "They say he knew about you, about the money, the fraud, the drugs."

"How could they think that? And why now?" Sorcha asked.

"They had a warrant; they searched his home. This happened yesterday. He was arrested last night. Gosh, what do we do? I don't know what to think, your father is on the phone trying to find out what has happened. Oh my—is it possible we were hoodwinked?"

Lacie heard the words but the blood rushing through her ears distorted their meaning. Pushing away from the couch, she strode to the window to process the new information.

"I can't believe this. I thought he was good," Ann cried. "I thought he was on our side."

Lacie left the window and went to the stairs.

"Lacie!" Sorcha stopped her in her tracks. "Where are you going?"

"To do what's right," she said. With her foot on the bottom stair, she took her attention to her mother. "Don't ever doubt him again, at least, don't do it in front of me. I owe him my life."

"How can you be sure he wasn't involved?" Ann asked.

"Because we promised no more secrets or lies," Lacie said.

Lacie left it that way and ran up the stairs to pack her new clothes into an old suitcase. She fired up the computer and booked the next flight, which gave her little more than an hour to get to the airport. Throwing her things together, she got back downstairs at the same time her cab showed up.

"You're going back?" Sorcha asked. "Back to the States?"

"Yes," Lacie said, putting on her shoes and jacket.

"You said you were home," Ann said. "That you were staying here."

"I have unfinished business," Lacie said. "He didn't abandon me when I needed him. I can't abandon him now. Maybe there's nothing I can do, but maybe there is. This is about me. He's in this because of me. I have to stand with him. I have to."

"Wait for me and I'll come with you," Sorcha said.

"No time, I have a flight booked," Lacie said, giving her mother and friend a kiss.

"I'm not sure I agree with this," Ann said. "You could be putting yourself in danger again."

"I can't think of a better reason to take that risk. Wallace was refused bail and he was the mastermind."

"And Ryder?" Ann asked.

"Privacy and loyalty," Lacie said. "His ideals are mine."

"Be careful," Ann beseeched as the cab honked again.

"I won't have to be," Lacie said. "He won't lose me again."

Departing her childhood home was liberating. Now she had a mission to get to his side. The cab driver put her suitcase in the back and then they were on the road to the airport. Why was this so important? Lacie didn't know. She didn't have a plan or know what she was going to do when she got there… or even where she was going to stay.

He was in trouble. Her soul compelled her body to follow her spirit to his side. Ryder had lost his best friend and carried guilt about her predicament. Now he found himself in need and alone… he wouldn't be for long.

FORTY-EIGHT

Lacie

LACIE CHECKED INTO a hotel. Every minute before and after her flight had been spent on the phone, trying to find out what was going on. Foremost was discovering where Ryder was and how she could get to see him.

After quickly unpacking and taking a short shower, Lacie was changed and in a different taxi, this one in another country. The journey took less than twenty minutes. After tipping the driver, she looked up at the cloud shrouded jail.

Not wanting to think too much about what lay ahead, she charged on. Security was thorough and took longer than she'd have imagined. Eventually, she was ushered into a bland, gray-floored room with a row of seats facing a Perspex screen. Each divide between the sections was created by gray privacy screens with an old-style black phone hanging on one side. She took a seat in the middle and waited.

The bland off-white walls left the place feeling stark and cold. As she sat there alone, she squirmed at the odd feeling of being watched despite being totally alone, in body at least. Noises from behind a partition told her that she wasn't going to be by herself for long.

After some clangs and bangs and a couple of shouts, she saw the flash of orange and leaped to her feet. A guard came in with him and stayed against the back wall. Ryder came over, displaying concern and surprise. He stopped on the other side of the scratched plastic.

Lacie lifted her hand in a static wave. He cleared a fraction of his shock to gesture at the unmovable stool on her side. He sat after she did and neither said a word as they examined each other. He gestured to the phone.

Lacie picked up at the same time as him. "Hi."

"I thought you were in the UK. What's wrong?"

"What's wrong?" she repeated. "I would've thought that was obvious given our location."

"Have you had trouble? Are you well?"

"Stop it," she said. "Would you stop looking after me?"

"You're still not eating or sleeping properly. You look terrified. If you—"

"You've been asking Sorcha about me?"

"I have, but she didn't tell me any of that," he said. "I can tell by looking at you. No one's looking after you."

"It's been difficult," she said. "I'm trying my best, but… it's been difficult."

"You're not telling anyone that you're struggling. Sorcha hadn't noticed."

"You noticed."

"I noticed that no one's looking after you," he said. "You should have support."

"No one has been looking after me," she said.

"I can see that."

"Because I ran away from you," she said. "Then you got yourself locked up. Who is going to look after me with you in here?"

His eyes narrowed. "I thought that was the point of going back to your parents. I thought they were supposed to look after you."

"It's not me we should be worried about right now. Look at you."

"There's nothing wrong with me," he said.

"Only you could say that at a time like this. Have you spoken to your lawyer? What is Gabe saying? How on earth could you get yourself into this mess?" she asked. "Surely as soon as they told you they had a warrant for SW you realized Wallace would've left something there for authorities to find. If he's going down, he'll take you with him.

"I spoke to Deacon, and he knows this stinks. The only thing connecting you to this is the drugs at the house. The detectives in charge say they're still collecting evidence. Nevertheless, the DA thinks there is a case. Wallace was refused bail because they said he was a flight risk. You're not a flight risk. I've been trying to get in touch with Gabe and I'm going to meet Shep this afternoon. I have a meeting with the DA tomorrow. There isn't a chance in hell that I'll testify if they're going to try to use my evidence against you. I won't do it—"

"Whoa," Ryder said, cutting her off. "Firstly, you're not going anywhere near Gabe or Shep. Secondly, you will testify against Wallace because he deserves to rot in hell for what he put you through. If all they can stick me with is a drugs charge, I'll take it as punishment for what I did to you. It's a small price to pay for your safety."

"I'll talk to whoever I want to, and you're not staying here, it's awful."

"Yeah," he agreed. "It is awful. But you're safe." He smiled. "After what I lived through when you were missing, the not knowing, the terror every minute of the day imagining what you were being subjected to… Yes, this stinks, but it's a walk in the park compared to what you went through, or what I went through missing you."

"You've given up?" she asked. "You're just going to take it?"

"I've spoken to a lawyer," he said. "I know I didn't do what they're accusing me of."

"You trust the system?"

"Not entirely," Ryder said. "But what's the alternative?"

"To fight," she said. "Give them hell, like I plan to."

"When did you get back into the country?"

"A couple of hours ago. I had to beg them to let me see you today. I've got a few ideas and I'll let you know how they pan out, but… I didn't want you to think you were alone in here. You should know there are people on the case to help you."

"I'm not comfortable with you going near the guys. We still don't know who was involved."

"I know who was involved," Lacie said. "And I know who wasn't. You can't let Wallace win. You can't let him take the people you care about from your life."

"He took the most important person," Ryder said. "You."

"I'm here," she murmured, sliding her hand toward the window. "I'm right here."

"You didn't ask me if I was involved."

"I don't need to ask you," Lacie said.

"When did you decide to come back to the US?"

"The moment I heard what happened to you."

His brows drew together. "You came back because of me? You could be at risk here."

"I missed you," she said. "You got me through my captivity. I want to try to help you, as much as I can, through yours… You're frowning."

"You didn't… when you were in the hospital after you were found… You didn't talk to me. You… I thought you wanted rid of me. I understood exactly why, and no one could blame you for it."

"I have a lot to work through, I'm not…" Thinking the words and saying them aloud were different things. No matter how deep she tried to wriggle into her stool, it didn't make it any easier. "I let you down."

"What?"

"We left Shep's office. When Sorcha got that call… we were out of there so quickly and… I didn't want to leave you."

"Don't blame yourself for what happened," he said. "It wasn't your fault."

"It wasn't yours either and yet here you are," she responded.

"I will get out eventually."

"That's not good enough. I want you out now."

"What difference does when make?" he said not expecting an answer.

"I'm thinking about your cock."

He choked on his own tongue. Even the guard jerked with astonishment.

"I love your mind," Ryder muttered when he'd recovered.

"And the way I speak it," she said. "I spent six weeks thinking about our night, about kissing you, about all the things we didn't get to do together. You told me you had time to have sex with me then left me hanging. Is that it for you? Are we over?"

"Over?" he asked. "I was giving you space. I thought you needed time to work through what happened. You left the country."

"You let me."

"If I'd known you wanted the big heroic gesture—"

"That's not what I'm saying," she said on a laugh. "I didn't expect you to stop me. I knew you'd respect my boundaries."

"Why did you leave?" he asked.

"Because I was scared and unsure. I suppose I wanted normality. I thought if I was over there, I could forget any of this had ever happened."

"You could forget me."

"That's not what I said. You weren't an option for me."

"Why not?" he asked. "You had to know I was crazy for you."

"I have things to work through, I didn't want to burden you, and…"

"And?"

"Wallace told me that you and Sorcha were having sex. I didn't want to make things awkward."

"And you believed him?"

"I had no reason not to," she said.

"How about us? Didn't you think I'd wait? Sorcha's not my type, you know that. We both care about you, why would you—sorry, it's not your fault. Every time I hear what he did, or said I—"

"You be careful about what you say in present company," Lacie said, eyeing the guard loitering behind him. "Do you know I've said more to you about my experience than I have to all my doctors and therapists?"

"Good," he said. "I want to help you through it. I want to be here for anything you need."

Lacie slid to the edge of her stool and leaned as close as she could while holding the mouthpiece near her lips. "I want you to hold me. I want to curl up in your arms and forget every second we spent apart."

Very slowly the corner of his mouth turned upward. "I've got my girl back."

"You're on that side of the screen and I'm on this

one."

"Are you staying at Sorcha's?" he asked.

"I'm staying in a hotel. Sorcha is still at my parents; she took too long getting ready."

"Phone Deacon. He owes me a couple of favors, he'll look after you. He's been a friend over the years and—"

"Your friend? I couldn't impose on him."

"It's not imposing," Ryder said. "I'd feel better if someone was watching your back."

"And I'm not welcome at your place?"

"I'm selling my place," he said. "The boys are still clearing it out. I'm not sure what happens now with all of this."

"I'm not staying with your friend," she said and carried on before he could object. "We have a lot of catching up to do… It's been so intense."

"Does that change things?" Ryder said.

"Right, folks, time," the guard bellowed and approached Ryder who stood.

Lacie scrambled to her feet. "We'll get you out," she said. "We'll fix this."

His lopsided smile slid up again. "Got my girl, there's nothing they can do to me now."

She kissed her fingertips and touched the plastic. "I'm here."

"Now I've got something to fight for."

After he hung up, he touched the screen at her fingertips before he was led away by the guard. With a last look over his shoulder, he was taken out. Once again, she was alone in the sad room.

The boost she'd had sitting with Ryder faded at the knowledge of what he was going back to. Having never spent time in jail, she couldn't identify with him exactly, but she could imagine.

Ryder shouldn't be caged; he was good and

deserved to be free. She resolved to do whatever it took to make that happen. He'd fought for her, and she planned to do the same right back.

FORTY-NINE

Lacie

LACIE SAW SHEP at his office. The whole experience was surreal, she actually looked forward to seeing his friendly face. The case had strapped them into a rollercoaster together and they weren't free of it yet.

Something as simple as locating a person had thrown all their lives into the dryer and turned it up to full. Booth was dead, Sorcha was still pregnant, and Lacie hadn't helped anything. All she had accomplished was to cause trouble and burden. She and Shep had been talking for almost an hour when he asked her to lunch, so they carried on their conversation on the walk to the mall.

While they walked, Sorcha called to say she was back in the country, in a cab driving away from the airport. Shep told her where they were headed, and Sorcha redirected her taxi for the mall.

Lacie was discussing Ryder's plan to liquidate SW, and his home, when Shep's phone rang again. After answering it, he held the phone toward her.

"It's for you," Shep said, handing over the

device.

Shep had spoken to Sorcha without passing the phone. Whoever was on the line now wanted only her.

"Hello?" Lacie asked.

"I heard you were back in the country," Gabe said.

"I don't have a phone yet."

"You've been looking for me? Have you heard about Ryder?"

"Yes. It's why I'm back," Lacie said. "I want him out."

"We all do. It's bullshit."

"I know that," Lacie said. "I'm with Shep and we're meeting Sorcha. Can you meet me tonight?" He didn't respond. "Gabe?"

"Are you sure?" he asked. "Ryder's not going to be hot on the idea of you with us right now."

"He doesn't mean to be hostile. Wallace burned him, he's being careful that's all. He's trying to look out for me even from behind bars."

"You've seen him?" Gabe asked with incredulity. "We heard you just got back."

"Of course I've seen him. I'll visit every minute that they let me. We have to get him out, Gabe. We have to."

"You trust us?" Gabe asked.

"Yes."

"Ryder doesn't."

"I know," she said. "I'm sorry about that. He doesn't trust himself after Wallace. We'll bring him around."

"Will we?" Gabe asked. "You left him. You left the country."

"Why are you pissed at me?"

"He's in love with you, Lacie. He was a mess every minute he spent without you."

"Everyone keeps telling me that."

"That he was a mess?"

"No, the other thing," she said. "I've seen him. We've talked. What goes on between Ryder and I is our business. If you don't want to help me—"

"I want Ryder out; we've been working on it. What I don't want is you pissing in his face when this is over."

"Before Wallace, Ryder told me I was part of the team."

"He did?"

"Yes, he said I had skin in the game… I suppose I have more now. I've told you that I trust you, but this will never work if you don't trust me."

"You're the key to this," Gabe said. "Ryder trusts you, and he doesn't trust us. As his girlfriend, you'll have more access than we will… I'll come and pick you up."

"Give me an hour," Lacie said then gave the address. "Sorcha will be joining us, and I want to fill her in."

"Ryder won't be wild about the idea, but if you want, I can have your things picked up from the hotel and brought to Ryder's bedroom."

"He said you were taking the place apart."

"We are," Gabe said. "But it's still more secure than being at a hotel alone."

"Okay. If you could do that, I'd appreciate it. I'll see you in an hour."

By the time Lacie hung up, she and Shep were arriving in the mall restaurant. Shep took his phone from her and sat to peruse the menu the waitress handed over.

"That was Gabe?" Shep asked.

"Yes," she said, reading her own menu.

"Ryder came to me because he didn't trust them."

"He doesn't trust you either," Lacie said.

"He trusts me more than he trusts his men," Shep said. "I was the one watching his back the night he came into that house. He wasn't coming in for you, at least that's what he said. But I knew if he laid eyes on you that he wouldn't come out emptyhanded."

"I'm talking to you too, doesn't that prove that I trust you?" Lacie said. "But I think we need as many hands to help as we can get. I'm going to stay at Ryder's. I'm sure you and Sorcha could stay too. There's strength in numbers."

"She hasn't told her parents," Shep said. "She's still avoiding them."

"She told you?"

"About the baby," Shep said. "Yes, she did."

"And you're still interested?"

"I don't know what I am. Your friend can be a complete bitch but… I keep going back for more."

"You can't mess around on her," Lacie said.

"Haven't you just got off the phone with Ryder's buddy who was warning you off?"

"The difference is I know how I feel about Ryder. I'm not about to become a single catholic mother with judgmental parents. If you're with her, then you're with her. If not, leave her alone." He didn't say anything, but a smile crossed his face. "What?"

"You two are unbelievable, do you know that? She's pregnant and terrified then she finds out the kid's father is dead. But her concern is you, so she jets to the other side of the world to make sure you're okay. But you, you do her a favor and find yourself taken prisoner and put through God knows what. You try to get yourself better, then you find out your boyfriend has been locked up for drug crimes, but here you are telling me not to mess with your friend."

"What's your point?"

"Even when your own lives are falling down

around your ears, you still pay attention and take time out of your lives to look out for each other. It's incredible."

"It's called friendship, are you going to listen to me? Decide, put it to her, work it out or walk away."

Their conversation had conjured her. As soon as the words were out of Lacie's mouth, Sorcha entered and was directed to the table. Time was short. Lacie wanted to call the police and the jail before Gabe picked her up. They had to fill Sorcha in and make some decisions. They needed a plan.

FIFTY

Lacie

BY THE TIME Gabe picked her up from the restaurant, Lacie had completed most of her tasks. The car journey was silent. That silence continued even after they pulled into the SW garage. Maybe it was because of trust issues, or maybe just shock at what they were facing, Lacie didn't know. Words were as scarce as movement when he parked.

"The last time I was in here…" she said, exhaling something of a laugh. "It's odd, isn't it? The turns in life that we don't expect."

"I usually find that they are the best ones," Gabe said. "Though I guess that hasn't been your experience."

"Being in that place… I wouldn't want to go back. It's changed me though I still haven't figured out how exactly. This situation started so innocently, I… Sorcha told me I wouldn't have to talk to Bruce but… I ended up watching his demise."

"Are you sure he's dead? Can you tell me what happened?"

As before, the memory made her shiver. No matter how tightly she squeezed her eyes closed, she couldn't erase the pictures.

"I've never seen… it was barbaric, and it wasn't—Wallace just snapped, I suppose."

"Wallace did it himself?"

"Why do you sound surprised by that?" she asked.

"He wasn't one to get his hands dirty. He'd delight in others torture but always stopped short of pulling the trigger if he could. I suspect it was more a case of deniability than sensitivity."

"He didn't do it himself," Lacie said. "He got the men into such a lather they were… It was like watching dogs pick off the weakest member of the pack."

"They turned on him? They beat him?"

"Yes," she said. "Wallace was taunting him and the men, telling them about how Bruce was the only one they couldn't trust. The only one who could snitch. Even when they started hitting him, Wallace carried on deriding him."

"Where was Eric for all this?"

"He was there," she said. "He was always there. He didn't say much. The only time I know he opened his mouth to say more than one word was… the first night."

"What did he say?"

"Wallace wasn't there… he told the men to…"

"To?" Gabe asked.

"He told them not to touch me," Lacie said.

"They were touching you?"

"Look, Gabe, I want to help Ryder. He doesn't deserve to be where he is, and I think if we all work together then we can exert enough pressure on enough weak spots to get him out of there for good. But I'm not there yet. I'm not able to get into all the nitty gritty of what did and didn't, happen.

"There were a dozen men working for Wallace. Booth was beaten to death at Wallace's urging. He sent Eric away to get rid of the body. I don't know where he is. I can't tell you where he's buried or even if he was buried at all. I've spoken to the police. I've been as helpful as I can. But I'm not going to tell you about what I went through. It's irrelevant."

"Stone won't see it that way when he gets out," Gabe said. "He'll want to know everything."

"He won't push me," she said. "I'll want to talk about it eventually, but not yet, not here, not with you."

"Understood," Gabe said with a nod. "Your things will be up in the house. I'll take you up and let you get settled in. There will be something on the go in the kitchen, come down to eat whenever you want."

"Thank you," she said. "I appreciate everything you've done."

"Just be ready for Stone to hit the roof when he hears you're here."

"I'm here of my own freewill, and Ryder has the most amazing Jacuzzi tub. If you guys decide to hold me captive, make sure it's up there."

Her joke had him smiling. "Understood."

When he got out of the vehicle, he came around to open her door. Just as he'd said, Gabe took her up to Ryder's room, turning on all the lights and checking all the corners and closets without her behest. She appreciated him being thorough.

When he left her alone, she focused on Ryder's bed, dominating the middle of the room. He'd kissed her on that bed. She'd felt the promise of him digging into her as he devoured her mouth. Only they hadn't got there; she hadn't enjoyed him in this room.

Looking out at the view of the city laid beneath the ledge that the house was situated on, she was hypnotized by the twinkling lights. She hadn't realized the late hour. It had been a long day. Stripping out of her clothes, she lay on the bed promising herself that she would just close her eyes for a moment.

One of those twinkling lights was on the building that he was currently in, on a hard single bed, probably staring at the ceiling without thought for sleep. She had come to be close to him. For now, this was as close as she would get. Tomorrow things would be different. She had to believe they would, she just had to.

FIFTY-ONE

Lacie

SOME SORT OF squawking bird jolted her awake the next morning. As Lacie tried to clear her vision, she sat bolt upright, completely at sea as to her location. His watch was on the nightstand, his boots in front of the closet, and she remembered. The smile that formed when she realized she was in his bed quickly cleared when she recalled why he wasn't there.

In an instant, she was up. Bypassing the bathtub, she went for the quickest shower of her life, changed clothes, and ran down the stairs looking for someone, anyone.

Gabe was in the kitchen laughing with most of the boys at a joke she hadn't heard. When they caught sight of her, the joke ceased to be funny. Each of the men examined her in turn.

"I fell asleep," she said to Gabe.

"Twelve hours ago," Gabe said. "You must have needed the rest."

"It's something about that bed," she said, making

her way to the center island.

The kitchen was huge, shiny, clean, and modern. A glass-walled corner was the location of the huge round table that had capacity for at least twenty.

"Doesn't say much for the boss man," Rocco said, nudging the man at his side. Sonny, at his other flank, turned beetroot red.

"I don't know you," Lacie said to the man who nudged Rocco back.

"That's Will," Gabe said. "Ty's on his other side, and you remember Toby and Rocco?"

"Sure," she said, vaguely remembering the men Ryder had introduced her to before they left for the meeting with Shep that fateful day.

"Guys this is Lacie Hart, who all the trouble's been about."

Lacie lifted her hand in a lame wave while they scrutinized her.

Rocco grinned and slung an arm around Sonny. "You remember our slave?" he asked, patting Sonny's chest.

"Yes," she said. "They're all so mean to you. I don't know why you put up with them."

"Not going to be a worry much longer," Will said. "What with the company folding."

"Don't look at her like that," Gabe said. "None of this is her fault."

"I don't think I said it was," Will grumbled. "But we're not thrilled by this state of affairs."

"You want to argue about this again?" Gabe asked. "Stone says it's done, then it's done."

"Yeah, 'cause we're all a bunch of criminals," Will said.

"He doesn't think you're criminals," Lacie said.

"Oh yeah?" Will snapped. "How else do you explain him firing us and selling the place from under us?"

"His best friend deceived him. He doesn't trust his own judgment at the moment," Lacie said, holding her ground.

"Yet his little woman is here," Will said. "Does he know you're here?"

"The way I see it you have two options," she said. "You suck it up, quit the moaning, and get on board to fix this situation."

"Or?" he prompted.

"You know where the door is," she said.

"You're throwing me out?" he asked.

"No," she said. "I'm telling you to get with us. If we can get Ryder out of jail and make sure Wallace stays there, something will come after this. StoneWall is done, but that doesn't mean Ryder will be going into retirement. You guys are a team, Ryder needs help. Is it your policy to leave a man behind?"

All exchanged looks. The tentative and uncertain became fierce and resolved.

"Do you have a plan?" Will asked her.

"We're not going to break him out in a hail of bullets if that's what you're suggesting."

"What are you suggesting?"

"I'm talking to the DA," she said, looking at Ryder's watch.

Lacie had put it on in the hope that having something of his against her skin would be comforting. It was way too big; she'd taken it all the way up to her inner elbow to fasten it. Still, it kept sliding down into view from under her three-quarter length sleeve.

"In an hour," Lacie carried on. "Then Shep and Sorcha are coming over and we'll regroup. Then I'm going to see Ryder. After that, I have a meeting with his lawyer."

"And two weeks ago, she was living in a squalid

basement without food," Ty said. "You know how to get things done."

"I've cleared up a few messes," Lacie said, thinking of Sorcha. "But this is important."

"You do know that you're the victim," Rocco said. "Are you happy running around like this?"

"A lot of people will think it's strange that you're fighting for the people who kidnapped you," Will said.

"Ryder had nothing to do with it. Wallace will go down for this, of that I have no doubt," Lacie said. "This won't be a walk in the park. But when I think of Ryder caged in a dark, depressing place, kept against his will… I have the inside on what that's like. I want him out."

Will smiled at the same time Ty did. She had a feeling like she'd just passed an undeclared initiation.

"Let's get to HQ," Gabe declared. "We'll get the war room operational."

The men got moving. She let herself be carried with them toward their shared objective. The group did this for a living. That was brought into stark focus when she entered their buzzing war room.

Toby stood near a bank of computers pulling something out of a printer and distributing it to each of the others that approached him. Sonny brought her a stack of sheets. As she flipped through them, she read biographical information on each of the men who'd held her captive.

Sections were added and some were highlighted. Their previous convictions, credit reports, known associates and aliases, everything was there. The SW men weren't only interested in getting Ryder out, they wanted to get the men who had wronged them. Lacie had little chance to sift through the histories and connections because Gabe and Rocco took her aside.

"We're going to work on the paper trail, the money," Gabe explained. "We know most of the men were grunts that Wallace hired for the dirty work, but there was a chain of command, a hierarchy. If Wallace is singing about Stone in there, we're almost sure that he'll have covered his bases and somehow linked Stone in."

"You think he's used Ryder's name?" Lacie asked.

"Maybe, but that would be heavy-handed," Rocco said. "The money will link back to Stone or SW somehow."

"And you're going to look for the connection?" Lacie asked.

"Yes," Gabe said. "So we can prove how bogus it is."

"Wallace was at the top," Rocco said. "We want to understand Eric's position in the chain of command. He got out of talking to the police because he's been in the hospital."

"He was one of the ones shot?" Lacie asked.

"Yes," Rocco said. "Now he's not saying anything because he wants to cut a deal."

"What kind of deal?" Lacie asked. "What does he know? Has he implicated Ryder too?"

"We don't know," Gabe said. "We're trying to find out, but he's been in hospital under guard."

"But if he's in jail now… can't someone go and visit, just ask him outright?"

"The police are still questioning him. I don't think they want anyone talking to him."

"Does he have family, or—"

"We can't influence his testimony," Rocco said.

"I'm not asking you to influence it," Lacie said. "I want to know what it is."

"We're going to work on that," Rocco said. "You're our girl on the inside with this."

"What do you mean?" she asked.

"We have to know what the DA's case is. The

evidence he has is what we have to debunk."

"He's not going to lay it all out for me," Lacie said. "But I'll do what I can."

"We can wire you, if you want," Gabe said.

"No, I'll remember," she said. "He can't have too much evidence against Ryder. He wasn't involved."

"Wallace is talking, and Eric might be too," Rocco said. "If they've got Stone's fingerprints on the money some place, that's the ball game."

"Okay," Lacie said. "Can I have a look at the histories?"

"You're part of the team," Rocco said, linking their arms and taking her to where the others were looking over their paperwork.

"We are going to get this done," she said to the group that appeared far more sinister and threatening in that setting compared to the bright kitchen. "Aren't we?"

None of them said a word, but conviction burned from each of them and scorched the air. It was a hell of a team and now she was one of them.

FIFTY-TWO

Lacie

DESPITE THE SITUATION, this event was the highlight of her day. The room she'd been alone in yesterday was teeming with people today. Seeing partners and children greeting their incarcerated father's and spouses brought tears to her eyes. The men were scary, some were bulky, others were wiry and sly, but few were the type you'd want to meet in a secluded alley on a dark night. Now Ryder had been lumped in with them.

When he came in and sat down, the rest of the room melted away. Her focus was him. She noted how tired he looked. They went for their phones at the same time.

"You look tired," he said.

"Thanks," she said.

"Have you eaten?"

"Have you?"

"Dusty—"

"I saw the DA today," she said. "And I've had lunch with Shep and Sorcha. We're getting forward movement. We're going to get you out of here, Ryder, I promise you."

"I told you to look after yourself."

"I'm here to get you out," she said, looking at the watch on her arm. "I'm meeting your lawyer after this. I'm trying to get time with the detectives on the case but they're—"

"Where did you get that?" he asked.

The flatness of his tone revealed she'd been busted.

"What?" she asked.

"The watch," he growled.

"It was uh… next to the bed I slept in last night."

"Goddamnit," he said, dropping his fist to the counter with enough force to shake it. A guard sidled up behind him. "I told you to stay away from there."

"And I said I'd go where I wanted to."

"I can't keep you safe, Lacie, I'm in here… Not that I did a great job of it when I wasn't."

"If you want to look after me, you had better work on getting yourself out of here. I'm sleeping in your bed. If you want me out of it, you have to throw me out yourself."

"There's a gun in the—"

"I don't need to know that," she said. "Gabe checked everything out last night."

"You were in my bedroom with Gabe?"

"He checked it out for me that's all."

"Why would he have to do that?" Ryder asked.

"You could ask me about what we're doing to get you out. You could ask me about my underwear, or ask to see my breasts, or something. But you choose to chastise me?"

"I want to see your breasts when we're alone," he said. "We're in a room full of people."

"And my underwear?"

"Rent an apartment," he said. "I'll pay for a hotel until—"

"Concentrate on getting out," she said. "I don't have the time to worry about semantics. All I need is a pillow for my head. When you're out, we'll argue about bedrooms. Can we get you on the same side of the glass as me first? Please?"

"I can't protect you from in here."

"You've said that already. But I know what danger is," she said. "I've seen what evil looks like. I'm okay. You concentrate on watching your back in here. Keep your head down, keep yourself safe, and we'll get you out soon. I promise."

The certainty of her words burned her throat, but they didn't seem to move him. Gradually the corner of his mouth slid upwards.

"It's so incredible to see you, Lace," he said. "I never believed that we'd lost you but... God, I could look at you for days."

"Get out of here, Ryder. I promise I'll let you."

During the rest of the conversation, he refused to give her any details about what life was like inside. The duty of talking fell to her, so she went on about Sorcha and Shep, and how nice Gabe and Rocco were being. She avoided telling him about her morning conversation with Will.

All too soon, the men were being filtered out, back to their confinements. Something about not being able to touch him wrenched at her gut. A tear skittered down her face when he stood to leave. His instant frown told her that he'd noticed. The guard was already ushering him away so all she could do was wave.

Ryder didn't deserve to be imprisoned, just as she hadn't. Still, they were kept apart. The injustice seared her with rage. But, for now, she would have to play the game.

FIFTY-THREE

GETTING BACK TO SW, Lacie was ready to carry on the work, to be updated with any developments, then to roll up her sleeves. The air in the war room was different when she arrived back, though the men were still bustling with activity.

"What's wrong?" she asked.

All the men stopped.

Gabe was the one to approach her. "Something's happened."

"What do you mean something's happened?" she asked, deliberately shifting out of Gabe's reach.

"Deacon just called. There's word of a deal."

"What kind of deal?" she asked, glancing from left to right for sign of a phone that could connect her to their allied detective.

"Eric," Will said from the background. "He's talking."

Fixing her attention on Gabe, she waited for an explanation. "What is he saying?"

"We don't know yet," Gabe said. "But…"

"But what?"

"We don't know for sure yet," Gabe said.

"Would you just tell me," she said. "I'm part of the team, remember?"

"It seems Wallace might have… his dirty dealings had been going on for months, maybe longer."

"Yeah, so? We had deduced that much—"

"He's implied that… Booth… he says he knows where he is."

"Yes," she said. "Wallace sent Eric to take care of the body when—"

"No," Gabe said. "He's saying that Booth is… that he's alive."

"Alive?" she murmured, her jaw swung loose. "But that's not… that's not possible."

"Apparently, it might be," Gabe said. "We don't know what's going on exactly yet but… if Booth's alive, with his and with Eric's statements, given that they don't imply Stone at this stage…"

"They can tell police what happened. They can get Ryder out," she said.

Hope bubbled to the surface within her, her smile spread.

"Be cautious," Gabe said. "We don't know yet, we don't know what they're saying. The police are trying to locate Booth. But if Eric's telling the truth, if Booth's alive… Wallace could be in trouble."

"I have to phone Sorcha," Lacie said.

Gabe took hold of her arm when she tried to pass. "Not yet," he said. "We don't know anything for sure. We have to hold position until we know. We keep working on the assumption that we have to get Ryder out ourselves. You can't tell Sorcha now, we're still not sure if it's true."

"Okay," Lacie said. "You're right. I don't want to

get her hopes up."

"Nothing changes," he said. "We keep working."

Lacie understood their sedate optimism and tried to follow suit. If she got her hopes up and Eric or Booth's testimony didn't work in their favor that could make matters worse.

So she'd follow Gabe's advice, his experience was what she relied on in this time of need. If she'd been working alone, progress would have been slow. Lacie would follow their lead and pray that they were going in the right direction.

FIFTY-FOUR

THOUGH SHE HADN'T been part of the team for long, when she looked around at the busy squad, something was very obviously missing. It didn't matter that she'd never seen how this unit ordinarily functioned. An aura hung around them emphasizing the conspicuous absence of a leader, their leader.

Gabe kept hold of the reins. He directed the men and tied the separate strands of their investigating together, weaving their individual findings into an increasingly strengthening rope. These men knew what they were doing. They were swift, efficient, and thorough.

From watching them work, Lacie concluded one major factor, all they needed was time. Once this group had an objective, an idea, a mission to follow through, nothing would get in the way of its completion. Whatever happened between now and then, Ryder would be out. He would be cleared. The sheer determination of these men was overwhelming. Being a part of such a group was humbling.

Her role wasn't defined, but there was plenty to do. Lacie followed the lead given to her by the men and ended up on the phone for most of the day. Being both victim of the crime and a close associate of Ryder's, she had access to areas that wouldn't otherwise be easily accessed.

Her queries were accepted as valid, where others asking the same questions may be seen as suspicious. Repeatedly, she was told to keep herself vague and not to refer to whom she was working with or why she was asking the questions. Her crash course in covert information gathering and espionage left her head spinning. They were all still going at it when Gabe told her to go to bed.

Initially, she objected but his reasoning did make sense. Hers was the face that had to be seen tomorrow. Being that it was after midnight, she couldn't work on the phone any longer. Deferring to Gabe's experience, Lacie left them working, not wanting to make a nuisance of herself.

Only after she'd filled the Jacuzzi bath, stripped naked, and slid into the still, clear liquid did she let herself think about Ryder again. Despite their fervor and devotion, Lacie tried to tell herself that she might never share this tub with the man it belonged to. So much had happened in such a short time. Her life had become unrecognizable, and she'd feared for her very existence, and now she feared for his sanity. Lacie got out of the tub almost as soon as she got into it. The calm silence wasn't an environment conducive to her own sanity.

Right now, she needed to be occupied, busy, thinking. As she crawled into his bed, she wished for normality. Only not normality as it had been. Her future had to include her work that she so desperately missed.

Yet he was the one she ached for and would give

up everything for. If only he could be with her. The sheets might have been cold, but if Ryder had been at her side there would've been zero chance she would have noticed the temperature.

Whatever happened next, all their lives had been affected. Nothing would be as it had been. But, right now, there was a mission to complete. She needed a game face, to be as stoic as the men she'd worked with that day, and she had to do it fast.

FIFTY-FIVE

LACIE AWOKE FEELING groggy and disorientated, so took her time in the shower, blasting herself with the coldest, highest-pressure setting. Plenty would be happening in the day ahead, but still she prickled against the force that pushed right back.

The job was worthy. Was she capable of the task? Wrapping herself in the fluffy white towel, she finger-combed her damp hair. Ryder's towels were clearly only meant to reach around his hips, they were so small that her breasts almost spilled out when she covered her behind, she'd never been so grateful for being small in her life.

Though she'd slept later than she intended to and showered for longer than normal, she knew the time was well spent in setting her up for the day. At least she could honestly tell Ryder that she was taking care of herself… omitting the minor detail that she hadn't eaten anything since yesterday lunchtime.

Her luggage had been brought there as Gabe said

it would be. The things that Sonny had bought her on her first visit here were hanging up in the walk-in closet too. Ryder had welcomed her into his home. Despite being absent, she had a place there, physically at least.

Leaving the bathroom, she was considering her day. The sight of a man sitting on the bed with his arms spread wide startled her backward. She remained frozen until the details sank in.

"Ryder," she exhaled.

Crossing the room without conscious thought, Lacie forged up the bed between his knees, snatched his face, and locked her lips to his.

His knees closed at her sides, his arms came around her, his kiss just as fierce as hers. He hadn't said a word. When he rolled her to her back and dipped his tongue between her lips, she locked her legs around his hips and sucked his tongue. A growl rumbled from his chest to hers, the vibration peaked her nipples.

Grabbing her hands, he pinned her to the bed. Kissing her jaw, then her throat, his heated, hungry mouth mimicked the chill she'd had the previous night, and it was nothing to do with the temperature. When he breathed her nipple to the roof of his mouth, her body arched automatically seeking out the solidity she needed to ground her, to fulfill her.

His hand skimmed the length of her torso, pinching her nipple on the way down. He separated her slick folds and dipped his finger around her opening. Lacie wriggled to attempt to urge him toward her clit, but he resisted seeming to enjoy her torture.

Getting her own back brought its own pleasure, her hands went to his jeans. Freeing him in an instant, his growl rumbled again, and she deliberately didn't let him capture her hands. Wrapping her fingers around him, she squeezed. Stroking him and cupping him, she caressed every reachable part of him. Dragging his teeth against her nipple, she squealed only to have the proceeding whimper swallowed by his mouth that plundered her again.

Just as she was lulled into his security, two of his fingers delved into her then he circled her clit giving her a blast of the pleasure that left her writhing at his mercy. Their night together had so often felt like an eternity ago. So much so that she would not let this perhaps isolated chance go by.

Keeping her grip on his thick member, she yanked him toward her, lifting her hips to meet the fat, blunt head she craved.

"Baby," he murmured into her.

Lacie plunged her tongue into his mouth and lifted her body again.

Increasing the pressure on her nub, his fingers slid in and out of her. On closing her eyes, her body undulated in time with that caress, except it wasn't enough.

"Please," she whispered against him. "Ryder."

With that word exhaled in ecstasy, his hands left her body, and then he was in her. Her scream was half sob, but she wrenched her body up to meet his, burying him to the hilt far inside her aching passage. She remembered this, him in a place within her body and soul, completion came in that union.

Their eyes locked and neither moved. Still, they hadn't spoken. There were things to be said. He was still basically clothed whilst she was completely naked.

Right now, there was no Perspex screen, no hooligans, or guns, or cars, or basement bars between them. They were joined together, no one and nothing between them. All these things were said without words. When he slid out, she moved away. When he plunged back into her, she shoved her hips up to meet him. The rhythm of their heart beats providing the bass of their merging.

Heat grew in her gut, forcing her chest to expand until breathing became a chore. But her panting increased, she wanted more. Their humid exhales fogged her skin. Their union, in, out, faster, more, deeper, harder…

Her whole body begged for his, for more, never would it be enough. Never had their attention strayed. To kiss him would slow their frantic action. The heat that burst shoved her into the precipice, dislodging his name from her throat again. Still, he battered into her, bruising her center with the onslaught of his passion.

On her final ripple, he slowed to press his fingers between them, massaging her still raw nerve endings. With that motion, his mouth closed over hers though his eyes remained open. A fierce flare shattered, sending her into another gasping explosion. In response, she dug her fingernails so far into him that she might have drawn blood.

The calm rhythm he'd adopted vanished back to the punishing pound that once again had her screaming his name. Forcing his arm under her hips, he smacked her g-spot until she yelped for mercy.

With a conquering roar, he slammed into her then stilled while shudders of bliss wracked her. Her inner muscles clamped him in position like a vice. If she could, she'd have kept him right there forever.

His arms buckled, bringing him down on top of her. The weight on her provided elusive security. The rightness of being under him, wrapped in his heat as he was still wrapped within her spread throughout her. After a dozen breaths, he rolled to the side keeping her body locked against his in the vice of his arms.

Stroking her hair from her cheek, he directed her head onto his tee-shirt clad shoulder. Turning her lips toward him, she kissed the cotton, then his jaw, and settled herself against him.

"Let me take this off," he muttered, urging her to sit up while he reached to the back of his neck to grasp his tee-shirt.

"We should get downstairs," she said, gathering her towel and wrapping herself in it again when she clambered off the bed.

"I just got out the joint, baby. I'm not through with you yet."

Glancing back at him, Lacie appreciated his presence once more then went into the bathroom to clean up. When she got out, he was sitting on the end of the bed wearing a new tee-shirt and pair of jeans.

"They released you," she said.

Retrieving clothes, she changed in the privacy of the walk-in only to about-face and see him leaning on the door frame watching her.

"Is it sexier if I tell you I broke out?" he asked.

"What happened?" she asked, stepping into him.

"They found Booth yesterday."

"Alive?"

"Yes," Ryder said. "He started talking in the car before they got to the station."

"What about Eric?"

"He got his deal."

"What does that mean? Did they drop all the charges against you?"

"They charged me based on what they found and Wallace's statement, which is unraveling. There's a lot of frustration. Booth's got the evidence. He laid it out… turned out he hadn't trusted Wallace from the start, he covered his back, which as it happens means he covered mine."

"I have to tell Sorcha," Lacie said, rushing forward only to be hampered by his obstruction. "What?"

His hand covered her cheek, his thumb traced her bottom lip back and forth. "I missed you."

Six weeks apart, a hospital stay, a foreign trip, and a visit to the slammer. Things hadn't been plain sailing. What she felt could be attributed to the intensity of events, but she wanted this feeling to last more than she'd wanted anything before.

"When are you moving?" she asked.

"I think we have a few things to clear up before we decide, don't you?"

"We," she said unable to stop her smile from spreading.

"Yes, we," he said, taking her hands and hooking them over his shoulders while moseying in closer. "Do you think I'll let you use me for my body without a commitment?"

"From me or you?"

"What do you think?" he asked, maneuvering her back to the wall.

"I couldn't make any promises," she said. "You are just out of prison. You'd be quite a risk for a girl to take."

"You put out the second you saw me. You're every guy's wet dream."

"Lacie?"

The voice from the bedroom interrupted their flirtation. Ryder let her slide free of his embrace to meet Gabe in the bedroom.

"What's wrong?" she asked.

"Something's happened," Gabe said.

"You're telling me."

Gabe's concern transformed to surprise. She surmised that Ryder had appeared from the walk-in behind her. His hand slipped to her shoulder, she tilted her head to press her cheek to his fingers thus ensuring nothing was miscommunicated.

"You're back," Gabe said. "We heard you got out. But we didn't know—"

"I thought security here was meant to be top-notch," Lacie said.

"It's his security," Gabe said.

"Man has a point," Ryder said.

His grasp drifted from her shoulder on his retreat to the walk-in.

"Sorcha's on her way over," Gabe said.

"They found Booth yesterday. Why didn't they tell us that—?"

"They were cutting the deal for Eric. The DA only approved it early this morning."

"He's talking now?"

"Yes," Gabe said.

"I don't understand how all this… I don't understand this. I thought Booth was dead."

"They got Stone out quickly. He always says it pays to have friends everywhere because you never know what you're going to need. Has he been here long?"

"Long enough," Ryder said, re-entering and kissing the top of her had when he passed.

"Going somewhere?" Gabe asked.

Lacie followed Gabe's line of vision to see Ryder dump a sports bag and a suitcase on the unmade bed they'd not so long ago enjoyed.

"I don't know, are we?" Lacie asked.

"We're getting out of here," Ryder said.

"No, I want to know what's going on," Lacie said. "We can't run away from this, we're part of it."

"It won't look too good, boss," Gabe said. "You go on the run the minute they let you out, and with the girl who's been abducted already."

"No one's abducting me," she said. "It's okay to be cautious, but we're safe here. I've been staying here and I'm fine."

A shrill buzz startled them all.

Ryder pointed at the phone on the wall. "That's the private line," he said. "Have you been phoning out?"

"No," she said. "I hadn't even noticed it was there."

"This has been Lacie's room," Gabe said. "And if she hasn't called out… someone wants to get in touch with her."

Lacie took the lead in going to the phone. If they wanted her, she'd deliver. Chances were the caller would want to discuss Ryder's guilt, or the prospect of his innocence.

"Hello?" she asked when she answered.

"Lacie!"

The sobbing fear of her best friend formed icicles around her heart. "Sorch?"

"He wants you to come! He says it's you. He wants you! But, Lace, oh God—"

Her scream stabbed at Lacie's heart. Lacie hadn't realized her legs had given out until Ryder caught her.

"Hello, Lacie," Wallace's voice drawled down the line. "Come and meet us. Sorcha and her baby would really appreciate it."

"You're crazy. Don't hurt her. Please, don't—"

"You better get down to the warehouse at West Hicks. You come alone and you come now. Tick-tock, Lacie, you know what happens when I'm out of patience… you haven't been behaving yourself."

Lacie didn't bother hanging up when the line went dead. She scrambled from Ryder's arms and went straight for the door, but his grip on her hand tugged her back.

"What?" Ryder asked at the same moment the bedroom door burst open.

Rocco stormed in. "He's out," he said not even blinking at Ryder who still had a hold of her.

"Out?" Gabe asked. "How the—"

"Something happened in the jail. Wallace was complaining of chest pains, he collapsed. An ambulance was taking him to the hospital and… Sonny got it over the scanner. We don't know what kind of head start he got, both paramedics are receiving medical attention. The guard that was with him is dead. There's a manhunt but—"

"He has Sorcha," Lacie said.

"She was on her way over here," Gabe said.

"He must have intercepted her," Ryder said. "Probably at the gate, if he was watching—"

"I have to go," Lacie said. "I have to get to her."

Rocco spoke. "We'll mobilize if—"

"There's no time," Lacie pleaded while trying to wrench her hand from Ryder's.

"I just got you back," Ryder said.

"He wants me to go alone," she said.

"You'll have me with you."

"No, he doesn't—"

"He probably doesn't know that Ryder's out," Gabe said. "Wallace won't mind the audience when it's Ryder he's trying to retaliate against."

"Retaliate for what?" Rocco asked.

"I have to go!" Lacie pleaded.

"No," Ryder said, tugging her into his arms. "Give me a minute to think about this."

"You can trust us," Gabe said. "You have to trust us."

"I trust you," Lacie said, twisting out of Ryder's embrace. "I'm going and I'm going now. He's at the warehouse in West Hicks."

"That complex has been deserted for years," Rocco said. "It's just four streets over."

"He knows the grounds as well as we do," Gabe said. "We did training exercises out there."

"But he doesn't have back-up," Ryder said. "Lacie and I will do the approach. You do not let him leave."

"You trust us?" Gabe asked.

"You've been looking after my girl," Ryder said. "We need your help."

The men immediately went into combat mode discussing plans and strategies. All of them got to the HQ building. While the men headed for the war room, Lacie diverted toward the stairwell. She stopped, glancing back at Ryder who spied her departure from the group.

"I'm glad you got out," she said. "And that we had this morning."

Ryder said something quietly to Gabe who disappeared into the war room with Rocco. "Let's go," he said, guiding her down the stairwell.

"You don't have to come with me," she said. "If you men have things to—"

"She's your best friend," Ryder said, taking keys from a coded panel on the garage wall. "Let's go and get her."

He'd proved she was his priority and now he showed that her priorities trumped his.

FIFTY-SIX

Lacie

GETTING DOWN INTO the basement garage and into the truck, they didn't talk. When he put it into gear, she covered his hand with hers, which stalled him.

"You've been incredible through all this," she said.

He curled his fingers around hers to take her hand up to his mouth. "Entirely selfish," he said. "I plan to make you pay me back for all my good deeds."

"You do, do you?" she asked.

His eyes trailed down her body. "Yeah," he said. "I'll take payment in frequent and exclusive access to your body."

"If your friend gets his way there won't be much of it left."

The reminder struck to the center of him. His expression became immediately stony. "We'll get her back and you're both walking away from this."

Her panic for Sorcha grew. "What about you?"

Ryder's lack of response did nothing to calm her.

His brutal navigation of the truck out of the garage and onto the road worried her. Now was the time she needed him thinking, level-headed, in control.

But he'd taken so much responsibility for Wallace's actions, she worried what the outcome would be if Ryder's irrationality continued.

Rocco hadn't been wrong about the proximity of the site; almost before the journey had begun it was over. Ryder put on the brake, inhaled, then looked at her.

"No risks," Ryder said. "I want you to stay behind me. I'll get Sorcha out of there."

"I won't take any risks if you don't."

Knowing he'd argue with her, and that they were on a clock, she got out of the truck and headed for the warehouse. Ryder was on her immediately, but she kept going, and he didn't try to stop her. He linked his fingers between hers. The show of support strengthened her resolve. Gently easing back, he slowed their pace, and tucked her behind him by moving their joined hands to his lower back.

In the past, a metal shutter would have covered the large goods entrance. The complex had been abandoned for so many years that it was gone. As they approached, Ryder closed in on the brick wall making sure she had cover while he exposed himself to the danger.

"You get everywhere, don't you, Stone?"

Lacie heard the echoing voice, but Ryder kept her on the outside of the wall behind him.

"What's your game now?" Ryder demanded.

His voice was firm but not half as menacing as Wallace's.

"Thought you were locked up," Wallace said.

"Thought you were too. Where's Sorcha?"

"Waiting for Lacie, did you bring her?"

"You don't want her. This is about you and me."

"You?" Wallace spat. Still she hadn't laid eyes on him or the interior of the building. "This has nothing to do with you."

"Yeah right, how did you get involved in this in the first place?"

"Money, you egotistical fucker! You think this is all about you? I've been doing this for years, little here, little there when the chance presented itself. Then I found Booth and regular income. The guy's a whimpering, sniveling idiot."

"Not such an idiot," Ryder said. "He's got you marked. He kept the details of every transaction, exactly where it went. Your fingerprints are all over it."

"Too bad he's dead then, huh?"

"Nope, got that one wrong too. Eric kept him alive. Booth's been hiding out… but the police have him now and he's singing their tune."

"Typical, looking after number one. I should've known it; can't trust anyone," Wallace said.

"That's the trouble with screwing people over. Everyone's waiting for when you'll do it to them."

"You never saw it coming," Wallace said, snickering. "You really bought all that "all for one" bullshit. You never saw it. You never saw it coming."

"No, but that's what trust is, isn't it? How many years did you chase after me?" Ryder asked. "Trotting around in my shadow."

"I did not! You! You think it's all about you!"

A splintering sound startled her. Ryder tightened his hold on her hand but didn't avert his eyes for a second.

"You've got a temper there, Jaim. Always struggled to keep your horses tethered didn't you?"

"Enough!" Wallace shouted. "No more talk. Where's the girl? Get the girl now!"

"Do you really think you're in a position to be

giving the orders?" Ryder asked.

"Yes," Wallace said.

A clatter preceded a scream that Lacie recognized. She darted around Ryder. Dropping his hand, she got at least three feet into the building when Ryder got a hold of her and pulled her back.

The building had bare concrete walls with pale flaking paint, and a rusting staircase to a questionably stable mezzanine floor. Old broken machinery littered the space along with sporadic greenery and a hearty scattering of rodent and bird feces.

Behind a stack of oil drums, beside an old production line, Wallace stood still in his prison coveralls. His wild eyes burned with an unfounded satisfaction. Except maybe it was founded. He held Sorcha in front of him, on her knees. Wallace's grip twisted in Sorcha's hair, Sorcha's hand went over his, but she couldn't free herself. She cried out and reached for Lacie but there was twenty feet between them.

"That's right," Wallace said. "Why don't you come over here, little Lacie? Come and join us."

"Let her go," Lacie said. "You don't need her."

"She's serving her purpose well," Wallace said. "She brought us back together, didn't she?"

"I'm here. You don't need her," Lacie said. "What is it you want? Why are you here? Why did you come back?"

"I came for you," Wallace said. "You're going to come on a trip with me."

"She's going nowhere," Ryder said, insinuating himself in front of Lacie.

"Not really your decision, mi compadre," Wallace said. "I think that's up to the girl."

"What do you want from her?" Ryder asked.

Wallace laughed absurdly given the situation. "Turns out some things are about you."

"You want her because you think I want her," Ryder said.

"The stupid girl started all this. She was the one who got you digging. None of this would've happened if it wasn't for her."

"You did this to yourself," Ryder said.

"You're obsessed with that girl. I've never seen you so… from the minute you met her you've been different."

"Are you implying if it wasn't for Lacie, I wouldn't have had a problem with what you're doing?"

"No, I did this for years. I'm telling you that if it wasn't for her, you'd never have noticed."

Wallace wrenched Sorcha back by her hair causing another curdling scream.

"Let her go," Ryder said. "We can work this out. Come on, we've never met a problem we couldn't fix together."

"You don't give a fuck about together, don't insult me! Now get over here, Lacie, or your friend will get a bullet in her brain!"

From his side, Wallace produced a gun and trained it first on Sorcha, then lifted it to aim at Ryder.

"You can go ahead and shoot me," Ryder said.

"Then I can have both the women," Wallace said.

"Let Sorcha go and I'll come with you," Lacie said, stepping into the path of the gun.

"Come over here," Wallace said.

Lacie began to walk, but Ryder got a hold of her again. This was difficult for all of them, Lacie turned to slide her hands up to rest on his neck and guided his lips down to hers.

"We can walk away from this alive," she murmured. "All of us. I'll find you, I will."

Ryder caught her for another kiss. The

determination in his eyes mirrored that of the day on the street when they'd lost each other before.

When she turned away, Lacie crossed to the mid-point between the men. "Let her go," she said.

Wallace dragged Sorcha to her feet. "You come here," he demanded.

Lacie moved closer with measured, gradual steps. When she was within reaching distance, Wallace thrust Sorcha away and snatched Lacie, pulling her body to his.

"Together again, Lace. I've missed our chats, haven't you?"

"Not for a second," Lacie answered.

Wallace spun her around. Lacie thanked the stars when she saw Sorcha clearing the building behind Ryder.

"Let her go," Ryder said.

Ryder whipped a gun from his waistband that must have been beneath his tee-shirt because she hadn't noticed it at all until now. Ryder moved in closer, leading with his gun.

"Are you going to be the bigshot now?" Wallace asked. "I've got your girl."

"You're going to let her go."

"Want to bet on that?" Wallace laughed, edging backward.

Lacie saw an ajar fire escape letting in a few inches of daylight. Their exit was imminent.

"Let her go!"

This shout came from behind them. When Wallace spun, she lost her footing and fell just before the pop of a bullet shattered in the air. Lacie stayed put on her face. Silence crackled until the thunder of footsteps closed in around her.

Sirens began to blare in the distance.

"There's a van outside, engine running," Rocco said.

Lacie rolled onto her back. Ryder was upon her

with Gabe and Rocco, the rest of the boys behind them.

"Baby, look at me, are you okay? Say something."

"What happened?" she asked.

"The guys surprised him through the rear exits. We got him."

"We…?"

The sirens stopped when the wheels screeched to a halt outside. Ryder helped Lacie to her feet and checked her for injuries. She spied Wallace's body prone on the floor not far from their position.

"Is he…?" she asked.

"Nah," Rocco said, rolling Wallace to his back with his boot. "Tranq dart."

"This guy's not getting out of doing his time," Gabe said. "We don't leave a man behind. This one's coming with us, all the way back to jail."

Lacie was aware of the uniforms swarming in. The SW men disarmed just as they were instructed. Gabe went to talk to the lead agent, and she couldn't help but notice how quiet Ryder was. He was preoccupied with Wallace who was being checked out by medics.

Each of the men was being interviewed. Rocco told her Sorcha was being checked out too. Just as Lacie was going to approach Ryder, she was side-lined to give her statement.

A couple of hours passed before the scene was cleared and they were allowed to leave. Shep had shown up and gone to the hospital with Sorcha though the medics had cleared her. But because of the baby, and the shock, Sorcha had agreed to spend the night in hospital for observation. At times like this, Sorcha's enjoyment of the attention paid off.

The SW men had been talking in a huddle for a while. Lacie took the chance to get outside into the fresh air. She'd believed that the drama was over before when she went back to the UK. She'd been wrong.

Now that he'd woken up, Wallace would be observed in the prison infirmary. Sorcha was safe with Shep in hospital. Eric had hidden Booth and between them, they held every fact needed to convict Wallace.

Sorcha was still pregnant. How her relationship with Shep would progress now that Booth was alive, Lacie didn't know. Although there would be a chance that Sorcha's baby daddy would be spending some time in prison, and still Sorcha hadn't told her parents any of it.

"Are you okay?"

Lacie spun to see Ryder approach as the men casually dispersed to their vehicles. "I think so," she said.

"The medics checked you out, they said—"

"What about you?" she asked, reaching for his hand. "You were in prison this morning. Your best friend took aim at you. Now he's going back to jail. I can't imagine how it must feel to—"

"Eric was a medic," Ryder said, ignoring her observations. "When he took Bruce out of Wallace's house, he took Booth to a cabin in the woods and put him back together. Booth got a deal too, he'll testify against Wallace, and he'll get immunity for the embezzling. Wallace won't be granted bail. Any men that he might have tried to lean on are all inside with him."

"Bruce will get out?" Lacie asked. "I have to talk to Sorcha."

"Do you want me to take you to the hospital?"

"Are you sure? It's been a long day for you—"

"Come on," Ryder said, directing her into the same truck he'd helped her into on the day their journey began.

The trip to the hospital was quick. When they got to Sorcha's room, Ryder tactfully removed Shep from the room so the women could be alone. Their privacy gave Lacie the chance to fill Sorcha in on the information

Ryder had gotten from the detective at the scene.

"He's out?" Sorcha said. "Bruce is going free? And he won't be charged?"

"What does that mean for you?" Lacie said. "Do you want me to phone your parents?"

"No, Shep's already talked about that."

"You have to tell them."

"I have to talk to Bruce," Sorcha said.

"What are you going to do?" Lacie asked.

Sorcha shrugged. "This all started because of the life in me. It's half Bruce too."

"Hasn't this shown you that you don't know Bruce very well? You have to be careful about what you're getting involved in."

"Everything I've heard goes back to Wallace and he's in jail now. Bruce is a good man, who made bad choices. We've all done that… well us mortals."

Lacie took Sorcha's hand and didn't respond to the joke. "I'm your best friend. I'll support anything you choose. Shep's been a good man through this. Yes, he has a crappy work ethic, and he's crude, but he stepped up for you. Your happiness is what's important."

"Shep was never forever," Sorcha said. "He doesn't want to be a father to another man's child."

"Have you asked him that?"

"I don't have to."

"There's no evidence that Booth would be a good bet for you, or a good father," Lacie said.

"There's none that I'd be a good mother either," Sorcha said. "We have to take some things on faith."

"If you think Booth's a better candidate to take to your parents—"

"The man who got mixed up in a stack of illegal activities?"

"So what do you want?"

Silence lingered for a score of seconds.

"Ask Bruce to visit," Sorcha said.

"Here?" Lacie asked. Sorcha nodded. "What about Shep?"

"I'll send him home."

"Do you want us to take care of that?"

"Us? Listen to you." Sorcha smiled. "But, no, thanks, I can do it."

"Okay," Lacie said. "Do you want me to come back later?"

"I'll phone you," Sorcha said. "When it's done."

"Okay."

"What about you?" Sorcha asked. "Are you going back to your parents?"

"I don't know."

"What has Ryder said? Has he asked you to stay?"

"We haven't had a lot of time to talk."

"Your happiness is what's important," Sorcha teased. "You decide what you want and make it happen."

"I can't make up his mind for him."

"That means you want to stay here, where he is."

"Maybe."

"I'm biased. I think that's an excellent idea," Sorcha said. "You should stay in the US with him… and me."

"I have a life to somehow cobble together."

"Talk to him, then tell me how it goes tonight when I phone."

"I'll try," Lacie said, leaning over to hug Sorcha.

When a wolf whistle joined the opening of the door, both women knew who had arrived. "Surely we can work out a time share agreement with our girls," Shep said to Ryder who was at his side.

Lacie kissed Sorcha and went to Ryder. "We'll leave you two alone. But if there's anything you need, just let us know."

Both she and Ryder said their goodbyes and then they were back in the truck.

"What did she say?" Ryder asked.

"She's going to talk to Booth."

"He knows about the baby, do you think...? Is she still considering marrying Booth?"

"I think so," Lacie said.

"What does Shep say to that?"

"We'll know by the end of the day," Lacie said. "But Shep's not a forever guy. He won't want to play daddy."

"I might have agreed with you a couple of months ago," Ryder said. "Now I'm not so sure."

He drove into the garage at SW and shut off the engine. The sat there a minute.

"Sorcha asked me if I was going back home."

"What did you say?"

"I told her I didn't know," Lacie said, then took off her seatbelt and opened her door.

After leaving the truck, she went upstairs, and walked through the yard to the house. Running through the foyer and up the left side of the double staircase, Lacie was in his bedroom, filling her suitcase, before Ryder found her.

"Are you running away now?" Ryder asked, slamming the door. "Because I'll follow you, I will."

"I'm not running away. You wanted to leave here, didn't you?"

"So we're going together?"

Dumping the clothes she'd been folding onto the bed, she swiveled to him. "What are we doing, Ryder? Are we it? Are you going to trust me? What about your men? Do you trust them? What comes next, Ryder?"

"What do you want?"

"My best friend is about to have a child. She's going to marry the man who knocked her up. Her parents will freak, she needs support, a lot of support."

"So you're going to stay in the US for your friend? For Sorcha? Is that what you're telling me?"

"No," Lacie said. "I'm telling you that she'll need a lot of my time and that we're going to have to make concessions for the difficult time ahead."

"We?" he asked, softening his anger.

"Yes, we," she said, lifting her hands to his shoulders.

"I want to make a go of this, of us."

"Let's see how we do without the drama," she said. "Neither of us have a place to stay. You don't have a job if you fold this place."

"I'm still going to sell," Ryder said. "But I've got a few ideas about what the guys and I can get up to."

"You and the guys?" she asked.

"They looked out for us today. You were right. I should've trusted them."

"Things have been difficult, but we're going to look out for each other from here on in, right?"

"You'll stay… with me?"

"With you," she said as he gathered her close.

"I love you, Lace," he said, tucking her hair away from her face. "I've loved you since… I need you with me, always."

"I know," she said, smiling at his frown. "Everybody keeps telling me… Love is easy, you make loving you easy. I've been falling for you since I walked into Shep's office. I love you, and I want to support you just like you'll support me."

The corner of his mouth curled up. "I love you, and you love me… that makes us lovers."

"You want to seal the deal?" she asked. "I suppose I do have a debt to repay."

Ryder walked her backward until her calves hit the bed. "You do," he said, tossing her down on top of her scatter of clothes. "It's going to take you years, maybe decades to clear it."

"Oh, what a shame," she said when he dropped on top of her. "You drive a hard bargain."

"I'm thinking about your body," he teased with his half smile.

"Yeah, I bet you are."

They sealed their agreement with a kiss.

Want more from Ryder and Lacie...?

Thank you for reading this tale!
If you can, please take the time to review.

~

Ask your local library for more Scarlett Finn
novels!

~

For all things Scarlett Finn
check out:

www.scarlettfinn.com

Mistake Me Not sequel:

SCARLETT FINN